GET ALL

WITH JUST ONE PROOF OF PURCHASE

$50 VALUE

◆ **Hotel Discounts**
up to 60%
at home
and abroad
◆ **Travel Service -**
Guaranteed lowest published
airfares plus 5% cash back on
tickets ◆ **$25 Travel Voucher**
◆ **Sensuous Petite Parfumerie**
collection ◆ **Insider
Tips Letter** with
sneak previews of
upcoming books

*You'll get a FREE personal card, too.
It's your passport to all these benefits—and to
even more great gifts & benefits to come!*

There's no club to join. No purchase commitment. No obligation.

SD-PP5A

Enrollment Form

☐ *Yes!* I WANT TO BE A *P*RIVILEGED *W*OMAN.
Enclosed is one *PAGES & PRIVILEGES*™ Proof of
Purchase from any Harlequin or Silhouette book currently for
sale in stores (Proofs of Purchase are found on the back pages
of books) and the store cash register receipt. Please enroll me
in *PAGES & PRIVILEGES*™. Send my Welcome Kit and FREE
Gifts -- and activate my FREE benefits -- immediately.

More great gifts and benefits to come.

NAME (please print)

ADDRESS   APT. NO

CITY   STATE   ZIP/POSTAL CODE

PROOF OF PURCHASE ONLY

**NO CLUB!
NO COMMITMENT!**
*Just one purchase brings
you great Free Gifts and
Benefits!*

Please allow 6-8 weeks for delivery. Quantities are limited. We reserve the right to
substitute items. Enroll before October 31, 1995 and receive one full year of benefits.

Name of store where this book was purchased_____

Date of purchase_____

Type of store:
☐ Bookstore   ☐ Supermarket   ☐ Drugstore
☐ Dept. or discount store (e.g. K-Mart or Walmart)
☐ Other (specify)_____

Which Harlequin or Silhouette series do you usually read?

_____

Complete and mail with one Proof of Purchase and store receipt to:
U.S.: *PAGES & PRIVILEGES*™, P.O. Box 1960, Danbury, CT 06813-1960
Canada: *PAGES & PRIVILEGES*™, 49-6A The Donway West, P.O. 813,
North York, ON M3C 2E8

SD-PP5B

▼ DETACH HERE AND MAIL TODAY! ▼

"Where Are You Going?"

Katherine looked down at him. "I'm going to the airport."

He caught her wrist, circling it, holding her a willing captive. "No, you're not."

"I'm not?" Her gray gaze was wide with innocence.

"Not like that." His eyes moved over her, lingering, needing.

She looked down at herself with an innocence even more pronounced. "My goodness, then where am I to go?"

Mitch tugged at her wrist, and brought her toppling down on him, his body shielding hers from the fall.

"Here." His fingers caught in her hair, bringing her lips to his. "Here," he muttered, "to me."

Dear Reader,

Are you looking for books that are fresh, sexy, and wonderfully romantic? Then look no more, because you've got one of them in your hands right now! Silhouette Desire, where man meets woman...and love is the result.

When you enter the world of Silhouette Desire, you travel to places where the hero is passionate...ready to do *anything* to capture the eternal affections of the heroine. He's a guy you can't help but fall a little in love with yourself...just as the heroine does. And the heroine—whether she's a full-time mom or full-time career woman—is someone you can relate to!

And in Silhouette Desire you'll find some of romance fiction's finest writers. This month alone we have Dixie Browning, Lucy Gordon, BJ James, Susan Crosby, Judith McWilliams and Ryanne Corey. And where else, but in Silhouette Desire, will you find the *Man of the Month* or a bold, sensuous new miniseries such as MEN OF THE BLACK WATCH?

Silhouette Desire is simply *the* best in romance...this month and every month! So, enjoy....

Sincerely,

Lucia Macro
Senior Editor

Please address questions and book requests to:
Silhouette Reader Service
U.S.: 3010 Walden Ave., P.O. Box 1325, Buffalo, NY 14269
Canadian: P.O. Box 609, Fort Erie, Ont. L2A 5X3

BJ JAMES
THE SAINT OF BOURBON STREET

SILHOUETTE *Desire*®
Published by Silhouette Books
America's Publisher of Contemporary Romance

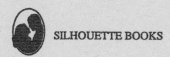

SILHOUETTE BOOKS

ISBN 0-373-05951-5

THE SAINT OF BOURBON STREET

Copyright © 1995 by BJ James

This edition published by arrangement with Harlequin Books S.A.

Printed in U.S.A.

Books by BJ James

Silhouette Desire

The Sound of Goodbye #332
Twice in a Lifetime #396
Shiloh's Promise #529
Winter Morning #595
Slade's Woman #672
A Step Away #692
Tears of the Rose #709
The Man with the Midnight Eyes #751
Pride and Promises #789
Another Time, Another Place #823
The Hand of an Angel #844
*Heart of the Hunter #945
*The Saint of Bourbon Street #951

*Men of the Black Watch

BJ JAMES

married her high school sweetheart straight out of college and soon found that books were delightful companions during her lonely nights as a doctor's wife. But she never dreamed she'd be more than a reader, never expected to be one of the blessed, letting her imagination soar, weaving magic of her own.

BJ has twice been honored by the Georgia Romance Writers with their prestigious Maggie Award for Best Short Contemporary Romance. She has also received the *Romantic Times* Critic's Choice Award.

Prologue

Mitchell wore rags.

Clean rags that would have been neatly pressed if he owned an iron.

If he could afford an iron, he wouldn't wear rags.

There was enough in his hoarded stash for closets of clothes, a dozen irons.

If he bought the clothes, the iron, he couldn't buy the child.

No choice.

No choice at all.

This child was small, almost delicate, and wonderfully younger than his years. Neither garish neon, nor the sickly yellow of anemic street lamps, nor the inky black of alleyways masked the ethereal innocence on his baby face. He was a towhead, with deep blue eyes, an upturned nose and perfect skin. At ten, no stubbled beard marred skin like satin. No teenage acne scoured fine pores.

A beautiful face despite the mascaraed lashes and painted lips.

His name was Billy.

A night would make mockery of Billy's innocence; a year

would destroy his beauty. If he survived to his teens, acne and
a beard would be the least of his worries.

The very least.

The boy stumbled over uneven cobblestones. A huge hand
weighted with diamonds lifted him with exaggerated concern to
his feet, the flawlessly manicured nails digging into, but not
marking, his throat.

There was no outcry, only lethargic compliance.

It was five minutes from the appointed time of his meeting
with The Mentor, as the boy's captor liked to be addressed, but
Mitchell Ryan's rage was too volatile to wait. He stepped from
the gloom of an alley into their path, halting the little parade.

"Mitchell, my man, you're early!" With a theatrical bow,
the hearty greeting boomed over the street, a performance only
furtively remarked by loiterers and strollers. Locked in private
miseries and desperate to make the latest score, none dared risk
overt attention to The Mentor's affairs.

"Then you'll be richer that much sooner, won't you, Isaac?"
Mitchell refused the self-appointed title, calling, instead, the
name he knew. The only name, for surnames were rare on the
street. No matter his rage, he spoke softly. He always spoke
softly when there were children.

A proprietary hand cupped the shoulder of the child as the
older man swept the ragged adolescent with a look of disdain.
Arrantly and brazenly aware of his own sartorial excesses, he
spared no contempt for those he considered less tasteful. "Must
you always look as if you found your clothes among the re-
jects at the Salvation Army? Gives the street a bad ambience for
customers to see young lads like you."

"Ambience?" Mitchell allowed himself a chuckle. A mechanical sound issuing from his throat, as grim as the line of his
lips, as stark as the chiseled angles of his thin face. "That's a
new word. Reading the thesaurus again?"

"Never hurts to improve oneself." Another look disparaged
Mitchell's garments. "And the street."

"As you do?" A gaze like mellow sherry, but far, far too old
for his sixteen years, never strayed from the black insulting
stare. "With bounty from kids like Billy."

"A man does what a man must do to make a living." An
elderly vagrant brushed by, thought of begging for enough to
buy a bottle, thought again, and shambled on. Waving a
handkerchief in his wake, The Mentor resumed his discourse.

"Take you, for instance. You're long in the tooth for my clientele, but in the proper dress, I could find something."

"Yeah," Mitchell agreed, "I just bet you could, but the answer's the same as it was when I was Billy's age."

"Ah, Billy." The hand gripping harder over the thin shoulder of the ten-year-old boy elicited no more response than the conversation. "You won't cooperate, and now you would deny me even his good services."

Mitchell risked a glance down, and was sickened all over again by what he saw. Blue eyes rimmed by clotted mascara stared vacantly at nothing. The painted mouth, with a false mole pasted at the corner, was slack. Drugs blocked out pain as well as fear and, ultimately, inhibitions. Mitchell had no idea where the boy came from, nor how The Mentor had gotten him, but he knew that stare should have life in it.

The eyes should sparkle and the mouth smile, as the boy did things boys do. Shag fly balls on a sunlit ball field, ride a bike, or a horse, or fish a bayou. Normal things for normal boys.

Abruptly, Mitchell looked away. His voice was strained when he spoke. "How much?"

"We do business now, eh?" A gold tooth flashed in Isaac's smile.

"Yes, now."

The sparring was done. Friendly overtures that had never truly been friendly were abandoned. Time to deal. With the cunning learned from years on the street, Mitchell knew it was the most dangerous time. A show of cash and Isaac might be stricken by an attack of greed, craving money and boy. Deciding to take both.

Others had tried, but not so many anymore.

Backing out of the pedestrian traffic, but not out of the light, Mitchell stood with his shoulders against a wall. His weight rested lightly on the balls of his feet. The packet of money, all large unmarked bills, was taped inside the tattered polo shirt. The switchblade, never more than inches from his relaxed fingers, lay like a weight in the hip pocket of his jeans. One wrong move from Isaac, and Mitchell would be out of there.

"This Billy, he is a fine lad." Like an auctioneer extolling the virtue of his consignment, The Mentor opened the bidding.

"How much?" Mitchell cut him off. There was no sport in buying a child. No pleasure in bargaining.

"I quoted a price before." Isaac stroked the blond hair. Riffling it with his fingers, smiling at the charming disarray.

"I'm sure it has changed. It always does."

"He's such a pretty boy. So sweet."

"They all are, for a while."

"And you would buy them all."

Mitchell held the mocking stare. "If I could."

"Returning them always, by way of our illustrious and unquestioning police force, to their grieving mothers' arms."

"Can the sarcasm, Isaac." No one knew better than Mitchell that there were no grieving mothers for most of the kids he took from the street. "Cut to the bottom line."

A gusty sigh accompanied feigned disappointment. Black eyes turned hard as agate. "Five hundred dollars," Isaac whispered in a voice as hard. "Five hundred above the quoted price."

It took every bit of control at his command to hide his shock. Mitchell expected an extra hundred, maybe two, but five? Where would he find five hundred dollars? Where within the next critical hours?

"A problem?" The Mentor grinned, showing the long, pointed eyeteeth of the parasitic vampire he rivaled.

"No problem," Mitchell lied. "None at all, but I don't have so much extra cash with me."

"A wise thing. It's never good to carry so much cash with one on the street, you know."

Mitchell looked down at the boy. He couldn't save them all. Not even many of them, but somehow it was important that Billy, who should be shagging flies in the sunlight, wouldn't be one he lost. "It will take several hours to convert what I have into untraceable bills."

Long fingers threaded through golden hair. Diamonds glittered in murky light. "There's great demand for a new commodity, I'm not sure I can wait."

"Damn you, Isaac, we had a deal. Renege, and I'll see that everyone on the street, and every street around knows it. How long, then, before word spreads to your customers? Who would trust The Mentor?"

Lie, cheat, steal. Twist a bargain, corrupt it, milk it for all allowed, but never go back on an accepted deal. Not completely. Thus was the peculiar honor among men without honor, on a street that had never known the word. Mitchell was counting heavily on it, and on the man's immediate greed. "We're talking instant profit. No upkeep, no drug tab. No risk on an untried commodity that might not be a success in the long run."

Commodity! Mitchell nearly choked on the word. This was the future of a child, hanging on the aberrant whim of a monster and Mitchell's own ability to raise an additional five hundred dollars.

The Mentor shot back a cuff to glance at a Rolex. "The evening's young yet. I suppose I have time. An hour?"

"Three."

"Two."

"Three." Mitchell wouldn't be moved. He couldn't. Any less time was impossible. "Three hours. Midnight, or it's no go."

Isaac liked money. He liked it in lump sums, with little outlay, and no gambling on the unknown. "All right, three."

"Done!" Mitchell didn't offer his hand. He wouldn't, not to The Mentor, who traded in the souls of children.

The street was deserted and enough street lamps had been broken out that it was nearly dark. Mitchell couldn't believe his luck as he stopped a half block from the gleaming Jaguar parked alone at the curb.

Who would bring such a car to this section of New Orleans? What rich yuppie would add idiocy to foolhardy by leaving it unattended with the driver's window down? The dark burgundy machine with its camel top literally screamed to every car thief in the city to take it.

Lucky Mitchell Ryan was first to discover it.

"Yeah, baby," he muttered. "One like you can buy six Billys from scumbag Isaac."

He moved closer, one careful step after another. There was no one in sight, but to be sure, he hugged the walls, dodging from doorway to doorway. His natural caution moved to a higher plane, for in his world an opportunity like this was too good to be true.

On his tools-for-survival list, on a scale of ten, caution ranked right up there. Along with nerve and a switchblade.

All three were firmly in place as he moved like a shadow within the shadows until he was adjacent to the car. On closer inspection he decided this was more than a car. It was a work of art. The temporary owner's savvy of motor vehicles commanded admiration, if his common sense did not.

Common sense? The fool had none, and a fool and his chariot deserved to be parted.

The open window didn't mean there wouldn't be alarms, but a hunch told him the driver hadn't taken time to engage them, any more than he'd taken time to close the window. Just in case, Mitchell would be thirty seconds of extra caution getting in. A little longer circumventing the lack of an ignition key and firing the engine. Then he would be home free.

Billy would be home and free.

Heart pounding, adrenaline pumping, Mitchell looked left, then right.

No one.

The street was eerily empty.

This caper was a go.

Sprinting across the sidewalk, he bent at the sleek, burgundy door. As easy as that he was inside. The mechanism was new to him—this was the first Jaguar in his career—and it required a bit more thought and took more than a bit longer. But with hands that could move like magic, he set out to conquer its intricacies. Then, success!

The ignition of the powerful engine ripped through the night, a sound far louder than he'd bargained for.

He laughed and ran his palms over the supple leather of the steering wheel. "Can't steal a Jag without the roar."

"Think again, kid." The grating voice with a peculiar inflection accompanied two brawny hands that lifted him bodily from the car. "You aren't stealing this Jag at all."

Mitchell found himself disarmed and dangling at the end of arms that resembled nothing as much as tree trunks, clasped by hands that could double for vices. The eyes that glared up at him from a lined, weathered face were peculiarly pensive beneath the savage anger. Far in their depths lay reason and strength the fiercest rage could not diminish. Thick silver hair, cut in an austere brush, contradicted the youthfulness of the strength and the clarity of the eyes.

"Who the hell are you, and what made you think you could steal my car?" The words spoke of outrage, the tone was level, composed. "*My* car, you little creep."

Mitchell was on the lanky side, but not what the average person called little. This wasn't an average person. He was a ghost, a strong ghost. How else could he come so swiftly and silently out of nowhere? "I was looking." The feeble excuse burst out. "Just looking!"

"Sure you were. You always hot-wire a car to get a better look. It's the best way."

A million excuses were running through his mind, but Mitchell knew before he tried one that none would work on this man. "All right," he screamed at the top of the silvered head. "I was stealing the stupid thing. What more would you expect when you practically hang an invitation on it saying, 'Take me, I'm yours.'"

Ironically, the burly man laughed and set him on his feet. The young eyes in the older face were no less savage for the laughter when he leaned close. "You've watched too many bad movies, kid."

Mitchell hitched up jeans, disturbingly light without the weight of the switchblade, and tried for bravado. "I'm not a kid."

Maybe the man would laugh again. Laughter was good for the soul, he'd read. Somewhere. Maybe it was good for the fury he saw, as well.

"How old are you, then?" In the gloom the face that would have been venerably handsome in better light was a sculptor's manque of eroded crevasses and bottomless chasms.

"I'm sixteen, near as I can tell."

Riveting eyes stared into him. "Near as you can tell, huh?"

Mitchell jutted his chin and narrowed his gaze, expecting an insult. "That's what I said."

"That means you don't know for sure?"

"You want I should draw you a picture?"

The older man ignored the brashness. "How long have you been on the street?"

"Long enough." Two words, speaking volumes.

A light flared in the cold gaze, vise grips closed over the broad, bony shoulders beneath the torn T-shirt. A flick of a thick wrist spun Mitchell around the car. Another flick and the passenger door opened. Before he could even consider resisting, a hand on the top of his head forced him down and inside.

"Hey," Mitchell protested. "Who do you think you are, and what do you think you're doing?"

"I don't think on either count, son. I'm Simon McKinzie and I feel the sudden, burning need of a cup of coffee. There's a diner a few blocks away that serves the best in New Orleans. We're going there. Now. Together."

This startling statement was punctuated by the solid thunk of the Jaguar's door. Seconds later the engine roared again and the car squalled away from the curb.

"Now—" Simon McKinzie set down his cup and leaned back against the tall banquette "—suppose you tell me."

"Tell you what?" Mitchell didn't want to sound sullen, he didn't want to sound afraid. It was difficult on both efforts, and just as hard not to stare. Giving the subdued magnificence of what appeared to be a private club the name "diner" was as much a travesty as calling Isaac "The Mentor."

"Start with who you are, why you're on the street, and what you planned to do with my car."

"What I planned to do was steal it. So call the cops and get it over with."

Simon stared at the thin face. Beneath the insolence he saw intelligence and courage and, he fancied, integrity. The clothes had seen better days, the deep auburn hair was shaggy and too long, but healthy and clean. The pale brown gaze was steady and direct, even when the boy was afraid. "I'll call the cops when and if I'm ready."

Before the boy could register his surprise, Simon lifted a hand to summon a waiter. "A *beignet* would go down well right now. Join me?"

"No, thank you."

Simon almost smiled. No, thank you? This from a kid with larceny in his heart and a switchblade in his pocket. Who would, no doubt, be meaner than two gators in a fight, but had honor in his eyes.

The tuxedo-clad waiter hovered at his elbow, never showing by the slightest look or inflection that the younger of the two patrons was a far departure from the norm.

"Never mind." Simon waved the waiter away. "I've changed my mind."

About the pastry, perhaps, but not about the boy. The gut feeling was stronger that this one had the qualities he was searching for, the qualities he needed.

Simon McKinzie always searched, he always needed, and he never questioned gut feelings.

"So talk, kid," he growled as he settled deeper into the banquette. "Start with who you are."

The command was low, flat, not to be denied, and it never occurred to Mitchell Ryan to refuse, or to lie, or evade. In the peaceful quiet of the diner, and in the relative privacy of their remote corner, his story was told. Haltingly, at first, for a scion of the street was not accustomed to speaking of himself or at such great length.

Four cups of coffee later, a silent Simon McKinzie knew Mitchell Ryan was sixteen—as near as he could tell—and as unlikely a Cajun as he'd ever met. Perhaps because he was only part Cajun and had never lived the traditional Cajun life. His father, an Irish sailor, if he was ever there for more than conception, was long gone. His mother succumbed years ago to alcoholic poisoning and even before that, the street was the only home he ever remembered. He could read because he had taught himself, and he survived because he was as tough as he talked, and tougher than he looked.

"That leaves one question," Simon said when the boy fell silent.

"Just one?"

Simon ignored the brashness designed to cover the embarrassment that was common when the focus of his interest realized that he or she had said far more than they'd intended. "Just one, for now."

"For now."

"That's right."

"Okay." Mitchell rested his folded hands on the table. He had refused coffee or soft drink and was thirsty from the long story. A goblet of ice water with moisture beaded on its curving bowl nearly touched his fingertips, but he resisted temptation. "Ask away."

"Why did you try to steal my car?"

Mitchell laughed. "For the money I could get for it."

Silver hair caught the muted light as Simon nodded. "Why did you need the money?"

"That's question number two."

"So it is," Simon agreed, unperturbed

Mitchell unfolded his hands, stretched his cramped fingers, and folded them again. He hadn't spoken about the children.

It wasn't something he liked to talk about. He shrugged, looking for the first time like a belligerent juvenile. "I needed the money."

"Why?"

"I just needed it."

"How much?"

"Five hundred." His response was as rapid-fire as the question, and as startling to him. But Simon didn't give him time to think on it.

"Why?"

"For Billy." The dam that held back the truth cracked. "A ten-year-old kid. To get him out."

"Billy, but not yourself."

"No."

"What will happen to the kid now?"

Mitchell stared down at his hands. "I don't know."

"Yes, you do. What?"

"Something awful."

"What?"

This time Mitchell couldn't answer. He shook his head and never looked up from his hands.

Simon McKinzie was not of the streets, but he knew them better than he knew his own world. He didn't need a blueprint to know what would become of a ten-year-old boy in the dark side of any city. He didn't need to know exactly what purpose the money would serve. He wondered if the boy sitting across from him understood how futile his efforts might be. That for every child salvaged, another would fall.

Sighing wearily, he closed his eyes, but only for a second. Hiding did no good, for the truth was always there. Waiting. For him. For Mitchell Ryan. For the boy called Billy. "When is your deadline?"

"Midnight."

Without a moment of hesitation, Simon took out his wallet. Before he put it away again, five crisp bills and a switchblade lay on the table in front of Mitchell Ryan. "You don't have much time."

Mitchell's hand hovered over the money and the knife. He looked into those cool, waiting eyes. "What about your car? The cops?"

"Nothing happened to my car." Simon watched one emotion chase after another on the young face. He was gambling.

If he was wrong he would be five hundred dollars poorer. But he wasn't wrong about this one, he was sure of it. "All I need is your word you won't steal anymore. Do I have your word, Mitch? No matter what."

Behind them two glasses tapped in a melodic ring. A man murmured a question too hushed to be heard. A woman's sultry laugh was his answer.

Lovers.

Somewhere beyond Mitchell Ryan's world of squalor and deceit lay another world of trust and honor and love. Tonight Simon McKinzie had given him a glimpse of it.

"Yes, sir," he said softly, gratitude beyond words expressed in the respectful title. His hand closed over the money, and next the knife, as he made a pledge that wouldn't be broken. "You have my word."

Then Simon was alone. He smiled a rare smile as he spun a cup in its saucer. There were those among his critics who would adjudge the driving of a high-profile automobile to a clandestine meeting in a stinking alley the epitome of arrogance. But the car was window dressing, to influence enemies who understood the show of wealth more than words. If along the way it won a friend, this visit to New Orleans was more than successful. And the Jaguar had served his purpose twofold. Perhaps three.

He looked up as his would-be car thief threaded through scattered tables, oblivious of staring diners, back straight, head high, thoughts centered on more important matters than clothes or stares.

Simon watched as he disappeared into the night that hovered beyond the door. The rare smile became an even rarer grin.

A closed deal. A boy called Billy. And Mitchell Ryan.

Ah, yes, the Jag had served its purpose and more.

One

"Katherine Mary."

A nervous stallion screamed and reared, tearing free of his trainer's hold. Hooves pawed the sky, flashing in the sun. Parched Carolina clay lifted from the corral floor in a dusty haze, hovering in the air, waiting to settle in a gritty red stain.

"Katherine Mary, Gran wants you."

"Not now, Rose." The strained admonition came from a slender woman dressed in jeans and boots, as she darted under murderous hooves to grab a trailing bridle.

"Katherine Mary, she wants you now."

Katherine Mary wasn't listening. She was much too occupied with twelve hundred pounds of terrified horseflesh fighting like a tiger and threatening to trample everything in its path. Mainly Katherine Mary.

"Whoa, boy. Nobody's going to hurt you. Not here." For her promise she was rewarded by a violent toss of the Morgan's massive head, sending her flying into the corral gate. She was winded, and in an hour or so her ribs would be one big pain, but she held the reins.

"Whoa, Juggernaut. Whoa, boy." Her words took on the mood of a crooning chant. Her tone was low. She might have been calming a baby, even as she dug her heels into the dust and fought. "Nobody's going to hurt you, not here."

"Katherine Mary, you'd better finish with that creature soon, or Gran's going to be in a snit."

"I'll be there when I can, Rose." She didn't look at the woman, dressed in chiffon and lace, fluttering by the fence like the incongruous flower that named her. To look away would be suicide.

The horse screamed again and tried his best to dislodge the woman dangling beneath his great neck, but the flower at the fence didn't notice.

"You know how upset she gets." A delicate hankie was plucked from the nether regions where a bosom should have been, and dabbed eloquently at a patrician nose. "Mercy! How do you stand the dust? A gentlewoman like you."

Juggernaut didn't think she was a gentlewoman. He obviously considered her a scourge to be crushed until she was an indistinguishable part of Polk County soil. It didn't help that he reacted to Rose's voice as he would a wasp.

Another toss sent his nemesis into the fence again, and though she couldn't breath again for what seemed forever, Katherine Mary Rivard held on. Grimly, as she pitted her slight weight against the rampaging animal, she wondered whatever had possessed her to agree to train him.

"My word! He is upset, isn't he? Almost as upset as Gran will be."

The horse reacted as Katherine Mary expected. This time she was ready, and this time she avoided the fence. "Go back to the house, Rose. I'll be along in a minute."

"How long is a minute, Katherine Mary?"

"Dammit, Rose," the younger woman snapped. "Go back to the house. Now!"

"You needn't be rude." With a sniff and a wave of her handkerchief the stick-thin woman with a washboard figure rambled back to the white-columned mansion.

"Rude? Ha! Try desperate, Auntie Rose." Grumbling under her breath, aware that later she would have to say twelve self-imposed Hail Marys to appease her conscience, Katherine Mary dug her heels a little deeper into the fabled red clay. Clay that still billowed, threatening to abscond to the neighboring county before the drought ended. Hell, from the looks of it, all her precious soil might well join the mists that painted the distant mountains and gave them their name. Wouldn't that be something? The Blue Ridge Mountains dressed in clay red. "I'll worry about that later, after I figure out how to let this equine freight train go."

"Talking to yourself, brat?" A new, very deep, very masculine voice drawled the question.

"No, Cam." She didn't look at the owner of this voice, either, for she knew exactly what Cameron Halsey, neighbor and lifelong friend, would be doing. She could picture his familiar face and hard, lean body perfectly as he lounged against a rail of the corral, his Stetson hat pushed to the back of his head, a devilish grin on his face. "I'm not talking to myself, I'm talking to Juggernaut."

"That's his name, huh?" Laughter rolled across the corral. "Fits, wouldn't you say? Almost as well as Jughead would."

"You enjoying this, Halsey?" She barely missed the fence again as the horse lunged left then right in a sly move calculated to set her on her rump.

"Nah, just wondering how many ribs you broke this time."

"None. Yet."

"Let's keep it that way." Cam vaulted the fence. His weight and strength added to hers quieted the tiring horse. Before it could gather a new head of steam, he tucked a bandanna into the bridle, blinding the wild, rolling eyes. "There." Then, with the keen appreciation of a knowledgeable horse trainer, "He's a beauty. When did you get him?"

"Someone from the consortium dropped him off this morning. He has a few bad habits that need to be broken."

"Yep." Cam Halsey grunted at the understatement. But if anyone could break these few bad habits, it was the woman at his side. "So, where are we taking him?"

"Last stall on the right."

Even blinded, the Morgan fought, but not so fiercely.

"What do you think the ladies want?" Cam asked when the beast was safely deposited in the barn.

"Only heaven and the ladies know. But I'm thinking seriously of changing my name. If I hear Rose say Katherine Mary one more time I'll . . ."

"What?" Cam grinned. "Run away from home? That'll be the day. Where would the revered Stone Meadow Farm and Rivard Stables be without your sweet nubile arms to hold it up?"

"At the moment my arms, which feel as if they've been jerked out of their sockets, which aren't sweet and haven't been nubile for a heck of a long time, don't care."

"That'll be the day." He pushed his hat back a degree and grinned the grin that promised mischief. "Anyway, turning thirty ain't so old. Your arms are just as nubile as they were when you were sixteen and every boy from six counties dreamed of a tussle in the hayloft."

Katherine Mary Rivard laughed as she was meant to, even though it set up a new ache in each of her ribs. At least Juggernaut got both sides, and when the color bloomed she would have a matched set. Something to think about other than her conscience and the growing list of Hail Marys. At least heck was a cheapie. "Ask me how nubile I feel tomorrow when this thirty-year-old body is declaring it's a century old."

Cam sobered at that. "You work too hard, Katherine Mary, and those sweet old things moldering in that great white elephant of a house can't see it. The little twit over at Saint Mary's School for more little twits doesn't care. Nor the playboy down in the islands."

At the oblique mention of her errant father, Katherine held up a staying hand and he stopped.

"Okay, I know I'd better not get started on your family and you've been summoned for an audience. Go on along. I'll finish up for you here, the Son of Satan and I should do fine. Just traipse on up to the big house and see what else they want to put off on you." His voice dropped to a low, sexy whisper as he leaned close. "But don't let anybody tell you that you ain't nubile."

"Thanks." She flashed him a smile and walked with him from the barn. Halfway across the curving drive that led to what had been the service entrance, she turned to get in the last word. Walking backward she called, "Help yourself to a nice sprig of hay to carry in your teeth, Cam. To complete the hayseed role you've adopted for the day."

Cameron Halsey laughed. "Scat, brat, your great-grandma is waiting."

"When did this happen?" With her fair hair caught in a clasp and still damp from her shower, Katherine Mary Rivard paced from window to window. Her long legs clad in tight fawn

trousers and tall black boots made short work of the great ex-
panse. In the unseasonable heat, a perfectly laundered white
shirt clung to her shoulders as she hooked her thumbs beneath
the wide belt at her waist to ease her arms.

This was not the rough dress she'd worn in the corral. She
would no more come to Gran with a red film of dust clinging
to her clothing, than she would with the sweat of her labor
turning it to mud on her body. "When, exactly, did Jocie decide to skip school again?"

"She didn't return for classes following spring break."

Katherine spun from the window, turning her back on
parched rolling hills that should have been brilliantly green with
a thick stand of new spring grass. Perfectly erect and unbending, Gran watched her from her wheelchair. With a will of iron,
Jocelyn Rivard refused to allow the arthritis that twisted her
hands and feet into useless malformed lumps to reduce her to
a crouching, mewling hunchback. Medical science would say
that her will had nothing to do with her untouched spine. But
Katherine decided long ago that medical science simply didn't
understand the Rivard will.

"Jocie's been missing for two months this time and I haven't
been told?"

"You had enough on your mind. I didn't want to worry you
with anything else." No emphatic gesture accompanied the
statement; Gran kept her hands tucked beneath an ever-present
lap robe.

"And, of course, you haven't called the police."

"Indeed, I haven't. When the school called, I engaged the
private detective."

"There's less chance of a scandal that way."

"Don't be smart, Katherine Mary. You haven't been guardian of this family's good name for three-quarters of a century,
as I have. In nine years I will be one hundred years old, and I
intend to live every one of those years with a clear name. When
I'm dead and gone, I expect you to continue my stewardship."

If she hadn't been so worried about her younger sister,
Katherine would have laughed. Gran knew as well as she that
the Rivard closets were so full of skeletons they would need to
build an additional wing to house any new occupants. "So, has
your detective found Jocie?"

"Not exactly. He knows that when she left here after the holiday she went to New Orleans rather than reporting for classes. Then she disappeared. There's been no trace of her."

Katherine felt sick. Every terrible thing that could happen to an adventurous and attractive teenager crashed down on her. Dropping into a chair, she fought a sense of dread that this time was different. More than a lark.

"I've contacted an old friend of the family," Jocelyn continued. "He has given me the name of someone who can help us. Simon does something dangerous and secret for the government, and he assures me that if Jocie can be found, his young man can do it."

"Wouldn't it be simpler to call the police for once?"

"No!" The old voice shook with her denial.

"Gran..."

"There's nothing the police can do that Simon's young man can't do better."

Katherine was disturbed by the violence of the objection. To force the issue could make serious inroads on the precarious health of this proud tyrant. She was shackled again by the stiff-necked pride of a dying heritage. But pride and heritage aside, she was a great-granddaughter and a sister, and she loved both. Putting the welfare of one over the other was more than she could bring herself to do. Jocie had been missing two months, she could only pray this delay wasn't disastrous.

"All right." She agreed by choosing compromise. "No police. We'll let your friend's young man try first. But, if after a sensible time he's found nothing, scandal or not, I will call the authorities, Gran."

"We'll decide that when the time comes."

"It isn't open to discussion. *I've* decided."

Jocelyn Rivard was unaccustomed to having her decisions challenged. But when she looked at Katherine, she recognized the same unbending determination that had been her own strength as matriarch of the Rivard empire. She hadn't intended relinquishing control, but perhaps it was time. And who better than this strong, spirited woman? Slowly she inclined her head, the nod was brief yet signified a momentous change. "As you wish, Katherine Mary."

Katherine was too caught up in her own distress to note the rare compliance. Abruptly she left her seat, it seemed wicked to be idle when her sister might need her. Might have needed her many times over the past two months. "I'll call this young man, I'll call him tonight."

"It isn't quite that simple." Jocelyn was startled by the heat of a blush. She wasn't accustomed to making explanations or excuses.

"I don't understand. Why isn't it that simple?" Katherine was shocked to realize her great-grandmother was uncomfortable. "What's the problem?"

"Simon only suggested that he might help us. In fact, he won't want to help. He'll have to be persuaded."

"How?"

"It's obvious, isn't it? He's staying outside Madison—that's less than a three-hour drive away. You simply have to go there and convince him. Take along an overnight bag, in case he's stubborn."

Katherine felt as if the world were tumbling in on her. She had responsibilities on the farm. If they were not met, it would affect many lives, as well as Jocie's. Perhaps the farm itself. "Gran, I don't see how—"

"It will work out. I've invited Cameron for dessert. Daisy made his favorite, and I'm sure that between us we can prevail upon him to see to our needs while you're away."

"I'm sure, too, but—"

"We can discuss this later, with Cameron. At the moment, Justin's flowers are holding dinner for us. Who knows, my dear, maybe all of this will look less black on a full stomach."

"Who knows? I think I do," Katherine muttered as she dutifully rolled the wheelchair toward the dining room, where Justin Rivard's flowers would be waiting. She wondered if giving his daughters their silly names was Jocelyn's son's one small rebellion against his mother. After all, most male members of the Rivard family bolted, in one way or another as her own father had, until there were only the women of four generations remaining at the mansion.

Gran, one daughter, three granddaughters, a resident great-granddaughter, and one missing. An insular lot with more eccentricities than Webster had words.

Katherine's shoulders were throbbing as she crossed the halfway mark of the long hall. Her ribs were aching by the time she passed the parlor. She wondered what more could occur to remind of her weighty responsibilities. When she crossed the dining room threshold to be greeted by the worried but hopeful and trusting smiles of Rose and Daisy and Violet, Justin Rivard's flowers, and his sister Bea, she knew.

Silently, wearily, she promised to make the world right again for all of them. "I'll pack tonight, and be on my way by dawn tomorrow."

Mitch Ryan laid down his hammer as the thrum of a heavy engine grew louder. Wiping sweat from his forehead with the band at his wrist, he shaded his eyes and waited for the lumbering car to round the last curve that led into the valley. His canny ear told him the approaching vehicle was a Rolls-Royce, an old one, thirty years or older. It moved as if the driver were unfamiliar with the rough mountain roads.

A glance at a hammocklike contraption hanging still and quietly from a nearby tree assured him all was well on that front, even though painted Indians skulked through the forest. Judging the speed of the oncoming vehicle, there would be time enough to worry about security once he caught a glimpse of who had come calling.

Collecting his tools from the grass, he put them away. His project lacked only the finishing touches, something he could see to in a matter of minutes. As soon as the impending intrusion was over.

That time was closer now, for the car was almost at the drive that led to the cabin. Mitch felt a small twinge of satisfaction that he'd been right. The Rolls sedan was a vintage model, thirty-five years old and well-preserved. The pearl gray finish was sleek and gleaming, even beneath a film of road dust. The woman at the wheel remained only a profile against the backdrop of the lowering sun, until she stepped from the car and strode across the drive.

She was tall and slender and younger than the Rolls. Her tawny hair was trapped in a no-nonsense coil at her neck, the severe jacket and skirt she wore were more suitable for a business meeting than an afternoon visit. Above the pristine drape of her creamy blouse her tawny features were exotic and striking, rather than pretty. As she moved closer, in an easy, long-limbed stride, with sun glistening on hair ribboned by varying hues of gold, Mitch decided pretty was far too mild to describe this woman.

Looking every inch the gracious gentlewoman, she approached the silent, watching man, stopping at the edge of the lawn where grass met loose gravel. "I'm sorry to disturb you, but I'm afraid I've lost my way. I was looking for McKinzie's Valley."

Despite an alarm that scratched at his nerves, Mitch decided he liked her voice. It was calm and composed and reminded him of a peaceful stream rippling over smooth stones. Chances were likely the alarm was no more than an occupational hazard. An overreaction to a perfectly innocent situation. After all, the whole area referred to this as McKinzie's Valley.

He wouldn't look for trouble. Yet.

"You haven't lost your way. In fact, you're right on target." A flick of his wrist directed her attention to the lake with mountains seeming to rise out of it, forests dressed in bright new foliage, and weathered cabins with shiny tin roofs. The McKinzie and Canfield cabins, identical, except in age, sitting side by side and surrounded by the gardens Raven Canfield tended. "This is McKinzie's Valley."

A small frown sketched a line between brows that arched like wings over cool gray eyes. "I'm trying to find a gentleman. A Mr. Ryan."

"You've found him, though few call me mister and no one has ever accused me of being a gentleman." Mitch put down the last tool and slipped into his shirt. Another alarm was sounding even as he counseled caution. Some of the local citizens knew his name and that he was the current occupant of the cabin adjacent to David and Raven Canfield's. He couldn't think why this regal woman would be looking for him, unless it was to deliver a message from the Canfields who were away for a day or so. No need to make an incident out of an innocent visit. "So, what can I do for you, Mrs...."

"It's Miss." She put in quickly. "Miss Katherine Mary Rivard."

On closer inspection he saw that the gold circlet on her left hand was embellished by a family crest. She would be one of Raven's customers, he decided. One of the wealthier collectors of the famed McCandless pottery. Smiling at the rightness of it, given the Rolls, her clothing and her manner, he bowed slightly. "What can I do for you, Miss Katherine Mary Rivard?"

Katherine's frown deepened before her rigid training asserted itself and her expression returned to the remote calm with which she faced the strangers of the world. But inside, doubt seethed. She wasn't sure of this. Not sure at all. Gran had driven into her that this man was dangerous.

Capable, but dangerous.

As she looked at him now, with the evening sun bearing down on him, turning his auburn hair to dark flame, he seemed lean and fit. A glimpse of his body before he'd slipped on his shirt assured he was as hard as Cam, or any of the temporary hands she sometimes needed on the farm. But dangerous?

Hardly, with his easy way and his quick smile. Particularly not surrounded by newly constructed playground equipment. Definitely not with a baby's bottle tucked in the hip pocket of his jeans.

"This must be a bizarre coincidence. I'm looking for Mitchell Ryan. He works with Simon McKinzie, and Mr. McKinzie sent me to him."

"I'm Mitchell Ryan, Miss Rivard." The alarms were screaming now, and not to be ignored. The change in Mitch was immediate and startling. The smile vanished. The easy manner was lost in a coil of tension. Sherry eyes that had sparkled with laughter, were hard and piercing as he glanced with a watchful gaze around him. There was menace in his quiet voice as he took a step forward. "Why don't you tell me who really sent you and why?"

"I beg your pardon?" Katherine took a step back. All the danger she doubted smoldered like a volcano. And it was directed at her. "There must be some misunderstanding."

"Not a misunderstanding, Miss Rivard. A mistake." Mitch took another step; his hand closed over her arm before she could back away. "You made it."

"What do you mean?" She didn't scream, for there was no one to hear. She didn't try to pull free of his grasp, for intuition told her the effort would be wasted.

"You're a cool one, aren't you?" Mitch had to admire her composure. She didn't show by even a grimace that his fingers were driving into her lightly muscled arm. For all the reaction she allowed herself, strange men might rough her up as a matter of course every day of her life. "Yeah, you're cool, all right, and a good little actress with your impeccable poise." His eyes narrowed, his grip tightened, and drew absolutely no response. "Sorry, your ladyship, your act didn't work, so why don't you tell me why you're really here."

"I just told you." Her tone was low, unruffled. An undaunted princess under siege, refusing to yield.

"Of course you did. Except Simon McKinzie wouldn't send you here. Not to me, and not now."

"If you are Mitchell Ryan, then Simon McKinzie sent me. Here. Now."

"You're a liar, Miss Rivard. A self-possessed, stunning liar, and a foolish one."

Katherine stood immobile in his hold. The change in him was startling and frightening, but if she could stifle her fear to pacify a half ton of rage on the hoof, surely she could deal with an angry man. "I have a letter."

"Sure you do," Mitch mocked.

"It's in my purse, in the car."

"Naturally."

The guttural snarl and the fierce eyes would have overwhelmed her struggle for serenity, but a move on the edge of the clearing caught Katherine's attention and her fear evaporated. "There's no need in this farce, Mr. Ryan."

"You think I'm joking, your ladyship?"

"No." She shook her head deliberately. "I don't think you're joking, but we both know you aren't going to harm me, so why don't you release my arm before you break it? Then I can get the letter from my purse, and we can get on with the purpose of my visit."

The lady had no quit in her. In another circumstance she would be an admirable adversary. "I said you were a cool one, now you're an arrogant bluff in the bargain."

"Not arrogant, Mr. Ryan. And not bluffing," she added pleasantly. "Just confident that you won't harm me."

Mitch moved a step closer, until his body brushed hers as he glowered down at her. "Suppose you tell me the reason for this great confidence?"

"You're the reason. You, plus the fact that there's a baby in the hammock, and two boys standing behind you watching every move you make." She lifted a questioning brow. "Your children, I assume, Mr. Ryan?"

He didn't look around as she'd expected he would. His gaze remained riveted on her. "No, Miss Rivard, not my children, but my charges and your salvation. For the time being." Releasing her, his hands palms up, signaling a small and temporary peace, he backed away. "Get your letter. If it's authentic, I'll listen to the explanation for your visit. If it isn't—" his expression was hard and unforgiving "—then you'll have more than a few questions to answer. And not just to me."

Turning his back on her, he walked away, signaling for the boys at the edge of the tree line to come to him. Katherine watched and found herself smiling as they descended on him with a fierceness that complemented fringed costumes and painted faces. Mitchell Ryan might be a dangerous man, but not to her, and not to the gleeful, make-believe braves he caught up in his arms.

Ignoring new aches added to those inflicted by Juggernaut with her customary stoicism, she was still smiling as she turned back to the Rolls. For the first time she'd begun to have hope for the wisdom of Gran's choice.

Katherine stood in front of shelves filled with a collection of pottery. Some were large. Some small. Some were white on white, some pure black, some painted. Each was unique. Through a favorite gallery in Tryon, she had learned of Raven McCandless and her work, and she recognized the dogwood blossom on each as her signature.

Mitchell Ryan had indicated this was the Canfield cabin, now she had a vague recollection that Raven McCandless had married a few years ago. Obviously this was her home. From a bedroom down the hall, the murmur of Mitchell Ryan's voice was punctuated by the giggles of her children as he read bedtime stories. Bath time had been even more fun as Simon and Colin, seven and five respectively, launched a campaign to keep their war paint intact. Tiny, baby Rhea, who was less than a year, spurred them on with her infectious giggles.

"Why doesn't it surprise me that the children won?" she wondered out loud as she moved to the window to look out over the lake.

"Maybe because a blind woman could see I'm a pushover for kids."

Katherine spun to face him. He'd taken the time to change after the boys' exuberant bath, and in khakis and a jade green shirt, he was most attractive. "Yes, Mr. Ryan." A smile tugged at her mouth at her droll double entendre. "A blind woman could see that."

"Since we've declared peace, could we try for less formality? Most folks call me Mitch."

Katherine laughed. "I'm afraid most folks call me Katherine Mary."

"A bit much, isn't it?"

"You should try listening to it for what seems a thousand times a day."

From servants? Mitch wondered. Old and faithful retainers waiting anxiously to do her bidding? "Then why don't we settle on simply Katherine, for the time being?"

"I'd like that." She gestured to the hall and the bedrooms beyond. "Will the baby sleep again so soon?"

"She'll sleep. I gave her another bottle, and she's tired. She was born dangerously prematurely. To make up for it she eats often and well, and sleeps most of the time. Little Rhea is a miracle baby, and one day she's going to be the belle of the countryside."

"And the Canfields trust you with their miracle baby?"

"This has been a rough time for Raven, and the boys are a handful themselves to say the least. David wanted to give her a break and I was available. They'll be back tomorrow morning."

Katherine held her tongue, but with what she'd seen and heard she suspected it was much more than availability that prompted the Canfields' trust.

"Enough about the children." He waved her to a chair and took one himself. "Tell me again about the letter, Katherine, and how you came to know Simon."

"Mr. Ryan . . . Mitchell . . ." Then, with an exasperated sigh, "Mitch, I've told you, I don't know Simon McKinzie. I'd never heard of him until yesterday when my grandmother, actually, my great-grandmother, brought up his name. He's obviously a very good friend of the family. It seems strange, even to me, that I would never have heard of such a friend. But no matter how many times you ask, nor how many different ways you phrase it, I still have not."

Not so strange, and more convincing that she was telling the truth, Mitch thought. Not strange at all when one knew Simon and understood the nature of his work. The nature of Mitch Ryan's work, as well.

He picked up the letter lying on a table where he'd tossed it the last time he'd read it. Simon had introduced Katherine Mary Rivard and asked, not commanded, that he help find her sister. Simon wouldn't command that he search for the child, especially not in the underbelly of a city he hated.

Especially not now.

"I'm sorry." He tossed the letter back on the table. "You've made the trip for nothing. I can't help you, Katherine."

"Can't, or won't?" Her cool gray gaze watched him.

"Does it matter?"

"I don't suppose it does." She reached for the letter, crumpling it in her hand. "Except to Jocie, and Gran."

"But not to you?"

"It matters to me," she admitted. "It matters a great deal, but I'm not the important one. And now I have to make a choice between them."

"Explain." He was puzzled by the sad resignation he heard.

"No." She stood, tucking the tattered paper in her purse. "You've made your decision. What I do now, the choices I have to make and their consequences are none of your business."

"Explain anyway."

"I have to be going. It will be dark soon and I don't know the roads. I didn't intend to be so late, but there were problems that delayed my departure at home, then there was the difficulty finding the valley."

"Sit down, Katherine Mary." His quiet insistence allowed no room for refusal. "Explain what you mean by choosing between them."

"It's a long story."

"I have all night."

"Perhaps you do, but I have to go."

"Why?" he asked implacably.

"Because I don't want to travel unfamiliar roads in the dark."

"Too late." He pointed a finger at the window and a mountain bathed in fiery light. "The sun will drop behind that range long before you can climb out of the valley."

Katherine shrugged. "I still have to go."

"Why?"

He was beginning to sound like a broken record. "There are people at Stone Meadow who depend on me, and I have obligations to meet."

"Dependents?" he mocked, but not scornfully. "Is that what you call your servants? And is it your obligation to give them their daily agenda?"

Katherine looked at him with astonishment written on her face. "Servants?" she muttered. "Daily agenda?" She shook her head, then she laughed. She laughed until her ribs ached, and her heart. Tears gathered in her eyes and sparkled on her lashes, but she wouldn't let them fall.

When she reached in her purse for a handkerchief, Mitch Ryan was there first, staying her hand, offering a handkerchief of his own.

"I'm sorry," she murmured as she accepted it. "I didn't expect the tears."

"Who are your dependents?" he asked softly. "What are your obligations?" The light was fading, only a lamp in the window held back the darkness. In its softer light her pale hair gleamed like a halo, and she seemed fragile and far more vulnerable than in the sunlight. Taking her unresisting hand he led her back to her seat. "You've told me about your grandmother and your sister. Now I want to hear about you."

"This isn't about me."

"Isn't it?" He sat by her. "The Rivards are a family, aren't they?"

"Yes, of course we are."

"Who is the center of that family?"

"Gran, of course. She's been our mainstay for seventy-five years."

"Has she? Is she?" He was watching her closely, noting every nuance, every rare, unconscious gesture. "Who keeps the household going? Who manages the farmhands and the servants?"

"Haven't you figured out yet that there are no servants and no farmhands? At least, not on a regular basis."

"All right, then, who bears the brunt of caring for the house and farm? Your gran is how old?"

"Ninety-one."

"Surely she doesn't work the farm."

"Of course she doesn't!"

"Then who does? Who sees to the crops and the meadows? I assume there are meadows at Stone Meadow, and animals to graze them. Who tends these animals?"

"I do," Katherine answered automatically. Then with a deprecating shrug she added, "There's no one else who can."

"Then this is about you and choices, and whether or not I will help you find your sister."

"Whether or not?" She looked up quickly from her hands folded quietly in her lap. "But you said—"

"I know what I said, Katherine. But now I want to hear about you and your family, before I make my decision final."

"Why would you change your mind?"

"Let's just say I have a passion for families, and yours sounds, shall we say, interesting."

"Eccentric would be a more accurate description."

"That sounds even better."

Katherine couldn't believe what she was hearing. It made no sense that he would reverse an adamant refusal on the flimsy excuse that she was the center of her family and he liked families.

The world was full of families, good ones, bad ones, and weird ones. Like the Rivards. Mitchell Ryan probably came from a huge family. And judging from his fondness for children, he would one day add to it.

A glance at the window warned that night was settling in in earnest now. But if there was even the slightest chance she could truly change his mind . . .

Her decision was made on a half-finished thought. "What do you want to know?"

"Everything."

Mitchell set his second cup of tea down and laughed. "He really did it? Justin Rivard, who had a sister named Bea, really named his children Rose, Daisy, and Violet?"

"He really did." Katherine grinned and brushed her loose hair from her face. At one point in her rambling and confusing story of her family, Mitchell Ryan had leaned over, plucked the single pin from it, commented that she looked more comfortable, then without missing a second beat, motioned for her to continue her tale of the mistakes and misadventures of the Rivards. "Gran was always so overbearing, I suspect it was his own small rebellion."

"There were other rebellions?"

"Heavens, yes! Justin's brother, who was my grandfather, Maxwell. And his wife, Katherine."

"Katherine, for whom you are named." He ticked off facts of her fascinating and convoluted family history, one by one. "Who hated your maternal grandmother, Mary, for whom you are also named. Who returned Katherine's hatred, until she and Maxwell absconded to South America never to be heard of again."

"As did a number of male and female Rivards in between. Abscond, that is, but not to South America."

"Some like the islands. As Lawrence Rivard and wife number . . ."

"I haven't the foggiest," Katherine said. "My father stopped informing us long ago. In fact none of us has had more than the erratic postcard since a month after our mother, Sylvia, was killed in a fall at a steeplechase thirteen years ago."

"Each event leaving you with the sole responsibility of caring for an aged tyrant, four dotty, old-maid aunts, and a baby sister. Now baby sister, at the wise old age of sixteen, has decided to decamp in the way of all the rebellious Rivards."

"Yes."

Mitch heard the pain she struggled to hide. Katherine Mary Rivard wasn't into playing the martyr. Sliding his cup aside, he stood. "It's late and you're tired. I assume you have luggage in the Rolls?"

"I packed a bag in case this took longer than I hoped."

"Give me your keys. I'll get it, then show you to your room."

"Show me to my room!" Her genteel calm slipped completely. "I can't stay here!"

"Of course you can. The roads are dark and unfamiliar and it's a long way into town. Besides that, where would you be safer? You said yourself that I wouldn't hurt you. Who knows, I might even help you."

Forestalling argument, he turned and left the room, closing the door carefully behind him. His footsteps faded from the porch and the stairs before the elegant, patrician Katherine Mary Rivard managed to close her mouth.

Two

Mitch Ryan drove well, as a simonized car thief should. The interstate was relatively straight and sparsely traveled in the midafternoon hours. With only the rhythmic clack of seamed concrete and the thrum of the engine filling the Rolls with their sound, he was afforded the luxury of a wandering mind.

His mind wandered to the woman who rode by his side.

Since she'd graciously yielded to his suggestion that he take the heavy automobile through the unfamiliar mountainous roads, she'd spoken little. Then, only in response to his questions. Yet her silence wasn't sullen or aloof, but introspective. Mitch suspected she was thinking of her sister, searching for reasons that might have prompted the girl's disappearance. He anticipated the direction of her thoughts.

"It wasn't your fault, you know."

Katherine turned from her study of passing scenery. "I beg your pardon?"

"It isn't your fault Jocie decided to take off," he explained in more specific terms.

"You can't know that," she said simply, returning to her review of the outside world.

Her hair was in that damnable knot at her nape again, a wealth of gleaming gold held by the single pin. When she turned back to the scenery, his fingers itched to pluck the spearlike adornment from it, letting it spill over her shoulders as it had in the evening shadows of the Canfield cabin. Instead he kept his hands firmly on the steering wheel and argued gently. "But I do. You wouldn't deliberately do anything that would drive your sister away."

"You don't know me, Mr. Ryan. You have no idea what I might or might not do."

"You're right, I don't know you very well, and I don't know what you might or might not do in a lot of circumstances. But in this one I know."

She faced him then, skepticism lying in her gray eyes. "Suppose you tell me the reason for this great confidence, Mr. Ryan."

Mitch saw the weariness that prompted him to suggest he drive at least as much as the unfamiliar roads, then refuse to relinquish the wheel later. She looked as if she'd slept only fitfully in days, but she probably wouldn't appreciate any comment on the observation. He smiled, realizing he knew her far better than either had realized. The smile turned to a chuckle as he realized, too, that she'd given back his own challenging words.

Katherine Mary was a wily woman and would, indeed, be an admirable adversary.

"That's twice," he murmured. Twice he'd thought of her as an adversary, but only in the kindest terms. The most intriguing terms.

"Twice?" Bewilderment joined skepticism and fatigue.

"Twice you've called me Mr. Ryan, and after our truce." It wasn't exactly a lie, just a small segue to the left of the truth.

"All right, suppose you tell me the reason for this great confidence, *Mitch.*"

If she hadn't been so worried, and so deadly serious, he might have laughed out loud. She would be interesting as well as admirable.

"You. You're the reason," he heard himself repeating her words as she had his. Then he added his own. "Plus my own primal instinct. I have a lot to learn about you, Katherine, but that much I know already. Until you prove me wrong, I'll trust in my judgment, in instinct. And in you."

She drew a long, slow breath, and with a nearly imperceptible nod, returned to the scenery flashing by. Both were going on faith, each believing the other to be the person he and she presumed. She hadn't been so quick to trust in years. Not since the early times when Gran's battle against arthritis was finally lost, and she'd assumed the management of Stone Meadow. When, at seventeen, she'd begun a thirteen-year odyssey of learning by trial, error and disappointment that it never paid to trust without caution.

Yet she'd thrown caution aside, putting Jocie's and Gran's lives, and ultimately her own, in Mitch Ryan's hands. She believed in him. She'd proven that to herself by staying the night in a cabin with a man who should have been a stranger, but was not. She'd trusted her own instincts then. She must trust them now.

"I'm going with you." Her refined voice rippled through an incipient hush.

"What?" Startled, drawn from his thoughts of the woman he was coming to know, he glanced from the road. It was his time to question, though not as politely as Katherine. "What the hell did you say?"

"I'm going with you," she said. "To New Orleans, to find my sister."

"You can't. There's no need."

"I have to."

"I can work better without you, Katherine, and there's no reason for you to go."

"I won't get in your way, and there is a reason."

He felt the cool gaze on him. Whatever the reason for her decision, it wouldn't be frivolous, and she wouldn't be easily dissuaded. "All right, let's open this for discussion."

"There's no need for discussion. I've made the decision."

"It's your dime, lady." Mitch shrugged. He'd heard of steel butterflies, but he'd never encountered one. Now he had. Later, when he understood her conviction, there would be time enough to dissuade her. "If you would indulge me, I'd like to hear your reasons."

"I have none, beyond a strong feeling that I'll be needed. We both believe in intuition. Call it that, or premonition."

"You'll be needed at home."

"Yes, I will, but I'll be needed more where you're going."

"Katherine." His hand tightened on the steering wheel. He would spare her what was coming, if he could. "It might be ugly. Worse than ugly. You have no concept of how bad it can be."

"Perhaps I haven't, but that doesn't matter."

"Don't." He couldn't bear for the grimness of his world to touch her. The world he hoped he'd left behind him. The very sight of it would taint her, sicken her. When she knew he was one of its citizens, he would sicken her.

Dear God, Kate, don't go. Please don't. The plea scourged his mind and was on the tip of his tongue when she silenced it forever.

"Jocie will need me. I feel it. I know it as surely as I know myself. If I'm not there I'll be failing her. By failing Jocie, I'll be failing Gran." She looked at him, their glances colliding for an instant, then moving away. "I'm afraid it would mean tragedy in the end. For all of us."

Mitch had no quarrel for that. Neither conscience nor common sense would allow it. Strong feelings such as Katherine's, gut instincts that recognized neither conscience nor reason, had saved his life more times than he cared to count. Matthew Sky, his sometime partner, always his friend, had taught him to believe in them. Had proven them. Now Mitch would let nothing dissuade him, not when the feeling was so strong. Neither would she.

He wouldn't try. Not now, not later. Katherine would be going with him.

"My plan was to be away by tomorrow," he said, accepting her decision once and forever. "I can delay for another day."

"There's no need. I can be ready tomorrow."

"What about the farm?"

"I can see to that easily enough. I've never defaulted on an agreement, this time I will. I'll explain. If that isn't good enough, so be it."

"Katherine, are you sure?"

"I'm sure." The worry was still in her voice, but now it was tempered by a ring of relief. The delay, the helplessness, had exacted its price, now the promise of positive action renewed her. "As sure as I've ever been of anything."

Once again he couldn't argue, once again he wouldn't try.

The habitual silence fell like a veil between them. For another half hour they rode side by side, surrounded by preserved splendor, each lost in private thought. The terrain changed from gradual slope to steep incline. The widely swinging, curving sort that made nervous novices cringe and truckers curse while the stench of burning brakes fouled the air.

The Rolls rushed along, hugging curves as it was built to do.

With this one last spectacular drop, they were moving another level down a geological staircase into the foothills. The retreating mountains were awash in a tender green sea of deciduous and evergreen, abounding with red maple and creamy dogwood. Valleys grew broader and more frequent. The ever-present mist scattered.

The view was awesome and stirring, but Katherine didn't seem to notice even as she stared out at it.

Mitch had decided that she almost certainly had no idea where they were when she proved him wrong by rousing from her preoccupation.

"The next exit is ours. Take it, then turn right," she directed. "A few more miles and we'll be on Stone Meadow property."

The interstate had been relatively quiet, but the roads she directed him through next were pastoral in comparison. Though they were paved and well-groomed at first, then later unpaved and still well-groomed, each seemed to wander aimlessly, without destination. Sometimes zigging between trees, other times circling a rounded hillock. Once, they splashed across a brook, a shallow one, but flowing water nevertheless. Mitch cringed at the idea of the fine old machine wallowing in sand and mud nearly to its hubcaps, but Katherine didn't turn a hair. No more than if taking the venerable antique for a quick dip was a common occurrence. Eventually even Mitch had to admit the Rolls took it in stride and never lost the tune of its lovely hum.

When they'd traveled a quarter of an hour with no sign of traffic, after the third hillock, the second narrow bridge, and another brook, he had to ask. "How much farther before we get to Stone Meadow?"

She looked at him in astonishment. "I thought you knew. We've been on Rivard land since we made the last turn."

"Katherine, that was miles ago."

"Yes."

"You own miles of land?"

"I suppose we do. I've never thought of it in terms of miles, we count it in acres."

"Pastures, farmland, forest. Miles or acres, whatever, still a lot of it."

"Don't forget stone," she added dryly. "Tons of stone. Most has been removed over the years, but if you look, there is still plenty lying about. Stone Meadow is not a misnomer."

"I believe we've dodged every one of them."

Something like a smile flitted over her somber features. "Maybe." Then she admitted, "There is a more direct and more civilized route to the house, but an hour farther."

"You're anxious to get home, to see about Gran and Justin's flowers, thus the shortcut through pastureland."

"They were worried when I left. By now they'll be frantic."

From her vivid description of stoic Jocelyn Rivard, Mitch doubted the grandam of the Rivards would ever be frantic. At least, not for public observation. The dotty old ladies, who sounded utterly wonderful to him, would be another matter.

"Much farther now?" he asked. "Just as a matter of interest."

"Only a bit." Her gaze was ranging over the terrain, the keeper of the land inspecting her sprawling legacy.

A hell of a legacy. A hell of a burden with no servants and only occasional farmhands. Mitch wondered how she did it. How any one human being could.

He looked around, admiring what he saw. Admiring Katherine. "The way the land lies is beautiful."

"There should be grass. Tall, rich grass, not this puny, brittle straw. There would be cattle here, and horses, but when the drought got so bad, the tenant gave up his lease."

"Then you don't tend all this?"

"We maintain the fences, seeing to their repair and paint. Beyond that, no. We keep little for our own use." Her laugh was humorless. "The Rivards haven't been true people of the land for years."

Keeping miles of fence in this excellent condition wouldn't be as simple as she made it sound. He wondered what hidden talents lay beneath the suit as classic as yesterday's. What hopeless yearnings did she hold in the brave heart beating its steady rhythm beneath a demure jabot?

"But you'd like to be a person of the land," he ventured. "You would be, if things were different."

"There's nothing I'd like better than to see Rivard cattle standing belly deep in grass, and Rivard horses racing along fences."

"Maybe someday you will."

"Maybe."

She didn't believe it. He heard the wry note in her voice. She retreated again, as was her habit, and they bumped along in a cloud of dust. The immaculate Rolls wouldn't be immaculate by the time they reached their destination. Someone was in for a long siege of scrubbing the dust away. He didn't question who that someone would be.

A winding curve took them near the edge of a forest. Or what had been a forest. "What happened there?" Mitch risked taking a hand from the wheel to gesture to the scraggly wooded area that lay like a wound in the midst of rolling terrain.

A look of distress crossed Katherine's face. Drawing a shaky breath, she answered, "That section was cut for pulpwood. The paper companies are hungry for trees and I sell off a section periodically. This is the first time for this side of the meadows. I'd hoped it wouldn't be so terrible."

"Pulpwood?" He was surprised. "Why would you do that?"

"For the money, Mitch," she answered matter-of-factly, with no effort at hedging.

For the first time, without prompting, she'd called him Mitch. He liked it. He liked what he hoped it meant. Katherine wore correct formality as her shield, a frail protection against the unknown. She trusted him already, now she'd gone a step further.

Mitch didn't know what she wanted from him. Or, indeed, if she would ever want anything more than that he should find her sister. But he knew what he wanted. He'd known since the moment that wonderful gray gaze had turned on him with that first flicker of trust and challenge. He'd known even when he'd tossed Simon's letter aside and refused her. He knew now, as she sat by him, weighted down by the worry and burdens of her life, but refusing to yield to them.

He wanted her.

He wanted tidy, proper Katherine Mary with her little suits lying in a tangle on the floor and her hair flying loose over bare shoulders in a golden cloud. He wanted that lean and supple body pressed against his. He wanted the full, firm globes of her breasts nestled in the palms of his hands. He wanted a rosy bronze nipple tightening to a perfect bud at the caress of his tongue. He wanted her to touch him and hold him as those lithe legs enfolded him.

He wanted her to need—

"Mitch?" Katherine touched his arm, her fingers curving briefly around the bicep beneath his jacket.

He turned a shocked face to her. It was as if she'd read his mind, finishing his thought for him. Because that was exactly what he wanted. He wanted her to need Mitch.

He wanted her to need Mitchell Ryan as much as Mitchell Ryan needed Katherine Mary Rivard.

"I'm sorry I startled you," she apologized as prettily as ever. "You were a thousand miles away, weren't you?"

"Not so far." He drew a ragged breath. "Not nearly so far."

"This is our last crossroad coming up." A ribbon of asphalt dissected their path. Just past it, another dusty, graveled avenue meandered through a wall of hedges. "I'll get the gate and catch up to you on the other side of the highway."

"Right."

When he slowed at the fence, she was out before he came to a proper halt. The gate looked impossibly heavy, but slid on what was evidently a well-kept track. Even in the slim skirt that hugged her hips and brushed the curves of her knees, she moved with an accustomed ease. Her high-heeled shoes, though not precisely the recommended footwear for walking pastures, deterred her no more than her clothing. Katherine was a woman who could and would make do, when and how she must.

Every minute with her was a revelation, and with each revelation, he liked and respected her more.

Liking. Respect. New dimensions in his life. Neither were often, if ever, part of Mitchell Ryan's desire. Maybe they shouldn't be now.

"Maybe I should have followed my first inclination and stayed in the valley," he suggested tardily as he shifted into gear and took the Rolls across the asphalt that split Stone Meadow in two. At the other side, he pulled to a halt, watching her in the rearview mirror. She closed the gate as competently as she'd opened it, and the view was no less spectacular. He drummed his fingers on the leather steering wheel and scowled at the mirror. "You're in over your head, buster. Way over. She isn't your kind of woman and you certainly aren't her kind of man."

Katherine slipped in beside him, a rueful smile easing the worry for a moment. "By now you must be wishing you'd never heard the name Rivard." Tugging her skirt over a tawny length of thigh, she tilted her head in warning. "I'm afraid it's going to get worse."

In spite of himself his gaze lingered on the hem of her skirt that only seconds ago had been a number of inches higher. It definitely was going to get worse, but not quite in the way she thought.

"I'm a big boy now," he growled as much to himself as to Katherine. "I've dealt with difficult situations before, I can handle this one."

"I think I'd better prepare you for the aunts. They aren't accustomed to having men in the house. Except Cam, of course, but he doesn't count."

Cam? Who the hell was Cam? he wondered as the Rolls took in stride a pothole that would send a lesser vehicle to the garage with a broken axle.

"They aren't accustomed to men, but they love them." Katherine searched for a word to describe to him how her aunts would react. No simple phrase would work, so she settled for the most direct and the least complicated. "When they find a man interesting, as they will surely find you, they flirt."

"They do, huh?" He found he was smiling, his unease temporarily set aside.

"Bea is in her seventies."

"If I remember right, she's Gran's daughter and Justin's sister." He was still sorting them out, committing names and generations to memory.

"You remember perfectly. The flowers are Justin's children. Violet is sixty-one, Daisy is sixty, and Rose is the baby."

"Let me guess." He was chuckling. "Rose is fifty-nine."

"A good guess."

"Justin was a busy man."

"Only in the bedroom."

"Am I to assume he was not only a scoundrel, but a lazy one at that?"

"A scoundrel of the first order, and good for only one thing."

Mitch laughed out loud. "Planting flowers."

Katherine laughed with him, then sobered. Gripping the seat by her side, she descended into a dark pit of guilt for laughing when her sister was missing. At his quick questioning glance, she forced a smile. "There are a lot of scoundrels in the Rivard family tree, along with a horse thief, a highwayman, and more than our share of ne'er-do-wells. The worst to the people of Polk County was that Royce, the first Rivard to settle here, was a damn Yankee. The Civil War had just ended a few years before and that was the popular term for the unforgivable sin of being from the North. Royce outfoxed them by becoming more Southern than the natives."

"Katherine." Mitch covered her hand with his and waited until she looked up at him. "It's okay to laugh. Laughing doesn't mean your heart isn't hurting, or that you've forgotten Jocie. Sometimes laughing is the only way to hold on to sanity."

Her smile was tremulous and, this time, real. "You're a kind man, Mitchell Ryan, and a gentleman, whether you admit it or not."

The last twist of the tree-lined drive was accomplished; a huge white house loomed at its end. The sheer size of it took him by surprise and prevented him from responding. Later, when he'd absorbed the shabby magnificence of the Greek Revival with its Tuscan portico and cast-iron balustered verandas, he would think it was just as well, for he wouldn't have known what to reply.

"Brace yourself," she murmured. "The welcoming committee is out in force."

Indeed they were. Even Jocelyn Rivard sat on the portico, her back straight, her head up, her hands and feet hidden by a lap robe. He would have known her even if Katherine's description hadn't been so fitting. The proud old woman was flanked by four other women. Two to a side, each dressed in pearls and bright, flowing chiffon.

"We're a half hour later than we thought we would be," Mitch commented. "Have they been waiting there, like that, the entire time?"

"Of course."

"But why?"

"There isn't that much that's exciting in their lives. Your arrival makes this a red-letter day. You're the first good news they've had since Gran told them Jocie was missing again."

The Rolls halted in front of the steps leading to the portico. Mitch took his hand from hers reluctantly. "You're home,

Katherine Mary. Do what you must to put things in order, to-morrow we begin the search that will bring your sister back to her family.''

"First you have to brave the garden." Her eyes were silver in the afternoon light. If there was no laughter, at least there was no guilt for a moment of levity. "Prepare yourself for one thousand and one questions." She climbed out of the car before he could even think of coming around to open the door for her. Waving to the ladies over the top of the car, she added, "Make that a thousand and ten, and then a few more."

"Katherine Mary, we thought you were never coming home. We've been waiting and waiting." The quavery voice drifted from the portico.

"I know, Violet. I'm sorry to be so late, but I'm here now, and I've brought someone to help us."

"We know," Daisy said in a voice as quavery.

"We've been waiting for him, too." Rose would always have the last word.

Katherine linked her arm through his, walking with him to the stairs. "Remember," she murmured in an undertone, her breath a warm, sweet rush against his cheek as she leaned close. "I warned you."

"More sweet potatoes, Mr. Ryan?"

Mitch looked up at Violet as she held a dish under his nose. Flashing his best smile, he had to refuse. "No, thank you, ma'am. They were delicious, but I couldn't eat another bite. Actually they were better than delicious. Best sweet potatoes I've ever had in my life."

"They're my specialty, you know. Won the blue ribbon at the county fair for many years." Violet preened and insisted, "Are you sure you couldn't eat just one teeny bit more?"

Mitch swallowed and wondered where he would put more food, but he hadn't the heart to disappoint her. "Maybe just a spoonful."

While Violet spooned a mountain of potatoes onto his plate, he risked a glance at Katherine. Over a candelabra of polished silver, her face was sober, but her eyes were dancing with the satisfaction of an "I told you so" sort of look. Their gazes locked and held, a feeling of warmth and respect binding them like gossamer in the candle-lit dining room.

Katherine was first to look away as Daisy and Rose vied for their share of his attention. As they had before dinner, even offering to unpack his valise, as they'd called it. Now one offered more homemade rolls, the other insisted he have another serving of pickled beets.

"For heaven's sake, girls, leave Mr. Ryan alone," Jocelyn Rivard's voice boomed through the simpering and the twitter. "You're going to do him in before he ever has a chance to find our Jocie."

"But, Gran," Rose dared to protest, "we're only trying to make Katherine Mary's young man feel welcome."

"Oh, damn!" Katherine muttered, and racked up another Hail Mary as she barely resisted the desire to slide under the table. She dared not risk a look at Mitch, but she knew he was hiding a grin. Maybe she deserved it, for only seconds ago she was laughing at him. "Rose." Clinging to her dignity, she addressed the aunt with more calm than she felt. "Mr. Ryan is here to help Jocie. Have you forgotten?"

"Of course I haven't forgotten." Rose was indignant. Setting the pickled beets down with a thump she returned to her seat.

"Don't blame Rose, Katherine Mary," Violet ventured. "It's just that the two of you look so good together."

"A matched pair," Daisy chimed in.

"How could we help but hope that you had let yourself have a young man at last." Rose, forever with the last word.

Katherine's face flamed in earnest and she wondered why she hadn't run away years ago. The blush paled as she thought of Jocie, and the pleasant evening turned grim.

"Bea." Jocelyn turned a haughty gaze on her daughter, sparing Katherine any more unwanted attention. "The man has had more than enough food, but I don't think he would say no to another glass of your summer wine."

While Bea beamed and shuffled to the sideboard and back, Jocelyn turned that same gaze on Katherine. "Katherine Mary, I believe you have a meeting scheduled for early tomorrow with Cameron."

Leaving Mitch to be fussed over by the aunts, Katherine had spent a desperate hour before dinner in her office on the telephone. One of her calls was to Cameron Halsey. "Cam will be here at six, to take the horse."

"You don't look as if you've slept well in quite some time, and I'm sure you have some packing to do, so why don't you retire for the night. The girls and I will see to Mr. Ryan's comfort."

There was nothing Katherine wanted more than to escape the dining room. But she couldn't bring herself to desert Mitch a second time. The flowers and Bea would kill him with kindness without some calming force standing between them. Mitchell, himself, was certainly no protection. He'd proven that over and over, taking what was thrust at him, never saying no. Smiling and flirting as unrepentantly as they flirted. He'd enjoyed himself immensely, a fool could have seen it. But too much of a good thing was exactly that. Too much.

"Gran, I don't think I should leave you to entertain Mr. Ryan."

"Fiddle!" Gran huffed. "What you mean is, you don't think you should leave him to our mercies."

"There's that, too," Katherine admitted.

"He's a big fellow and a handsome one in the bargain," Gran declared. "I'm sure he's done more than his share of handling women. Of any age."

"You're tired, Katherine." Mitch rose, circling the table to help her with her chair as he added his encouragement. "I'll be fine with the ladies, and I'll see you early tomorrow."

"You're sure?" She looked up at him. Gran never allowed electric lights at dinner, and in the flicker of candlelight he seemed even stronger and more handsome than before. Handsome and intriguing enough that he'd probably had vast experience with women. So, who was she kidding? He didn't need her to protect him. He didn't need anybody.

Mitch saw doubt play over her face, followed by a frown. She was softer and more vulnerable than ever. As he had, she'd changed for dinner. Her gown was pale gold, a match for her tawny skin, a compliment to her shining hair, and of a style from another era. Burnished pearls spilled from her throat and lay against her breasts, dipping into a breathtaking hint of cleavage. Like the pearls, the gold fabric that skimmed her body was as lustrous as a misty sunrise as it drifted and clung, playing an innocent game of hide-and-seek.

Hiding and seeking quite enough to drive a man wild.

He touched the column of her throat, stroking it with the backs of his fingers, wondering if the gold of her skin was a reflection of candlelight or the dress. Or if every inch of her would be as golden when one was snuffed out and the other stripped away. But he couldn't let himself think of that. Not now. Not yet. Perhaps never.

"Katherine Mary." Gran's voice intruded on a lost moment. Two pairs of eyes turned to her, slowly, reluctantly, then almost in surprise, as if they'd forgotten she existed. When she had their full attention, the grandam of the Rivards inclined her head, narrowed eyes moving from Mitch to Katherine and back to Mitch. "Mr. Ryan is correct, he will be fine with us, so, go along now. Rest for tomorrow and the days to come."

No one denied Gran when she used that soft, thoughtful tone. Not even Katherine. She excused herself with only a glance at Mitch, and hurried from the dining room. Somewhere in the far reaches of the tremendous house, a door closed before Gran spoke again.

"Mr. Ryan, I feel the need for a breath of fresh air. Would you be so kind as to take me to my sitting room for a wrap?"

"My pleasure, ma'am."

The crippled hands that had appeared only briefly during the meal, were tucked under a shawl when he wheeled her chair down a hall to the room she indicated. The flowers and Bea were busily scurrying about the dining room and the kitchen before a second door closed in a totally different part of the house.

"Well, Mrs. Rivard," Mitch said when he faced the old woman. "Shall we continue the farce, or address the real reason you asked me to bring you here?"

"Pretending doesn't suit either of us, Mr. Ryan, so why don't you begin by telling me why you decided to help find Jocie. Is it Katherine Mary?"

"You aren't one to mince words, are you?"

"Mincing words wastes time, at my age there's so little of it left, even a second is too precious to waste. It is Katherine Mary, isn't it? Only a fool wouldn't know, once one saw how you looked at her, and she at you."

Mitch folded his arms over his chest. "How is that, Mrs. Rivard?"

"Are you falling in love with my great-granddaughter?"

A massive clock ticked off the seconds of the night. A cricket chirped by the window. His long-held breath rasped from his lungs as a hard hand raked through shaggy auburn waves. "I don't know."

"Then you've never been in love?"

"Never."

"Neither has Katherine Mary."

Mitch's hand dropped to his side. When he would have spoken, she silenced him with a wave of a gnarled, knotted hand.

"To look at her, one would find it hard to believe her experience with men is negligible. Even as a teen, she rarely dated. To be blunt, thanks to all of us, she was never allowed to be a teen. Katherine Mary shouldered far too many burdens, far too young."

"She doesn't resent it."

"No, she doesn't," Jocelyn agreed. "She loses her temper, and when she forgets completely, she curses. When she curses, she imposes a given number of Hail Marys on herself. She doesn't know we hear and she doesn't know we are aware of the self-imposed punishment. But, through it all, she never resents us."

"You love her."

"We all do. I wager that before this is done, you will, too." She pinned him with her piercing look. "What then, Mr. Ryan?"

He didn't bother to deny her observation. "I don't know."

"Then you'd better decide, for it's already begun. The essence is there, the attraction. Where it goes, what it becomes, will be up to the two of you."

"There's more to it than what Katherine and I might want."

"Such as?"

There was no escaping her directness. His teeth clenched, a muscle rippled in his jaw before he answered. "Such as who I am, what I am," he said gruffly. "And where I came from."

"I know who you are, Mitchell Ryan. I know what you are. I know you come from the streets of New Orleans. I know you are a fine young man, or Simon wouldn't have sent us to you."

"Do you know what I do for a living?"

"I know."

"Then you know why I was in the valley, relieved, perhaps temporarily, perhaps permanently, from my duties."

"At your own request. You're a dangerous man and I know it. You would have to be to work for Simon."

Nothing daunted the woman. If the earth shook beneath her she would sit there calmly asking questions. "When Simon said I came from the streets, he truly meant the streets. I lived there, Mrs. Rivard, for most of my childhood and in my teens, until I was sixteen."

"When you tried to steal Simon's beloved Jaguar, and he ended up recruiting you for his organization," she finished for him.

He would spend time later being surprised that the closed-mouthed Simon had told this old matriarch so much. At the moment he was too busy trying to make her understand that he wasn't the man Katherine needed. "So there's your answer. I've been a vagrant and a car thief." A gesture encompassed the house and the grounds. "Katherine grew up with this."

"That matters to you?"

"No, it matters to you, and would ultimately to Katherine."

"Come here, young man." She indicated that he should take the stool at her side. "It hurts my neck to keep looking up at you."

"Wouldn't it be better if I simply excused myself? You've had a long day, as Katherine has."

"Sit down, young man. I have a story to tell you. One that few people ever knew, and those few are dead. When I'm dead, only you will know."

Intrigued, Mitch took his seat beside her.

"Before I begin, I must have your promise that the story will go no further."

"Not even to Katherine?"

"Especially not to Katherine Mary!"

He covered her hand with his, the shawl only magnifying the fragility of twisted fingers and swollen knuckles. "You have my word."

Again the piercing look bored into him. "Simon says you never break your word."

"I don't."

"Then before I begin, I must have one more promise."

"What would you have me promise?"

"I need your promise that, after my story, if you still feel the differences in your life and Katherine Mary's are insurmount-able, if you're really sure, then before morning you will walk out of this house and never see her again."

"What about Jocie?"

"There are other ways of finding her. We'll go to the police, if we must. But I won't sacrifice one great-granddaughter for the other. So, do I have your word?"

Mitch had no idea where this was going. At first he thought only to humor her. Now he knew it was far too serious for that. Could he walk out of Katherine's life? If he gave his word, he would have to.

"Well," Jocelyn said softly after a long while. "Do I have your word?"

His chest heaving in a low sigh, Mitch said, "If I'm sure, you have my word."

She nodded, accepting. Then, in a rare show of trust, she slipped her hand from the shawl and laid it over his. When he turned his hand over, holding hers gently, she smiled and there was a glitter of tears in her proud eyes.

"The story I have to tell you, the story we have agreed no one else will ever know, is of Byron Rivard and the girl he found in a backwoods brothel and took for a wife."

"You were that girl," Mitch ventured quietly.

"Yes." She didn't flinch or look away. Her posture was as ramrod erect and unyielding as ever. "I was that girl."

Three

Mitch leaned over the engine of the Rolls. As much an enduring work of art as a marvelous piece of machinery for a man whose innate talents and survival were predicated on things mechanical. Just after dawn he'd admitted defeat and risen from his sleepless bed to tiptoe down an uncarpeted grand staircase, telling himself he was answering the lure of the auto. When he'd driven it from the protective cocoon of the coach house, to wash it and see to any minor repairs, he'd expected to be fascinated, losing himself as only he could in machines. Instead he discovered that in these early-morning hours his attention was riveted on the corral a distance away.

Katherine was on his mind, in his heart, and constantly in his sight.

A Katherine such as he'd never seen, with her face shaded by the brim of a battered Stetson hat, and the wealth of her hair tumbling down her back, tangling in a length of ribbon tied at her nape. The proper suits had been discarded for a broadcloth shirt and trousers cinched at the waist by a wide black belt. Sturdy clothing that had seen hard use and suffered many launderings. The shirt had faded from rich to pale emerald, the trousers from fawn to cream. Even her tall boots showed the toll of wear, but only enough to make them truly comfortable, and not even the stirring dust dimmed their oiled shine.

He was inordinately pleased that Katherine knew and observed the first rule of survival for any sensible farmer, cowboy, soldier or laborer worth his salt. Wars and lives had been lost by soldiers with sore feet. So could a struggling land-poor empire in the piedmont of North Carolina.

But not by Katherine Mary Rivard, who was deep in conversation with a man dressed similarly. A lean, hard man, who gestured and argued, and did everything but shake her.

Mitch could hear the rise and fall of their voices, but could not distinguish their words. He didn't need that to see their argument was a ripsnorter. He'd wanted to step in more than once, but the instinct he credited with his life kept him on the prudent path. Though he'd resisted the temptation, nothing could still the curiosity that kept him watching and questioning.

The imposing man was Cameron Halsey, her early-morning appointment, and he argued with the heat and familiar verve of an old friend. Or lover.

In her discourse on Katherine's negligible experience with men, Jocelyn Rivard had dismissed this neighbor with an offhanded comment. She hadn't mentioned that he was dynamic and rugged. A hard, determined man who could easily have stepped straight from the pages of a popular cigarette ad.

The familiarity and rapport shared even in the midst of a fierce discussion conducted in the middle of a corral disturbed Mitch. Far more than he wanted to admit. Time and again he'd reminded himself that beyond finding Jocie, he had no right to interfere in Katherine's business.

Closing the hood carefully, he took up the cloth he'd used to polish the newly washed Rolls. If their route to the airport didn't include another shortcut across pasture trails, it would be the most splendid machine on the road.

The meeting with Halsey was in preparation for this trip. A journey to the city of memories Mitch had hoped to leave behind him forever.

He could still back away. It wasn't too late.

Or was it?

"You're still here, Mr. Ryan."

Mitch forced his attention from Katherine to the woman who sat with her wheelchair nearly touching the rusting balustrade of the encircling veranda. In his fierce concentration on the battle of wills taking place in the corral, he hadn't heard the whisper of the rubber-tired wheels. "Yes, Mrs. Rivard, I'm still here."

Jocelyn sat as rigidly as ever, but the night had taken something from her. In the unforgiving light of day she was wan and tired. "Since we have agreed you are a man of your word, does this mean you want—"

"It means I'm not sure," he interrupted gently. "I gave you my word I would go if I knew for sure. I don't know what I want from Katherine, nor what she wants from me. Only time will decide that, Mrs. Rivard. Not you, not Katherine, and not I. But I promise you that I'll do everything in my power to see that nothing hurts her. Even me."

He saw that there was still spirit in the unrelenting gaze, still a keen edge in the aged mind. After a long while an abrupt jerk of Jocelyn's head ended the appraising stare. "No one could ask more than that.

"You're a strong man, Mitchell Ryan. I envy Katherine Mary that. Unfortunately, contrary to a self-perpetuated myth, the Rivards were rarely strong. Neither the women nor the men. Especially the men. Weakness was their one dominant gene, even in my husband."

"I won't dispute that, I can't," Mitch said. "But no one can fault their one particular intelligence."

"What intelligence would that be?"

"The ability to recognize a remarkable woman. To love her and realize her strength. Possessing the wisdom to marry her, with no concern for what she might have been, or where she came from."

Jocelyn Rivard inclined her head, accepting his words as the compliment he intended. She didn't smile, but the creases and wrinkles eased a bit around her mouth and eyes. "She's the best of us, you know." Lifting her gaze to the scene by the barn, Jocelyn might have seen a thousand such quarrels from her lack of reaction. "Katherine Mary is what all the Rivards should have been, and few were. The strength, the honor, the determination. She's what we all have needed, but she came too late to us. After her there will be no more Rivards. She and Jocie are the last of the line.

"It's quite unintentional, and quite without her knowledge, but she's the reason Jocie ran away." At his look of shock, she finally smiled. "You'd assigned that distinction to me, hadn't you?" Before he could agree or deny, she commanded, "Look at her."

She waited until he obeyed. "Look at her and think of all you know of her in your short acquaintance. Think what it would be like to be her younger sister and walk in her shadow. Jocie is mature enough to recognize that she will never be the woman Katherine Mary is, yet not enough to understand and accept that few will ever be."

The young-old eyes returned to him. "But you know, don't you, Mitchell Ryan? You know very well what kind of woman your Katherine is."

He drew a long, slow breath, watching the young woman standing in dry, powdered clay. Clay that held the dream she fought for, even as it blew in the late spring breeze. She was tall and slender and golden. Delicate, but not frail. Proud, but not arrogant. Refined, but not pretentious. Responsible, but not a martyr. Gentle, but strong-willed.

A rare woman.

His Katherine?

Realizing he held his breath, Mitch exhaled slowly, murmuring in a low undertone, "Only the young and foolish couldn't recognize what she is."

"Jocie ran away from what you're seeing. Will you run, too?"

"I don't know."

Once again Jocelyn nodded in that peculiar, satisfied jerk of her head. "If you find Jocie..." She paused, correcting herself. "*When* you find Jocie, Katherine will know why she ran away. Can you help her deal with that?"

Jocie Rivard's reasons for running away could well be the least of Katherine's worries, but this grand old lady needn't know. "I'll help her, as much as I can."

"We're expecting a lot of you, Mr. Ryan, and now I have even one more favor to beg of you." For once she seemed unsure of herself, and uncomfortable in what she would ask. But, taking his silence as agreement, she plunged on. "I'm ninety-one. I speak often of living to be one hundred. Anyone with an eye unblinded by love can see that it isn't to be. There's a plot there on the hill, where my beloved Byron lies waiting for me. His wait won't be long now. What I would ask of you is that you help Katherine then.

"No matter what is, or isn't, between you, whether you are simply friends or if you are lovers, will you be here for her?"

"I'll be here, if I'm needed." He tried a grin that didn't quite work. "But I won't be. You're going to live forever."

"No." She shook her head. "I'm tired, and I'm ready. Katherine is the strength of the family in all but name. Soon she will be that, as well. Be here for her. Promise that you will."

"I promise," Mitch said, making it the qualified promise it had to be. "But only if I'm wanted."

"By Katherine Mary?"

"Yes, by Katherine."

"You're quite the diplomat, aren't you, Mr. Ryan?"

"Only a man, Mrs. Rivard, doing the best he can."

"Is there anything better to be?"

"I don't know."

"I know, Mr. Ryan." She smiled and a bit of the weight of her life lifted momentarily. "I know."

Like magic, without being summoned, one of the flowers appeared. And, as quietly as she'd come, the fading grandam disappeared into the shadowed recesses of the house.

Distressed by the looming specter of death, he turned back to the corral in time to witness Cameron Halsey sweeping his hat from the dirt where he'd thrown it. Without a word, the neighbor-friend-lover-whatever, turned on his heel and stalked through a gate and headed for Mitch.

"Ryan." He stopped a yard away, eyes hot and narrowed. "You are Ryan, aren't you?"

"That's right, Halsey. What can I do for you?"

"You can talk some sense into the brat."

"I suppose you mean Katherine."

"Who the Sam Hill else would I mean?" he groused. "This horse she's agreed to train is the devil's own horse from hell, but he's the chance of a lifetime. He could save the farm and Katherine. If she goes off on this wild-goose chase, it won't happen."

"I can't talk her out of going, Halsey. I've tried already."

"Don't talk, then. Simply refuse."

"Sure." Mitch tossed the cloth aside and hooked his thumbs into the pockets of his jeans. "Just like you refused her? You did refuse, didn't you?"

"That's different." Halsey bristled.

"How is it different?"

"I'm her neighbor. I've been riding herd on her in one way or another since the day she was born. Even if I don't agree with what she's doing, I can't welsh on her now."

"Neither can I, Halsey," Mitch said mildly.

"Hell's bells, man . . ."

"I can't," Mitch repeated, discovering he liked this man, who might or might not be Katherine's lover. He liked him for his frustrated caring. He liked him very much. "I can't any more than you could just now. But I'll make as quick work of it as possible. How long can you cover for her?"

Cameron Halsey studied him, seeing an ally when he expected an adversary. "A week. I can give you that much. Beyond that—" he shrugged "—we'll have to take it a day at a time."

"Give me two, if you can."

"Done, by God!" Halsey offered a hand as callused and weathered as old leather. One way or another, he would find a way to give Katherine Mary Rivard the two weeks she needed to save her crumbling empire. "Find that silly little twit. Drag her home by the hair of her head, if you have to. But whatever you do, have Katherine back in two weeks. Three at most."

"I'll give it my best shot."

Mitch found his hand enveloped in a bone-crushing grip. Halsey made no effort at friendly pleasantries. Neither man needed them. "You take care of her, I'll take care of the farm and the ladies, and maybe between the three of us we'll save Stone Meadow yet."

"Maybe."

By the time Halsey was gone, so was Katherine. Mitch went looking. It took no great effort to find her, for she was exactly where he'd expected she would be.

When he stepped into the barn, he waited just inside the doorway until his eyes adjusted from blinding daylight to its cool shade. The musky scent of hay enveloped him. A mouse rustled in the loft, a mourning dove grumbled a sad note from the rafters. The blackened tin roof ticked and popped in the heat of the sun.

Five horses stamped their feet and snuffled quietly in their stalls. Only one, the sixth horse, thrashed restlessly even as Katherine crooned to him.

"Good morning," Mitch said as he folded his arms over the top of the stall. "I missed you at breakfast."

"Sorry." She didn't take her eyes from the horse. "I skipped it this morning."

Actually, so had he. But one of the flowers had brought coffee and freshly baked pastries to the coach house. "Miss Daisy told me. She's worried a puff of wind is going to sweep you away."

"Daisy's always worried about something."

"I suspected as much." He returned his attention to the horse. A magnificent animal, truly, with the look of the devil in him. "So this is the horse from hell."

"That's Cam's name for him. Officially he's called Juggernaut."

"Which fits?"

"Both."

"You're going to train him?" The horse was massive, seventeen hands of powerful muscles, and more than half wild. He wasn't sure he wanted to see her linked with this awesome, frightened beast with only the fragile control of a leather lead.

"I was. Now Cam will. He swears not, but he will. He'll take Juggernaut to his place and fulfill the obligation I can't."

"These other horses—" Mitch jerked a thumb toward the other stalls "—you trained them?"

"Some of them. Others I board for people who love to ride but haven't the time or the space to keep their horses."

"It's a sizable part of your income?"

"The major part."

Mitch turned back to Juggernaut, regarding the horse carefully, wishing he didn't see such a dangerous animal. "Why is this particular horse so important?"

"He represents an opportunity to establish a working relationship with one of the larger consortia. One that buys or breeds fine young horses of good bloodlines, has them trained, then sells them. A good horse that's well trained brings a good price. An excellent horse, excellently trained, brings an astronomical price.

"I'm good with horses." She spoke as a matter of fact, not out of arrogance. "I was riding almost by the time I could walk, and training before my teens. Stone Meadow has always been perfect for what they were looking for. It offered the facilities and the pasture the consortium has been hungering after for years. The only drawback was the trainer.''

"Because you're a woman.'' He could have added young and stunning and too gentle for it to be conceivable that she could successfully take on the beast that paced the stall with furious energy. Katherine was the woman a man wanted decorating his arm and gracing the head of his dinner table rather than training a horse.

Katherine nodded without rancor. "Finally they've given me a chance to prove my skills.''

"By giving you the meanest horse in their lot? You call that a chance?''

"I wasn't given Juggernaut. I chose him.''

"You what!''

"He's a hard case, but he's also the best I've ever seen. If I can make of him the horse I think he can be . . .'' She shrugged and plucked a stray straw of hay from a splintered board. "But there's no sense in thinking about that now.''

Taking her by the shoulders, Mitch spun her to him. He'd rarely touched her, but when he did there was the tingle of a low-level current. It was there now, his tantalizing response to the feel of her. "There is a solution,'' he suggested softly. "You could stay here.''

Katherine knew he was trying to help, just as Cam tried with his frustrated arguments. When she'd resisted Cam's persuasion, he hadn't understood, and nothing she could say would change it. Mitch was giving it one last-ditch effort, but he would accept her final answer as irrefutable.

She looked into sherry eyes darkened by the shadows of the barn. "I have to go.''

His hands moved gently over the taut muscles of her shoulders. "You would do this even if it means losing the chance to prove yourself to the consortium?''

"Jocie's my sister,'' she said simply.

"It isn't a choice, is it?''

"No.''

Mitch's heart ached for her, wishing he could do something. Anything. She'd struggled so long for this chance, now it was gone. Whisked away by a family crisis, as he suspected most of her life had been whisked away. By crisis after crisis, in one way or another. "I'm sorry, Katherine. So sorry.''

A sudden rush of tears startled her. Ashamed of this display of weakness, she turned her head away. But not quickly enough.

"What's this?" With his palm curving around her cheek he turned her face back to him.

"Don't." Katherine tried to resist the insistent pressure he exerted, but he wouldn't allow it.

"There's no shame in tears, Katherine. They're as much part of keeping sane as laughter. I've shed my share."

"You?" Surprise swept away her resistance.

"Yes."

She almost voiced her doubts, until she remembered a brawny man with sweat on his brow and a nearly constructed swing set scattered around him. She remembered a baby bottle in the hip pocket of jeans, young gleeful faces painted with his version of war paint. Bath time, story time, and bedtime. A fragile preemie entrusted to his keep. The return of grateful parents. Tearful goodbyes. Bear hugs, exuberant kisses. Wheedled promises that he would be back again, soon, to play.

"You aren't just saying this to make me feel better." Her statement had no ring of question in it. "You really have, haven't you?"

"Many times."

"For the things that matter," Katherine surmised.

His hand was still at her cheek, their gazes met and held. She was mesmerized, entranced by this intriguing man unlike any man she'd ever known.

A horse whickered in a nearby stall, disturbing a coterie of doves. The turbulent flapping of their wings sent particles of hay and dust sifting from the loft. As the brief tempest subsided and the normal quiet returned, the only evidence that it had ever happened was the dust. Bars of sun slanting through shuttered windows caught at the tiny motes, turning them to a spangled haze.

That was how she saw him, a shadowy figure of mystery wrapped in a rare and splendid cloak of gallantry. A man who looked at her as a man looked at a woman he wanted.

As no man had ever looked at her before.

Her heart lurched beneath her breast, shivered to a standstill, then lurched again into a galloping rhythm. She wanted to rest her hand against it to calm it, but she couldn't move. Couldn't look away from what she saw in his face. Strange sensations, warm, sweet and exciting curled up from the pit of her stomach. And down.

In a lucid moment Katherine discovered she was trembling.

God help her! She was acting like a schoolgirl. She, at thirty, a maiden lady threatening to swoon over a man who was as beautiful inside as out. Simply because he looked at her as if she were beautiful, too.

She'd known him for little more than a day. But was there a timetable for emotions? So many days to like or to hate? So many more to care? How many days to feel this wonder-filled magnetism? This hunger?

Would time change anything? Would it matter?

He had shed his tears for the things that mattered. What were those things? she wondered.

"What matters to you, Mitch?" she heard herself asking in a voice not quite her own.

The thumb that had traced the line of her cheekbone almost absently grew still. He didn't move, hardly seemed to breathe. When she was sure she'd overstepped herself, that he wouldn't answer, he smiled and sighed. A weary sound of resignation and defeat, as if the things he cared about were beyond his control.

"The list is simple and short."

"Will you tell me?"

"Why, Katherine?"

"Because I want to understand you." She caught her lip between her teeth, then released it as she rushed on. "Because I *need* to understand you."

"I know." With both hands, he framed her face for an instant, then threaded his fingers through her hair, dragging the ribbon from it as he let the heavy strands drift through his fingers. He was captivated by them. One strand would be pure gold, another nearly platinum, another dark and rich with a hint of chestnut. He watched her hair fall to her shoulders in a shimmering mass, only to thread his fingers through it again.

"Children matter to me," he said, not looking at her but watching the play of light on her hair instead. "Hurt children. Children without hope. Little children whose lives are ruined before they ever really live. Lost children. Foolish children, like Jocie."

His hand grew still in her hair, tightening in it, dragging it back until her face was tilted to his.

"You," he whispered, settling for a lingering bittersweet kiss at her throat, when it was her mouth he wanted. Wanted desperately. "God help me, Katherine, you matter. Maybe more than you should."

"How much is that?" she asked unsteadily, not really quite understanding what she was asking, or even what she wanted to know, as she was engulfed by the deluge of unfamiliar sensations his chaste kiss unleashed.

"I don't know. I've never met anyone like you. Never felt like this." A muscle rippled in his jaw as he grappled for control. "I'm not good at this, Katherine." His voice was harsh, strained. "I've never walked away from anything I've wanted as much as I want you."

"No one's asking you to walk away. I'm not asking."

"You don't know what you're saying. I'm a stranger. You don't know who I am, or what I am. You don't know what I need."

"Don't I?" She brushed a strand of straw from his hair.

"You can't know."

"Then show me. Show me here. Show me now, Mitch."

"You would regret it. I'm not—"

Rising on tiptoe, she stopped him with the fleeting pressure of her mouth. "You're not a lot of things, and neither am I," she murmured, her words a sensual breath more than articulated. Her fingers curved around his neck, her lips brushed again over his. "But in the scope of things that matter, is what we are, or what we aren't, important? Does any of it figure in what we feel for each other?"

"Katherine . . ."

"Does it?" she demanded fiercely, shocked and wondering where it all came from—her daring, the words, the pragmatic wisdom, the innate knowledge that guided her. "Does what I might have done ten years ago, or ten days ago, keep you from wanting this? Could it?

"I don't care who you were, or what you might have been. It's enough that I know who you are now. I know what you are, Mitch."

He heard the ring of his own words to Jocelyn again in hers. His desperate resistance that was hardly any resistance at all was crumbling with her seduction. For that's what the lovely and demure Miss Katherine Mary Rivard was doing—seducing him with gentle persuasion that set his mind and heart reeling.

"What am I, Katherine?" he managed between labored breaths. "For both our sakes, tell me what I am."

"A kind man, a gentle man, a man of trust and honor. A reluctant gentleman, a friend." She smiled, a subtle curving of her lips. "A lover."

"Katherine, sweet Kate." The chant was a cry, a groan, a plea. "Do you know what you're doing?"

"Haven't the foggiest." She was almost giddy. No, she *was* giddy, and couldn't have been more so if she'd drunk a magnum of champagne. "But it seems right, doesn't it?"

He caught her hands in his as they wandered to his chest and the open collar of his shirt. "Have you done this before? Seduced a stranger in your barn, I mean."

"Never." She kissed his knuckles, grazing her lips over their roughness, refusing to let herself think of Gran or the flowers, or Jocie, or even Stone Meadow. For just this one isolated moment there was no work, no worry, no pressure, no fear of losing all that the Rivards before her had founded.

To the world that depended on her, she was Katherine Mary. But to Mitch who expected nothing, she was simply Katherine. Simply Kate. She liked that. No one had ever called her Kate. It held the ring of freedom.

So, for this one small interlude, she would revel in being Katherine and sometimes Kate. For Mitch, who was kind. Who looked at her as a man should look at a woman. Who had given her this special moment, when nothing else mattered.

Suddenly Mitch laughed and pulled her to him. His hands at her bruised ribs brought a sharp stab of reality, but the pain was gone as quickly as his hands, which were soon buried again in her hair.

"Who would have thought it? Who would believe it? Cool, aloof Katherine Rivard is a wanton in her soul. A lovely, wonderful wanton. An ice maiden with a wild heart." With sudden and astonishing ease he swept her into his arms and kissed her hard and long and deeply. Pulling away at last, a rueful smile flickered over his face. "A woman no man on earth could resist."

The steps to the loft were wide and well-built, and in perfect condition. She was light in his arms, a welcome burden. The hay was deep and fragrant, the perfect bed for lovers who needed no frills. Lovers who needed only each other.

Lovers who found even the pull and tug of taking tall boots from a shapely leg and foot a time of excitement and sensuality. A time of shared laughter that drew them deeper into the magic. Clothing was discarded in a haphazard heap as one delightful discovery led to another and then another. Until he wore only briefs, and she only the lacy scrap of a bra and tiny panties rising high over her hips, making wonderfully long legs seem even more wonderfully long.

Mitch backed away to look at her, to let himself see the treasure he had discovered. Her breasts were full with nipples dark rose beneath the veil of lace. Her waist was slender, blooming into hips hardly wider than a young boy's. But there was nothing childish about her, nor masculine. Not when her skin was like burnished gold. Not when it was taut and firm, not when it was...

A shadow shifted as a breeze whispered in the trees outside the open loft door. A burst of sunlight poured over her and the word *unblemished* vanished from his thoughts.

"Dear Lord, Katherine! What happened to you?"

For a moment she was puzzled, there were no bruises in the world he had taken her to. Then she looked down, remembering and dismissing. "Juggernaut happened to me."

Mitch went down on one knee, his hands spanning her waist only inches below the rainbow of colors that painted her body from ribs to her underarm and over her chest. Skimming his lips over the smooth, battered skin, he looked up at her. "Does it hurt?"

"Not anymore. Not when you kiss me like that."

"Like this?" His mouth moved over her, his tongue touching, tasting, soothing. The path of bruises led to her breast. Releasing the catch of her bra he slid the scalloped, weblike fabric from her, slowly, inch by inch, savoring each new revelation. When it fluttered to the floor, he traced the line of a fierce welt with a cautious finger.

With a muttered curse he leaned to her, rising a bit to retrace the same line with his lips until it merged with a blue band that guided him to a nipple. Perfect, unblemished, but waiting for his kiss. Katherine cried out then, her hands burrowing in his hair, clasping him tighter to her.

When he sat back on his heels after a while, he was so grave and solemn, Katherine felt suddenly shy. No one had ever seen her like this. No one had ever stared at her so fiercely, so wholly absorbed. When she would have shielded herself, he caught her hands in his.

"No," he muttered. "Let me see."

She stood pliantly then, amazed at the look of anguish and reverence she saw in his face. If she hadn't already been more than a little in love with him, she would have loved him then. It was madness, she knew that. Some tiny part of her remembered he was virtually a stranger, but her heart had known him.

How many days to like or to hate? How many days to fall in love with the man she'd been waiting for for years?

One.

And if one was all she could have, it was enough.

He touched her, his palm gliding over her, wishing he could take the hurt as his own. "Juggernaut."

"Yes."

"Damn that horse," he snarled savagely. "He'll be the death of you."

"No." She took his hand from her side, drawing it again to her breast. "You will be the death of me, won't you? The sweet, little death?"

"Yes."

He pulled her down to the bed made of the first and the last of castoff clothing.

Down to the waiting hay.

Down to him.

"Kate."

"You'd never done this before." He leaned over her, one leg lying over hers, one hand caressing the body he would never tire of touching. For a woman who had lived life as roughly as Katherine, there was no physical evidence of virginity. But a man knew. Mitch knew. "You've never made love to a man before. You should have told me."

"I did. You asked, remember?" She laughed up at him, more content than she'd ever been.

"I asked if you had ever seduced..." He stumbled and took her hand from his hip, trapping her exploring fingers so he could think. "I asked if you had ever seduced a man. If you'd ever seduced a man in the barn."

"I said no."

"Katherine, I asked you."

"And I answered." Mischief danced in her eyes as she pulled free to stroke his cheek. "I answered the question you asked."

"Next time I'll be more specific," he growled.

"Next time?" Undaunted by his play at irritation, she raised her face for a kiss. "How about now?"

"We have a plane to catch."

"Our plane leaves in just over two hours. The airport is sixty miles away. The speed limit is sixty. If you drive sixty miles an hour, we'll be there long before departure." She laughed and teased his mouth with hers. "That gives us plenty of time."

"It doesn't work out quite that easily."

Her fingers danced down his body, lingered at the curve of his ribs, dipped into his navel and brushed over his hip. When he drew a quick, sharp gasp, she sighed and murmured, "Too bad."

In a fluid move, she was rising to her feet, taking her shirt with her.

"Where the hell are you going?"

Katherine looked down at him, the shirt clutched to her breasts but not concealing them. "I'm going to the airport, silly."

He caught her wrist, circling it, holding her willing captive. "No, you're not."

"I'm not?" Her gray gaze was wide with innocence.

"Not like that." His eyes moved over her, lingering, needing.

She looked down at herself with an innocence even more pronounced. "My goodness, then where am I to go?"

He tugged hard at her wrist and brought her toppling down on him, his body shielding hers from the fall. "Here." His fingers caught in her hair, bringing her lips to his. "Here," he muttered, "to me."

"We have a plane to catch." She loomed over him, astride him, sunlight from the window cascading over her.

"I'll drive seventy." He was captivated by her breasts, by the half-moon shadow beneath them, wondering if any woman was ever as lovely.

"You'll get a ticket." She moved against him, her hips undulating in soft, easy circles.

Mitch made a comment about what could be done to tickets. A comment that should have shocked her, but she laughed instead, throwing her head back, never losing the cadence of temptation.

"It must have been difficult, washing the Rolls and tinkering under the hood."

"It was." He wished he was a sculptor, that the feel of her breasts in his palms could be captured to keep for all time.

"You must be tired." She paused, waiting for his answer.

"I am. Terribly, terribly tired," he whispered. "You'll have to help me."

"I will." She rose only slightly to guide him, leaning forward for one more kiss.

She made love to him. Slow, erotic, hypnotic love. With her newly learned expertise she teased, she tormented, gleefully, wickedly. She gave him pleasure and took her own, moving in a delicious rhythm. Halting, beginning, then halting and beginning again. Each cessation and each new beginning drawing them closer to the brink, until trembling became shudders and whispers became cries. Until the love she wanted to give him could be delayed no longer.

With her hair whipping over him, in the throes of her passion she rode him. Fiercely, without mercy, with the scent of hay around them and sunlight pouring down, until the exquisite fulfillment of the little death was done.

Keeping him with her, she cried out and tumbled into his embrace. Lying in his arms, the sweat of their bodies mingling, she savored the stroke of his hand at her back. Sounds of the outside world crept into her mind, but she held them at bay.

In a minute, maybe two, she would think of Stone Meadow, and Gran, and Jocie. This was her time and she'd left one thing undone that would make it perfect. "Mitch."

"Hmm?"

Folding her hands on his chest, she propped her chin on them with a tranquillity that surprised her. "I have a confession."

"You do, huh? Let me guess." He chuckled. "You have a rabid desire for the traditional cigarette."

"In a hayloft?"

"Uh-oh, I guess that leaves just one thing. You hate red hair."

"Wrong again. I love red hair. In fact—" she slanted a mischievous look at him "—I love you, Mitchell Ryan."

Mitch's body convulsed. His wandering exploration of her body ceased. "Kath—"

Katherine stopped him with a palm closing over his lips. "Don't say anything. Not yet. Promise me that you won't until we find Jocie."

"But . . ." he began as she moved her hand away.

"Wait."

"It's too soon. You can't."

"Please."

Mitch was shocked and not sure what he thought or felt, but he couldn't deny her when she looked at him with her heart in her eyes. Doubt warred with wonder and a touch of fear, but he did as she asked. "You have my promise."

"Thank you."

His face was grave, the banter gone from his tone. "Where do we go from here, Katherine?"

"To the airport, and New Orleans," she said simply as she rose to re-collect her shirt. "To find Jocie."

Four

Katherine looped a finger at the edge of a sheer curtain and brushed it away from the window. From her lofty tower she looked out at New Orleans, a city that never seemed to sleep. Even in the small, first hours of morning the streets were busy.

Distracted, with half a mind, she watched streams of revelers moving in gay pantomime, while she listened with her heart to the restless rustlings drifting through the open door of the adjoining room.

Since their arrival in the city, Mitch had been pensive, introspective. The hint of boyishness in his handsome, chiseled face had turned to grave, disciplined formality. The flash of his smile was a forced caricature of the beguiling grin that had first warmed her heart, then enchanted, then swept her breath away. His dancing, sherry gaze that had teased her as it encouraged and comforted, looked at her without really seeing.

He was troubled. So badly he'd withdrawn from her, leaving her alone even when he was close by her side. Time and again in the last hours, she could have touched him, could have felt the shape and substance of muscle and bone, and sensed the latent strength of body and mind. But she wouldn't be touching Mitch.

The part of him that made him Mitch had gone to ground, beyond her reach.

He'd gone through the motions and played his part. And, certainly he'd been attentive to her needs and considerate of her comfort. So attentive and considerate that he'd reserved a penthouse suite far grander than she expected or required. In the bargain he'd been informative, as informative and impersonal as a trained and polished tour guide.

In flight, on the way from the airport, in a quick journey through the city, then prior to settling for the night in the palatial hotel, she'd been inundated by facts, figures and points of interest.

All by a man who talked to keep from thinking.

Along the way she'd learned casually, too casually, as if it were a guarded admission, that New Orleans was his birthplace. Then, in a rush forestalling any comment, he added that the city had fondly been given the feminine gender by her natives. She was the Crescent City to some, for obvious reasons. To others, the Queen of the Mississippi, lying as she did at the mouth of the river one hundred ten miles inland from the Gulf of Mexico.

That was a good one to know, if ever she played Trivial Pursuit, Katherine thought with a wry smile.

Geographically, the city was almost an island surrounded by streams, lakes, and by giant oak and cypress swamps. Physical conditions contributed to the rich uniqueness of the city's culture by isolating it from the mainland for more than two hundred and fifty years.

That one should win her a point or two.

Then, for good measure, she could add the bit about flood walls taming the meandering course of the river, and levies controlling its level.

The pièce de résistance could be the tidbit about abandoned river channels that created the famed and splendid bayous.

Violet wouldn't have a chance at her own favorite game. If ever Katherine found the time to play, and if the subject were New Orleans.

Tired of her own effort at distraction, and not the least amused, Katherine abandoned her attempt to keep a sanguine outlook. Folding her arms beneath her breasts, her fingers clasping her bare arms, she breathed a discouraged sigh.

She knew so much, yet so little.

Jocie was out there, somewhere. She could be one of the euphoric revelers, happier than she'd ever been in her life. Or in a dark alley, sick and afraid and needing her older sister.

New Orleans sprawled at Katherine's feet, the end of Jocie's trail, yet she was no closer to finding her than she'd been at Stone Meadow. The one person who could help her prowled his room like a restless tiger in his battle with secret demons called up by the city.

She felt lost and helpless and useless. Mitch hadn't wanted to come here, yet he had, for her. Now he was paying the price for something she didn't understand.

If she understood, could she help?

"I can try."

Leaving the window she caught up her robe, sliding it over the slender slip of a gown that brushed the floor. On bare feet she padded to the open doorway of the sitting room. Pausing there, she watched as he stared out over the same city view she had forsaken.

He hadn't undressed. In the glow of a reading lamp, she saw his only concession to comfort had been to toss jacket and tie aside. The sleeves of his shirt were turned back, but the tail was still neatly tucked into the belted waist of his trousers. With his head resting in the crook of an upraised arm and a glass in the hand hanging limply by his side, he leaned against the steel window frame. For a short while he'd stopped his fitful pacing, consumed by what lay beyond the window.

As she gazed at his broad back, the muscles tensed and flexed beneath the fine cotton of his shirt. He lifted the glass to his mouth. Ice cube rattled against ice cube as he drained the last inch of liquid from it.

Katherine took a tentative step, then stopped, suddenly uncertain of her purpose. Company might be the last thing he wanted.

"Mitch?" Calling his name, she made the choice his. He could tell her to leave or stay.

Mitch looked away from the window, his gaze sweeping over her. Over the simple negligee that draped her body in the subtle gleam of gold. A color that was one of her favorites. She wore it often, she wore it well. A sudden ache deep inside him proved how well she wore it.

"Katherine," he said softly. "Come join me."

"Would you mind?"

"Why should I?" He lifted the glass in a tribute she was too modest to understand. "I would offer you a drink..." His voice was rough with her effect, and from the ordeal of his night. "But, surprise, surprise, it's only water."

He could use a drink about now, but he wouldn't risk it. Not when the next day was so critical. Not when he needed his wits about him now.

God help him, how many times had he wanted to go to her, needing to take her in his arms and lose himself in her? How many times had he stopped himself a heartbeat from the threshold of her room and the perfect peace only she had given him?

Staring at her, drinking in the sight of her, he wondered if she could ever know that she'd given him the most beautiful moment in his life.

Too beautiful to be sullied by the evil that clawed at him in the darkness. Even as it waited to take back one of its own.

Only Matthew Sky, the Apache, his friend and partner in their work for Simon, would understand. As shaman to his people, Matthew believed that evil could become so real it was capable of exerting just such power as Mitch feared.

Matthew would understand. And with him, Simon.

They would know the dread that descended the moment Mitch had agreed to return to the place of his childhood. At Stone Meadow and with Katherine he'd managed to keep it in the back of his mind. But each mile closer to New Orleans, Mitch had grown surer he could never leave his past behind again.

But now, with a lifting heart, Mitch knew he was wrong. The evil of the street wouldn't keep him. One look at Katherine and he knew it couldn't.

Moving away from the window he set the glass, carefully, on a table. Wondering at her effect on him, and blessing the day Simon sent her to the valley, he said the first thing that came to mind. Softly, thoughtfully, hardly aware of his words or the sound of his voice. "I'm sorry if I disturbed you with my nocturnal prowling."

"You haven't." She bit her lip and sighed as she abandoned the deception. "At least it isn't just you."

"You're anxious about tomorrow when we begin our search for Jocie."

"That's part of it."

"That, plus you're concerned and worried about me." A bitter laugh rumbled deep in his throat. "Considering my behavior in recent times, only a fool wouldn't be."

She made no effort to deny her concern. "Can I help?"

"No, sweet lady, but thank you for asking." With a backhanded gesture he indicated the window and the city beyond. "I was just saying hello to another lady who wasn't so sweet to me once. No one can help with that."

Katherine crossed the room to him. Laying a hand on his arm, she murmured, "I'm sorry."

"Why should you be sorry, Katherine?"

She didn't have an answer. She had no idea what was tormenting him, except that it had to do with his memories of the city and his past. That was her answer, the only one she could give. "For all the things you can't forget."

"It has nothing to do with you."

"It has everything to do with me. You came here because I asked you to come. More than that, anything that concerns you concerns me, because I care about you."

He laughed quietly and took her hand from his arm. Lifting it to his lips, he kissed her palm. "You're so accustomed to shouldering everybody's troubles that now you're going to take on mine, as well?"

"If I can, at least a share of them." She lifted her chin a degree. "If you'll let me."

His laughter faded to a bittersweet smile. "You've helped already, just by being here. And that's enough, sweetheart, the rest is my problem. I hadn't taken into account that I'm a lot older and wiser and stronger than I was when I left here. My memories aren't pleasant, but I can handle them, now. Maybe not gracefully, but better than I thought I could."

Taking back her hand, she moved away, flushed by her presumption. "Of course you can. I've intruded. Forgive me, please." Then, accepting his evasion with a detachment she didn't feel, "I should've warned you I'm proof of the cliché about old habits."

He was shutting her out. There was nothing she could do but wait and hope that one day he would trust her enough to share all of his life with her. Even the ugly parts.

"Old habits die hard for all of us, Katherine."

"That must apply to the Rivards in spades. Why else would I keep making the same mistakes?"

He took her by the shoulders and brought her back to him. "There's nothing to forgive, for you haven't intruded. And the only mistake you make is giving too much of yourself, to anyone who needs you."

His fingers moved down her spine beneath the wild, glorious flow of her loose hair, and back again to her shoulders. The burnished silk she wore was like her skin, soft and tawny and bewitching. Touching it was like touching her. Feeling the heat rising from her skin to warm it recalled the heat of a loft and the scent of hay. And a laughing, teasing woman gilded by sunlight pouring over her like liquid gold. A woman who gave herself joyously, without reservation.

"Even to me," he whispered, holding her tighter. "Especially to me."

But that was another time, another circumstance, in her clean, familiar world. Tomorrow she would venture with him into one like she'd never seen. Where cleanliness was a forgotten word, and nothing would be familiar.

He had to prepare her, as much as anyone could be prepared. He'd delayed as long as he could, thinking that the morning would be soon enough, but now this timing seemed right.

Katherine sensed the change in him as the tensions that had begun to ease were rekindled by dread. Stepping out of his embrace, she looked up at him, bewilderment in her eyes.

"We have to talk," he explained before she could question. "I have to tell you some of what you can expect tomorrow." A rueful grimace curled his lip. "I don't suppose I could persuade you to wait for me here, until I come back?"

Before his speculation was complete, she was dismissing it with a shake of her head.

"Right." He caught a long, harsh breath. "That's what I thought."

"But you had to try."

"Seemed like a good idea. If I found Jocie, this wouldn't be so far away. When I find Jocie," he corrected.

"You're that sure she's here?"

"Aren't you?"

"Yes." Her answer was emphatic. She went to the window, the view was no different than from her bedroom. Nor would it be from his at the opposite side of the sitting room. "It feels right. As if she's out there somewhere.

"She could even be one of those celebrating the night." Katherine looked again at the milling street, then at towers of commerce and business reaching toward the quiet night sky. Like jagged teeth they rose out of the neon maw of a city that on another occasion would have been enchanting.

"Jocie could have a job in one of the offices. She could be fine." Katherine bit back another disheartening speculation and covered her lips with her fingers.

Mitch moved behind her, folding his arms around her as he pulled her back against him. He felt the long, slow shudder that shook her as she faced reality. "Shh." He kissed the side of her throat, his lips lingering at the rushing pulse. "Don't think about it."

Katherine turned in his embrace. Sliding her palms over his chest to the open collar of his shirt, she grasped the cloth as if it were her anchor. "I have to think about it. I have to face the truth and admit that if she were working and everything was fine, the detective Gran hired would've found her. He lost her trail. That can only mean she's in trouble of some sort.

"She isn't out there with the merrymakers, Mitch. You know she isn't. Jocie's walking the dark side, where we must go tomorrow."

"We could be wrong, Katherine."

"We could be." She looked from the throbbing hollow of his throat to his pained gaze. "But we aren't. I'm not a fool, Mitch. I know it isn't going to be pretty and it won't be safe, so I think we do have to talk. I don't want to be a burden."

"You won't be." He took her hand again and, linking his fingers through hers, led her to the sofa. When he began to speak he held nothing back. He spared her nothing, nor himself. He confronted old memories, and silently, apart from their discussion, faced the conviction that he'd abandoned the very children he'd once dedicated himself to helping.

When he spoke of what he'd done, children became child, and he told her only of Billy. Then of Simon. And finally of his belief that he should have stayed to do more.

"You didn't abandon an obligation, Mitch," Katherine insisted quietly when he fell silent at last. "You were only sixteen, but wise beyond your years when you chose another and better path to the same end."

"How could you know what path I've chosen? You don't know for certain what I do, Katherine."

"I can't deny that I don't know, at least, not specifically. But you've avoided the subject so adroitly I would be a fool not to realize your work is secret and even dangerous. Why else was Gran so reticent about her friend Simon? And why would you be so suspicious of me in the valley?"

When he slanted a startled look at her, she only smiled. "You told me about Simon McKinzie's splendid Jaguar, and that you needed money to help a friend. Why would you be any different now, just because you have a law degree you've never used? Whatever this clandestine work is that you do for Simon McKinzie, it would be good, because you're good."

"You have it all figured out, haven't you?" He wondered what she would think if she knew taking Simon's Jaguar wasn't just a one-time occurrence. Could she cope with the knowledge that helping a friend was his idiom for buying a child he hardly knew from a pimp or a pedophile?

No matter what connotation she tried to give it, he committed crimes for the purpose of trading in human life. "You're being idealistic, Katherine."

"Am I? Just because I see a decent human being in you? If that makes me an idealist, what does it make Simon? Funny, from the little you and Gran have told me of him, he didn't strike me as either a simpleton or a garbage collector."

Touché. With no specific knowledge of The Black Watch—the clandestine organization formed and controlled by Simon, and the focus of Mitch's own life for more than a decade—she'd drawn the right conclusions. Katherine was neither a Pollyanna nor anybody's fool. Just naive in the ways of the underbelly of society.

Tomorrow and the days after would change that.

"Tell me what to do, Mitch." She touched his cheek to pull him from his thoughts.

He pondered that for a minute. How to keep the grotesque and violent from her? How to keep her safe?

"Stay close. So close we could be attached at the hip. Don't ever stray away from me, or be distracted. Listen, but don't speak, not even when someone speaks to you.

"For all appearances you're deaf and mute. I'd throw in blind, if I thought I could get away with it. If you have a question, wait until we're alone to ask it." He took her face between his palms, his gaze bored into hers. "Whatever happens, I want you only a touch away."

Katherine accepted his rules with her silence, and waited for more. When he leaned back in his seat, with nothing to add, she asked one last question. "What time do we begin?"

"At nine."

She glanced at her watch. "Six hours."

"Eighteen." At her startled look, he explained. "We begin at nine tomorrow night. The vultures we have to see only fly at night."

"Vultures?"

"My name for them. Except they don't feed on carrion. They prefer the weak and the innocent. The children."

"Girls like Jocie."

Mitch buried his face in his hand, letting his fingers squeeze the ache that thundered in his temple. Exhaling heavily, he took his hand away and returned her anxious look. "Yes, girls exactly like Jocie." He didn't mean to be cruel, but she had to know. His voice was gentle as he restated in forewarning, "Especially like Jocie."

Katherine folded her hands in her lap to still their shaking. She stared down at them for a long while, allowing herself to admit what the vultures were, and what they wanted from children and young boys and girls. "I hoped it wouldn't be like that." Her voice was a hoarse whisper. "I prayed it wouldn't be."

"There's a chance it won't."

"A very slim chance."

He covered her hands with his. "It's better than no chance at all."

"Eighteen hours is a long time to wait." She didn't look at him, she didn't want him to see the horror in her eyes. "What do we do in the meantime?"

"First of all, I have some more telephone calls to make, some old contacts to reestablish, if they still exist." He didn't add that the most important contacts couldn't be reached by telephone. "After that, we go shopping."

She looked at him as if she'd suddenly begun to doubt his sanity. "You're joking." Then, in response to his unwavering look, "You aren't joking."

"Not for a minute."

"Shopping? What on earth for?"

"Clothing."

"We have clothing, Mitch. Suitcases of clothing."

"But none of it proper dress for the street."

Forgetting that she wore a slim column of a gown and a bell-sleeved negligee, Katherine looked down at herself, then at Mitch. Granted, she couldn't go on the street dressed as she was, but her luggage was filled with what she considered proper clothing. "What's wrong with what I wore on the plane and brought with me? Or what you're wearing now?"

"We look like the establishment."

"That's wrong?"

"The people we must try to talk to have dropped out of society and the establishment. They don't like it, each for reasons of their own. They've learned not to trust those of us who are part of it, and refuse to have any contact with us. If we come at them, looking like a couple of yuppies, no one will give us the time of day."

"So, how should we look?" She was at a loss. Her clothing was presentable but not on the cutting edge of fashion. Some were more than old-fashioned—the dresses and gowns worn by the Rivard women of other eras and more prosperous times, then stored with care that preserved them in tightly sealed chests and closets lined with cedar. Styles like her favorites, the sleek and uncomplicated lines of the twenties that appealed to her more than modern styles.

"We have to look like we belong," he clarified. "As if each of us is one of them and can be trusted. As much as anyone trusts anyone on the street."

"When do we start? Where do we begin?"

"The afternoon will be soon enough, and we begin at some of the secondhand shops a few blocks over. If we don't find what we need there, there's always the Salvation Army."

Katherine didn't flinch at the prospect of wearing used and discarded garments from a secondhand shop. After all, other than her work clothes, they comprised the major part of her wardrobe. She didn't have quite the reaction to clothes intended for charity. Instead she wondered how many Hail Marys would be needed for taking something someone far more unfortunate might need.

"Counting Hail Marys?"

"What!" Then, with a disbelieving gesture, she asked, "How could you know about that?"

"Gran told me." He smiled at her. A smile that was almost real. "She says you don't realize they know, but both she and the aunties see how hard you are on yourself. And they hear the punishments you inflict when you don't live up to the standards you've set for yourself."

"For the most part, the penance is reserved for when I curse. I know a lady shouldn't. I know it's childish to let myself be that frustrated. But sometimes it's like a volcano erupting and one mean and rotten word is the lava. Occasionally more than one," she admitted. "Bless her heart, it's usually Rose who drives me to it."

Mitch chuckled and understood. Sweet, batty lady that she was, Rose could drive most anyone a little batty, too. "Ah, Katherine." He took her hand in his and kissed the tender flesh at the base of her wrist. "Who would ever believe that a wonderful family like yours exists?"

"Most people would thank heaven there's only one." At the sound of his laughter, Katherine knew she'd accomplished part of what she'd come to do. If she didn't understand, completely, what demons he fought, there was a glimmer of light she could follow.

If those demons were not laid to rest, at the moment they were quiet and her intentions were served. She rose from her seat, meaning to leave.

Before she could say good-night, he caught her wrist. "Don't go."

"You're tired, Mitch. Tomorrow will be a busy day for you, and a difficult one."

"Until tomorrow, tomorrow doesn't matter. Don't go, Katherine. Stay with me."

"Mitch..."

"I'm not asking anything but that you stay. Talk to me, tell me things. Tell me about growing up in a family like yours."

"A crazy family like mine."

"A wonderful family." He pulled her back down to him. This time to his lap, to hold her in his arms.

Katherine heard a hunger in his voice and she wouldn't deny him. She couldn't. "Where would you like me to begin?"

"The first time you sat a horse. Do you remember?"

"I remember."

"Start there."

Katherine was silent for a minute, gathering her thoughts. Her head was resting on his shoulder when she began. "I was three. The horse was Alexander, fifteen hands and as big as a

Clydesdale to me. It was Gran who put me in the saddle and kept me from being afraid.''

''Is that when you got the scar on your elbow?''

''No, that came from falling off the first horse that was really mine. It was my sixth birthday and Sugar was my gift from Gran. Cam picked me up and wiped away the blood, but it was Gran who kissed away my tears and put me back in the saddle.''

If Gran hadn't, Katherine would have gotten back on alone. Even at six. Nothing could persuade Mitch differently. It didn't escape him that it was always Gran who was there for her. Gran who was the center of her life. When Gran wasn't there, it would have been Cam.

Mitch didn't need to ask to know that her mother was too busy with her own riding, and her father was just too busy. Katherine had come to terms with their neglect and didn't dwell on it. Neither would he.

''When did you get the tattoo on your tush?'' There was a mischievous note in his sly question.

Around a grin, without missing a beat, Katherine retorted, ''I don't have a tattoo on my tush.'' Just to keep it interesting, and because for a little while she had the wonderfully wicked Mitch back, she added, ''Good guess, wrong location.''

''Then you do have one, huh?'' He played her tease to the limit. ''Funny, I didn't see it.''

''Naturally, you didn't. It's black and blue, the color of bruises.''

''Ah, a clue! I'll have to look again, when you're a little less colorful.''

''I suppose you will. Later.'' She caught a roving hand pretending early exploration in hers. ''Now,'' she said with mock seriousness, ''where was I?''

''You were three, and then six.'' And very much her greatgrandmother's granddaughter.

''So I was.''

Mitch realized, if Katherine did not, that this detour into the ridiculous was a natural retreat for a mind too heavily burdened. He'd seen exhausted men laugh and joke together while they stood knee-deep in horror. If they hadn't laughed, they would have cried, even died. Or if there hadn't been someone to share the madness, they would have descended into madness themselves.

So he held her, listening to her ramble. Laughing when the time was right, and holding her closer when it hurt.

She spoke without rancor of Sylvia Rivard, her mother, and of her absorbing, excluding passion for riding. She spoke of her father and his absorbing, excluding passion for nothing but passion.

She talked about Cameron Halsey, her best friend in all the world, who filled the empty spaces Gran could not. Cam, her champion, and sometimes her nemesis and conscience since she was a newborn and he was three.

She spoke of her second best friend, and answered questions that Mitch hadn't and wouldn't ask.

"Lianna is Cam's wife. I was ten, she was twelve, and Cam was thirteen when her family moved to Tryon. It was love at first sight and there was never anyone else for either of them. They were married the summer after she graduated from college. Lianna could have had a modeling career. There were agents waiting to sign her, but all she wanted was Cam.

"For six years they were happier than any two people could be. All they needed for their marriage to be perfect was a baby. They'd tried for years, and just when they were ready to give up and simply be happy with themselves, Lianna discovered she was pregnant.

"If they were happy before, they were delirious then."

"But it was too good to be true." Mitch interpreted the sadness in her and knew that tragedy had visited the perfect union.

"Lianna suffered a stroke in her seventh month. The baby, this little boy who was wanted more than any child had ever been wanted, died before he ever really lived."

Mitch held her closer when her voice broke, and said nothing as she wiped away a tear.

"Lianna survived, but she can't speak or move," Katherine continued in a bleak voice. "She sits in her chair, day after day, staring out a window at nothing. Her doctors have told him it's hopeless, but Cam has never given up. He never stops waiting for the day she will look at him, and see him, and be his Lianna again.

"He's waited for five years, he'll wait the rest of his life or Lianna's if he has to."

Mitch found himself listening for any nuance of more than friendship for Halsey, yet all he heard was regret for a lost friend, and for a dear friend's loss.

Katherine was silent for a bit, then began again to speak of her family, from damn Yankee, to horse thief, and eccentric maiden ladies. As time passed her words came slower and farther apart. She relaxed against him, saying less and less.

"That's all there is," she roused to say at last. "There's absolutely nothing more to know about the illustrious and infamous Rivards."

"I think there is," he murmured into her hair. "At least about this Rivard."

She didn't answer. Her breathing was measured and even.

He waited until he was sure this was more than a catnap, then carried her to her bed. For a long while after he'd slipped the robe from her shoulders and tossed it into a chair, he sat at the edge of her bed, watching her sleep.

He'd pulled the sheet to her chin, but he needed only his memory to recall every inch of the delicious body wrapped in a gown that caught the light like smoldering embers.

She slept as a child sleeps, deeply, innocently. He was reluctant to leave her, but it was time. He would need a clear mind when he began the search for Jocie. The bit of rest he might salvage from the night would be a beginning.

Rising carefully from the bed, he smiled as she muttered and turned on her side. The sheet tumbled to her waist, revealing her barely covered breasts. As carefully as he could he pulled the covers back to her chin, leaning over her just for a moment to kiss her cheek.

"Good night, Katherine," he whispered. "Sleep well."

He was at the doorway when she sighed and muttered again. She'd swept the sheet away as she had before, and he allowed himself the exquisite luxury of looking at her.

Her room was dark, but the light falling from the doorway to the sitting room was enough. Enough that her hair shimmered as it rippled over the pillow and tumbled down her breasts. Enough that her skin gleamed like pale amber and her lashes lay like a veil against her cheeks. Enough that his body ached with desire and his heart filled with the need to protect her and keep her safe.

He'd never wanted to protect anyone so badly in his life. And he would, as much as it was in his power to protect her. As much as she would allow.

Protecting Katherine wouldn't be easy. She was headstrong and independent, and played whatever hand life dealt her alone.

''But you're not alone now, Katherine.'' Mitch understood then why he hadn't gone when Gran had given him the opportunity.

Katherine Mary Rivard was everything good in his life. She was beauty and honor and innocence, and he was in love with her.

No one could take away the beauty that came from within. Nothing could compromise her honor.

But as Mitchell Ryan turned away at last, away from the golden woman he loved, he wondered sadly what the future held for her. In spite of all he might do to protect her and keep her from harm, could he keep the insidious ugliness from touching her?

After tomorrow would Katherine ever be innocent again?

Five

―――――

"**W**ell?" Katherine spun from the mirror and back again, her arms lifted from her sides to reveal the lines of her costume. "What do you think? Do I look like a lady of the night?"

From his chair by her bedroom window, Mitch looked at Katherine wearing what she considered, in her genteel terms, her street-walking finery, and wasn't certain what he thought, or how he felt.

After a long morning of making quiet last-ditch inquiries through proper and legitimate channels, then some not so legitimate nor so proper, and turning up not one single clue, he'd accepted the inevitable.

Jocie was out there, every instinct told him she was. Dead or alive, on the street or in a house, city or bayou, she was there. But beyond proper and legitimate channels.

Chafing at the interminable but necessary delays, first at the farm and now the city, Katherine had spent a quietly restless morning prowling the confining spaces of their suite waiting for him while he was away, or listening while he spoke on the telephone. Though he knew she understood the need for the tedious process of uncovering every shred of information, and for thorough preparation, she was feverishly relieved to escape the hotel in their first, visibly positive action.

In their afternoon visit to a consignment shop, among row after row of used clothing, he'd left her to make her own choices with only a suggestion or two from the shopkeeper and another one or two from himself. He leaned to the more conservative. The shopkeeper, a reformed lady of the night, with an eye for mischief and his rising blood pressure, pressed for the risqué. Katherine, with a suddenly calm purposefulness and a startling sense of what worked for her, chose from both.

The result was a heady mix of class and trash. Now she'd stepped from the dresser's screen and stood in front of a mirror, biting her lip and looking at herself, Mitch's inclination was to tear every piece of the costume from her. What he wanted to do most was stuff it back into its respective bags and toss it down the incinerator.

First to go would be the formfitting bodysuit. A sultry scrap of black satin that at first appearance—except that it was unquestionably formfitting and cut daringly high over her hips—seemed only moderately provocative. Until one became aware of the subtle razor-thin slit that plummeted from banded choker collar to the tight waist of skimpy spandex briefs.

With each breath the clinging fabric of the bodice lifted and buckled, teasing with a glimpse of the shadowy undercurve of her breasts, whispering promises of more. Mitch had never realized how seductive the completely but intriguingly clothed breast could be.

The modicum of comfort he'd found in the slim skirt she'd wrapped and tied at her waist was short-lived. Nothing could have prepared him for the glorious flash of long, lovely legs bare from the tops of tall, glossy boots to her hips. A man could suffocate holding his breath watching the tulip curve of the wrap, waiting for it to part in the next revealing step, and the next.

Just in case some poor fool should miss the subtle tease, a band of sequins and jet beads circled the tight collar and marked the cleaving borders of blouse and skirt.

Sure, Mitch thought, just in case some poor, *blind* fool should miss it. For that's what any man would have to be not to see and want her.

"Good Lord!" Katherine muttered, unmindful of his stunned silence as she surveyed the results of her choices back at the hotel. "I didn't know I could look so...so...earthy."

Earthy wasn't quite the word for it. Mitch had several others he could name. Just as he had several colorful and picturesque words for the idiot who would dare look at Katherine tonight as he was looking now. Yet short of locking her in her room, he knew he couldn't stop her from going with him. But there was another tack he could take.

"Katherine, maybe I was mistaken about this."

"Mistaken?" She turned to him, the skirt flaring, the beaded cleavage beguiling. "How so?"

"I don't think the costume is necessary. Your own clothing should do as well."

"My prim, safe, establishment clothing?"

"Right." Prim and safe, that was the key.

"But you said the people who live and work on the street wouldn't trust us unless we looked like one of them."

"They'll talk to me."

"Because you look like a gangster who stepped out of the thirties?"

The pinstripe shirt, the vest, the flashy tie with its rhinestone pin were the ultimate in campy style. All he needed was a bottle of Vaseline for his hair, a gold chain for his neck and a diamond stud for his ear. "They'll talk to me because I can speak their language."

"*If* they let you get close enough to speak any language with Miss Prim and Proper on your arm." She shook her head, and her hair drifted about her shoulders like a mist at sunset. "I'm going as I am, Mitch."

"Katherine, you don't understand."

"You're wrong, again. I understand." She was moving toward him, slowly, seductively. As a streetwalker would, displaying her wares. "I understand perfectly. You think I can't play my part." A slow tug at a fluttering loop of satin sent the skirt skimming to the floor. "But I can."

Mitch wanted to stop her. He wanted to wrap the skirt back around her and scold her for playing games. Instead he watched, with pounding pulse and dry mouth, mesmerized by her lush body, the sensual, gliding step.

She halted in front of him, an inch from his knees, and lifted his head with a finger under his chin. When their gazes met and held, her smile was sensuous, provocative, and wicked. "Let me show you."

Mitch lost the thread of argument as she took a single step forward and in a sinuous, feline move sat astride his knees. Linking her arms around his neck, she silenced any abiding protest with a brush of her mouth over his. A breathy laugh flowed like a purr out of her and into him, filling him with the essence of her as she teased his rigid lips with the tip of her tongue.

With each bend and twist of her body, the perfume she'd chosen enveloped him in its dark, erotic scent. Sequins and jet beads glittered and danced with each rise and fall of her breasts. The heat of her naked thighs against his ravaged his last remnant of sanity as each kiss grew bolder, deeper, sweeter.

Hardly remembering if there was a point he needed to prove, or why, Mitch fought to resist. A pulse throbbed in his temples, strain furrowed his brow as his fingers curled around the edge of his seat as he struggled for a steady breath.

Laughing softly, indulgently, at his stubborn resistance, Katherine pulled away. Her eyes were heavy-lidded and veiled as she brushed a wayward shock of hair from his forehead. From his hair her fingers danced a path over the pulsing temple to his cheek; from his lips to his chin, to his throat. In moves so languid they were hardly moves at all she slipped his tie from its knot. Slowly, in delicious increments, as a stripper would the prerequisite long white gloves, she pulled it from his collar.

The buttons of his vest were next. And his shirt. As slowly, as deliciously languid, one button at a time. Her gaze kept his, never straying, never wavering. Until her task was done.

Her eyes were like elusive smoke, dark, rich, ever-changing, as she watched the changes in his.

As she watched him watch her.

A naughty smile curled the corner of her mouth. A taunting fingertip skimmed the open edge of silk as it lay against his bare skin. From the hollow of his throat to the snap of his trousers, she drew a path of fire.

Mitch shivered and gripped the chair tighter.

With a delighted ripple of triumph, she slipped her hands beneath his shirt and pushed it away from his chest. Then, and only then, did she let her look follow the path her hands had taken. A look as lingering as a caress, as tangible. Leaning forward, she let her hair glide over him as she blazed a second trail over his ribs and shoulders, caressing the tiny buds of his nipples with the bite of her teeth. Letting the tips of her own swaying breasts soothe the pleasant hurt as she lifted her mouth to kiss him again.

A gentle kiss that found his lips softer and yielding, but without surrender. A kiss that nipped and plundered as joyfully as a child, as wantonly as a woman. A kiss that drew him to the last boundary of his strength, the last of his resistance, only to back triumphantly away...to begin all over again. This time slower still, artless in new expertise, lingering over each caress. Keeping him waiting there at the brink, anticipating the next touch, the next kiss.

And the next.

"Katherine." Her name was a cry, ripped from him against his will. "Damn you, Katherine."

She lifted her head, her feverish gaze returning to his. "Damn me, or love me, Mitch," she whispered. "The choice is yours."

"Witch." His hands closed in a punishing grip in her hair as he dragged her back down to his kiss. Hot, hard, taking and yielding. A shift of her body turned her in his embrace, allowing him access to the charms she'd used against him.

His kiss was savage with the venting of frustration and denial. He became a marauder taking what he wanted. What he needed. A renegade stepping from the charted course. A lover whose kiss would mark her, brand her, make her forever his.

As her laughter marked him.

As her wonderfully wicked delight in loving him made him forever hers.

His kiss softened in a smile, as wicked as Katherine's, as delighted. A sound that was half laughter, half groan, rumbled in his throat as his kiss deepened and teased as she'd teased him. His hands stroked her, journeying over satin and sequin and bead. As she had, he drew a finger the length of the opening of her blouse, brushing the cleft of her breasts, then moving away.

As frustration became enchantment he stroked her body, cupping her breast in his palm, drawing the bloom of a satin-covered nipple to taut bud. Then hungering for the wonders the garment promised, he parted the beaded fabric to touch flesh softer than any satin, and nestled the wondrously exquisite crest in his palm.

As she whimpered against his mouth, he was only half aware of the passage of time. Only half aware that as he kissed and caressed her the setting sun played hide-and-seek behind taller buildings, filling the room with suffused light and bars of darkness.

The day was slipping away as afternoon turned to twilight, and the night beckoned. But darkness was hours away, and in the fading light there was Katherine.

Sweet Katherine.

He could never have enough of her.

Not if he lived forever.

Sighing softly, he took his lips from hers, but only to end one kiss and start another. His hand left her breast to rove across her stomach, and he was pleased when she quivered beneath his touch.

In experiment, and simply because he wanted more, needed more, he pulled his hand down her hip, circled the top of a boot, and up the inside of her thigh. She was trembling, almost violently, as he traced the gathered leg of the French-cut brief from inner thigh to the flare of her hip and back again.

She gasped, her mouth opening to his, and her body lurched against him at the intimate caress. He laughed softly against her lips and moved away to look into her heavy-lidded eyes.

Katherine was a neophyte femme fatale. A woman just shedding the chrysalis of her naiveté, discovering her sexuality. Reveling in the newfound power of it.

The untold pleasure of it.

"So, Miss Katherine Mary Rivard." He dragged her hair from her face and cradled her head in his grasp. "Whose choice now?"

"Mine." She didn't look away from a gaze that blazed down into hers.

"What do you choose, sweet Kate?"

"Damnation. Love." Her fingers slid from his arm to his shoulder, to curl around his neck. "You."

She drew him back to her. "I choose you."

"Katherine." Mitch moved to stand behind her in what had become her habitual spot. In quiet moments he would find her here, staring down at the twisting maze of thoroughfares and nooks and culs-de-sac that held the key to finding Jocie.

"It's almost time, isn't it?" She didn't turn to him as she spoke. She seemed frail now in the golden negligee she'd slipped into when she'd left her bed and his arms.

"Almost," he agreed as he slid his hands beneath the open lapels, pulling her back against him to kiss the top of her head. "We need to dress in a little while, but first we need to talk."

Katherine crossed her arms over his, clasping his hands to her bare breasts. "About this?"

"About this and other things."

"Are you afraid that I'm feeling guilty?"

"I thought you might be worried."

Katherine shook her head and turned in his arms. Even in her pensive thoughtfulness she appreciated the irregular handsomeness of his face, the rugged look that was far more interesting than the perfection of classical beauty. She liked the way that brows, shades darker than his auburn hair, arched almost wickedly over his eyes. Eyes that were by nature compassionate and warm, but in perception of danger or cruelty could grow bitter and cold in the space of a heartbeat. She liked his nose with its tiny bump and slight crook, and was given to wondering in odd moments what it was like before it was broken the first time, or the second.

She was solemn as she touched his face, cradling his cheek in her palm. "I'm not worried, at least not about what you think."

A fingertip stroked his mouth in a fleeting caress and moved away. She liked his clever mouth, the fine shape of it, the quick, flashing smile.

She liked the things the clever mouth did to her, the things it made her feel. The love it made with a kiss, a sweet whispered word.

She liked everything about Mitchell Ryan. Honorable spirit, kind heart, virile body. Beautiful, masculine body, as fine as he, clad now only in briefs. And she could find not one regret in loving him.

"There are no Hail Marys lying in wait for me, Mitch," she said with a calm resolve that surprised him. "I don't feel guilty, not for this. Jocie's lost and it hurts. It hurts that something was so wrong in her life that she ran away. It hurts so much I feel sick inside. But hurting for Jocie doesn't mean I can't love you. That I shouldn't.

"You taught me not to feel guilty, remember? I would change things for Jocie and for Gran if I could. But I can't undo what's been done. All of us will have to live with the outcome of this, disastrous as it is, and as difficult as the days ahead may be. Because of you, I can.

"Because of you, I know that each of us must find our own moments of peace and forgetfulness. In good times and in bad, through laughter and through love. To survive and do what must be done. How could that be wrong?"

"It would only be wrong if wrong things happen as a result." He threaded a single finger through a lock of her hair and tucked it carefully behind her ear. He looked away, unable to meet her questioning look. "Sweetheart, we weren't very sensible or responsible. I least of all," he explained. "Neither of us gave any thought to caution."

"I know," she said quietly. "If this were another circumstance and we were different people, it could be disastrous and even deadly. But there are no other circumstances, and we are who we are. Both of us are healthy. I, because I was that ancient cliché, the virginal old maid. You, because you are a man of uncommon honor. No passion would have been too great, if you thought it would hurt me."

Mitch met her look then, and saw utter trust. His heart careened, then plummeted. Such belief could be a burden as much as a precious gift. What if he disappointed her? Could he bear to see that trust tarnished?

Had he tarnished it already? "There could be more to think of than health and virginity and honor. Something far more important."

"A child." She laid her palms over her stomach. "Our child."

Our child. His and Katherine's. Mitch was shocked at the thrill of hearing his thought spoken aloud. Hearing it made it seem real. Possible. He loved children; they were his first priority from his first sentient days on the street. Yet he'd never thought of having a child of his own. The time had never seemed right for it. His life in The Watch—the constant threat of danger, the long days away on assignment—were not the life a father should lead. He had a thousand and one reasons, but he knew now that it was simply that he hadn't met the right woman. The woman he wanted to give his children to.

Until now.

Until Katherine.

The thought of her filled with a part of him astounded and delighted him. Her body blooming with a son, a daughter—*his* son, *his* daughter—swept the breath from him. But it was only a pipe dream, for Katherine was moving her head from side to side with an expression of dismay.

Right woman, wrong man. They were from different worlds and all the love in both worlds couldn't change it.

"I should have told you," Katherine said in a low, shaking voice. "Of all the people in the world I might have loved, I should have told you."

"Shh, it doesn't matter, sweetheart." He'd never thought of himself as a coward, but he didn't want to hear this. He wasn't sure he could endure it.

"You don't understand," she insisted.

"I do, truly, I do. I'm a stranger, from a strange place."

"No." She was implacable, and her next comment proved how wrong his assumption had been. "I've known you all my life, for my life only began when I met you. And where either of us comes from is of no consequence. If I were from New Orleans and you from Stone Meadow, you wouldn't care. We both know you aren't the sort of man who would.

"Because you aren't there's nothing more I would ask than to have your child, if it were what you wanted. But the odds are that I never will.

"It isn't impossible, just unlikely." Her hands were clasped between them, the knuckles white. "Too many falls from horses. A kick or two that left more than bruises. Horses are a way of life to the Rivards, but a life that hasn't always been kind."

The specter of bruises marking her ribs in bold, ugly stripes rose in front of him. The violently reddish purple of hemorrhaging beneath skin like shimmering gold. The blue-black of emerging, deep-seated injury. The mottled, green-tinted yellow as they faded at last.

Grievous injury to a body that should have only fine care, and she dismissed it with the diffidence of common occurrence. Part and parcel of her life.

"You're a man who should have children, Mitch. Lot's of them. A houseful." There were tears glittering like diamonds in her eyes as she looked up at him. Tears of regret, not self-pity. "Chances are I can't give them to you."

Mitch didn't know what to say, so he simply wrapped her in his arms and pulled her to him. The contact was electric as her nearly naked body twined into his. It would always be this way with Katherine, for as long as he lived, but his passion for her was tempered by heartbreak, for the longing he heard in her voice, for the despair.

"I'm irrevocably tied to Stone Meadow and the past, with little hope of a future." Her arms were around his waist, her cheek lay against his chest. The powerful beat of his heart thrummed through her, a reminder of his strength, his energy. "I should have told you."

"No." He moved her from him, but only a little, to kiss the soft skin at her temple where a fine blue vein disappeared into her hairline. "You told me all that mattered when you said you love me."

"But—"

He shook her gently. "That's all that matters."

"Once you told me that children mattered."

"They did. They do. They always will, but not as my own, and not as much as Katherine Mary Rivard." Wrapping his hands around her waist, he looked down at her. "I never figured on children of my own, but I never expected to meet a woman like you. I didn't think a woman like you existed, or if she did, that she would ever care for someone like me."

He smiled, a comforting smile with a touch of wonder. "So you see, Katherine, my love, proof positive that nothing is impossible."

The tears were there, sparkling in her lashes, but they didn't fall. There was so much to talk about. So much in the present to resolve if they were to have a future. The present was her sister. "Even finding Jocie."

"Especially finding Jocie. So you can go home," Mitch murmured, "to Stone Meadow."

Mitch slid his newly purchased car into a space by the curb. A vehicle with a many-colored body of rust and an indeterminate make, destined for the junk heap years ago. But with an engine that growled its power in a low, rumbling purr. An expensive purchase made in the hours he'd left Katherine alone in their suite, but perfect for their needs.

A street car with little worth stealing.

He sat for a moment flexing his fingers on the steering wheel, waiting for Katherine to speak. For all she'd seen to sink in.

Lights flashed from a sign in front of a building, filling the interior of the bastardized car with its harsh light. Most of the bulbs were broken or burned out, leaving a different message than the dilapidated building intended. Blinking a hot pink reminder, in case they could forget, that they had come to hell. Minus one L.

Mitch waited as the jarring clamor of the street seeped in, but Katherine kept her silence. Drawing a breath as harsh, he forced himself to look at her, and found she was pale even in the garish light, and trembling.

"Katherine? Kate?" He wanted to reach for her, to make the ugliness go away.

"I didn't know," she whispered, staring straight ahead through the stained and scarred windshield.

"No one can know until they've been here, or the countless places like this."

"Countless places," she repeated numbly. "Most of us live lives of quiet desperation, where each day is a struggle. But not like this. Never like this. Dear God! The filth, the human suffering. The degradation."

The light flashed its reminder.

On. Off.

Hel.

On. Off. Endlessly.

Mitch waited.

"The dirt in my life is sweat and horsehair, mucky stables and red dirt. But this..." She bowed her forehead to her clasped hands, blocking out the sight, wishing she could purge it from her memory. "God forgive me, I didn't know."

Mitch ached for her, and for an innocence lost.

She hadn't understood that dignity was a luxury beyond reach on the street, and degradation a way of life. Nothing in her life prepared her for the sight of women working their little territories in transparent clothing, stopping cars and trucks, making their pitch. Offering fifteen, twenty, thirty minutes of true love in the back seat, or the nearest alley. All under the watchful, greedy eyes of protectors. Pimps who would take most, if not all, of what they earned with the only commodity they had. Their bodies.

She'd known, but hadn't been ready to face that all who peddled themselves wouldn't be old, or teens, or women.

She hadn't been ready for the shuffling, mumbling zombies that had been once human. Or beggars in filthy tatters, lifting clawed palms for a nickel or dime to buy the next hit, the next drink.

She hadn't really realized the squalor of the life that spawned Mitchell Ryan.

He wanted to hold her and shield her, but how could he shield her from what he was?

"Katherine." He risked touching her shoulder, and waited until she lifted her head from her hands. "Would you like to go back to the hotel?"

"No!" She was vehement in her denial, and her eyes blazed like hot coals in her haggard face.

"I can do this alone."

"No, Mitch."

"There's no need for both of us to stay."

"I said no." She turned from him to the horror she'd found. "If Jocie's out there, she'll need me more than ever."

"I can bring her to you, to the hotel, when I find her."

"I need to know, to understand. I'll be with you when you find her."

"Please, Katherine."

"I'm not going to fold on you. I'm flesh and bone, not spun sugar that will melt in the rain, or crystal that will shatter with the first assault." There was the steel of Gran in her. In the unbending spine, the stubborn tilt of her chin, in her steadfast tone. "This was a shock, but I've been shocked before. No doubt, before we're done, I will be again. But I'll be all right."

She would be, he knew it now. She'd tapped that rare reserve of strength hidden deep inside her. Strength that would help her deal with what she must, as she must.

Katherine Mary Rivard would be all right.

Until they found Jocie.

A fist banged the window at her side. Katherine cringed and barely smothered a scream. Despite her bravado the minute before, she turned a shade paler at the cloudy eyes that peered at her from a pockmarked face of a man dressed as an overstuffed scarecrow.

"Easy," Mitch murmured, much as she would have to a skittish mare. The sound of his voice and the grip of his hand over hers were all that kept her from recoiling when the ravaged face broke into a green-toothed grin and a three-fingered hand touched the window as if it were touching her.

In mesmerized horror she watched as the face, only inches from the glass, tilted this way and that, studying her from all angles. Tracing the shape of her cheek and brow on the glass, pursing lips in a pantomime of a kiss.

"Dear Lord!" she muttered through clenched teeth and stiff lips. "What does he want?"

"You."

"Me!" Only the greatest effort kept her from turning to stare at Mitch, with all the revulsion pouring through her.

"You," he repeated grimly. "When he makes his offer, let me handle it."

"His offer? You're joking." She was staring at the stooping creature who hadn't had a bath or seen a toothbrush in years. "You are joking, aren't you?"

"There are no jokes down here, Katherine."

Proving his point, the scarecrow looked to Mitch, rubbing the tips of his fingers together in a common sign that asked how much.

Mitch gripped her hand tighter and shook his head.

The scarecrow persisted, this time drawing a packet from the nether regions of a puddle of clothing. From the packet he took a roll of bills. The first he peeled off was a hundred.

Mitch shook his head.

Another hundred was peeled from the rest.

Mitch shook his head again.

A third bill joined the first and second.

Mitch shook his head.

An angry fist smashed at the window. Katherine blinked, but didn't move. She couldn't.

Mitch jacked open the door and bailed out of the car. Leaning on the rusted top, he glared at the would-be john. "Move on, old man, the lady's not for sale."

"She for sale, man, or she don't be down here."

"Not tonight."

A laugh like a string drawn through a rusty tin can accompanied the baring of white gums.

"She's mine." Mitch tapped the top of the car with an emphatic finger.

"Tonight?"

"Every night."

The rough face tilted, the murky eyes narrowed. "Why you be bringin' her here, then?"

"We're looking for a girl." Mitch took a picture from the pocket of his shirt, and scaled it over the roof. A grubby hand scooped it up and brushed away flakes of rust.

The man, who could have been thirty or sixty, or somewhere between, gawked at the picture that nearly touched his nose and whistled. "Pretty lady, she."

"Have you seen her?"

Picture in hand, he bent to peer again at Katherine, his face pressed to the glass. "Two pretty ladies."

"Yes," Mitch agreed. The creature might be dense and dirty, his eyes might be ripe with cataracts, but he wasn't blind. Yet. "Have you seen her?"

"Sister?"

"Yes."

"Sorry, man, myself, I don't see her." He thumped the picture with a fingernail. "I keep this, yes?"

"Keep it. There's a number on the back. If you see her, or hear of anyone who has, give me a call."

"I call, myself, it change things with the lady?"

"She's my lady, I said, only mine. Nothing changes that."

"Then I don't see her." The picture fluttered to the sidewalk as he shuffled off in a twitch of multilayered clothing.

The drifter had been swallowed by an alley before Mitch slipped into his seat, closing and locking the door behind him. Katherine was still pale, shock lingered in her eyes, but her hands were steady as they lay in her lap.

"Not exactly an auspicious beginning." But a telling one. The scarecrow was the dregs of the dregs. Katherine had been appalled, but she hadn't panicked.

"He had so much money. Where did he get it?"

"Who knows? Maybe he stole it. Maybe he earned it selling drugs, or running for bookies. Maybe it was his. Not everyone is here because of poverty. Granted, most are destitute and trapped. Some few are here because they like a life that imposes few rules and requires nothing of them.''

"It's sad.''

"Yeah?''

"That he thinks his money can buy someone.''

Mitch laughed, bitterly. "Honey, it can.''

Katherine looked at him as if he'd lost his mind. "No one would be that desperate.''

"Being desperate has nothing to do with it. It's a buyer's market out there, Katherine. The seller has no say. Particularly when his or her pimp is watching from a few feet away. How dirty or clean, how old or young, counts for nothing as long as the color of the client's money is right.''

"There was a little blonde, she couldn't be a day over twelve.''

Mitch nodded, he had seen the child standing on the corner a block back. Her hair done in an elaborate coiffure, the nipples of her flat breasts rouged to show through her sheer blouse. Thin satin shorts clinging to hips too narrow to tantalize any but the sickest mind. He would put her age at ten. An ancient ten.

"If the scarecrow wanted her,'' Katherine's tone was brittle, stilted, "what would happen, Mitch?''

Mitch didn't have to ask who she meant. Jocie and the child had become one in her mind. "He could have her.''

"If the child refused?''

"She wouldn't.''

"But if she did?'' Katherine persisted, unable to let it go.

"She wouldn't. If she had enough mind to care, she wouldn't have the spirit to dare.''

"Enough mind. Surely you don't mean someone would be cruel enough to put a retarded child on a street corner for any monster to take.''

"Pimps don't care about intelligence quotients. All that's required is enough mind to know how to perform.'' Mitch drew a long, disgusted breath. "But I was speaking of drugs, not mental abilities. The first thing a pimp does when he gets his hands on a novice is turn him or her into a druggie. Cocaine, crack, whatever designer drug is current. Addiction and fear are his weapons. In the end, addiction is the strongest.''

"By then they will do anything for the drug," Katherine whispered in a voice that nearly failed her.

"Anything," Mitch said with a chilling finality. Telling her what she had to know.

Katherine shuddered and lifted her gaze to their wretched surroundings. The sidewalk was littered with human flotsam. The trapped and the damned.

She was thinking of Jocie.

Mitch laced his fingers through hers and waited, giving her the time she needed.

Six

The Rust Runner sat at the curb. Its usual spot. The usual time. Perhaps the name of the street was different, perhaps the sign that shone into the windshield spelled another name less completely. Or more. But in any guise, under any name, it was still hell.

For Katherine there was no escaping it.

Each morning, as the grip of darkness slipped away, while honest, upright citizens hadn't even begun to think of their honest, upright day, she walked away from it to climb to her clean and pretty tower in the sky. But the taint of the night still clung to her. No matter that she scrubbed until her skin was raw, and the shower of her immaculate bathroom in the immaculate suite sometimes ran with blood. No matter that Mitch was with her in the bed they no longer made any pretense of not sharing.

Sometimes he only held her and comforted her, watching as dawn painted the sky in perfect light. Watching with her the promise of days bright and undefiled, so far above the city. Other times, he made love to her. Answering needs spawned by nightmares of horror and anguish that caused her to thrash and shudder and cry out. When, in the restless desperation of sudden wakefulness, she would reach out for him with an urgency that distressed and disturbed him. Until, in her soft, frantic murmurs, he understood that making love with him, to cry out with a different urgency, was ablution.

Forgetfulness. For the hopelessness. For the pain. For the despair and ugliness the act called love had become in this netherworld.

In the beginning she would be distraught, with muscles taut, tendons like wires, skin clammy. A ravenous lioness with her hair streaming over him, binding him to her. He let her set the pace. Whatever she wanted, however she wanted it. Sometimes, when the dream was particularly bad, there was a lasting violence in her. As if by violence, violence could be purged.

Then their coupling would be furious and brutally swift. He would pin her slim, feverish body to the spotless mattress, covered with fine spotless linen, and pump himself into her until her harsh, futile sobs became ragged whimpers. Until her tormented mind ceased its grieving. Grief, diminished for a little while by the bittersweet comfort of oblivion.

There was healing in the blessedly mindless mating. Enough that out of an aftermath of silent accord that was balm, if not contentment, desire would kindle. True desire. Like a gentle fire it would begin, with a sigh, a brush of her fingertips over his stomach, the touch of her lips against his shoulder. Hesitant, shy, incredibly tender. As if the first had never happened.

He would make love to her then. Gentle love that knew nothing of anger or grief or urgency. Love that was slow, lazy, heartbreaking sweetness. That eased the heart of the lioness, bringing forgetfulness more than any fury. Then when she shuddered it was from the delight of his mouth at her breast. When she arched to his caress it was only in pleasure. Exquisite pleasure that sought more. More of Mitch.

She was like a child, exploring, delighted, and each time was like the first time. Katherine never ceased to be surprised by the wonder of him. Her unworldly fascination never dimmed.

She understood with a tacit knowledge that there had been women in his life. For a dynamic man like Mitch there would have been. Exciting women, erotic, exotic. Women accomplished in the art of seduction. But she was too unworldly to perceive that no one, not even the wonderfully clever, had ever delighted in him as she. No one made the breath leave his body as she did, nor left him hungering for the next touch, the next kiss. None responded with her natural abandon and trust.

She accepted that there had been others before her. Nameless women with faceless bodies, women beyond compare. But when passion demanded its release she didn't think of them. When he reared up over her, filling her, taking her with him into ecstasy, it was her name he cried. Only hers.

Only Katherine. Then . . . Kate.

And, in the fiery new beginning of a day, she was content.

For a while, lying with him in a penthouse that reached for vanished stars, there was fragile peace. But, no matter how safe or perfect her glass-encased tower, no matter that Mitch was strong and good, a thoughtful, gentle lover, in the end there was no escape.

It was always there, burned into the back of her mind. Her reminder. The improbably named Heliotrope Hotel. A wilted flower. A shabby burned-out sign with letters lost like shriveled petals. A banner that branded her thoughts, becoming her omen of perversion and obscenity.

All she had to do was close her eyes.

The sign blinked its revelation.

On.

Off.

Faded red bulbs staining the night tawdry pink.

On.

Off.

Hel.

It waited for her to close her eyes.

She sat quietly now, in the Rust Runner, waiting for Mitch to decide if they would go or stay. Her eyes were open and calm, with no betrayal of revulsion. Her silence was not alarming—she never spoke in these tense times. The grim moments when he watched the doorways and alleys, probing the darkness and the light, judging in some mysterious way the temper of the milling mass beyond the protection of their shabby cage of steel.

The car was a cage well named by Mitch. Rust for apparent reasons. Runner for the snarling power of the engine beneath the dented hood. An engine that purred beneath the mastery of his hand.

Once in passing, as he adjusted some abstruse intricacies within its armored valves and plugs, Katherine observed that it was the perfect getaway car, given his skill at the wheel. His abrupt, absorbed reply was that she was wrong. Though the car was a hoax, hiding the secret of its capacity in a shabby body, and perfect for the street, it would be too noticeable in places worth robbing. Banks, he named for one. Jewelry stores for another. The stark and busy convenience stores that were springing up on every corner.

To her teasing rejoinder that he knew an uncommon lot about thievery, his second, seemingly as absorbed answer had simply been yes. An answer that left her bewildered. But, Mitch, who was a perplexing mix of candor and diversion, said no more.

So she wondered, sitting in a car that drew attention like cats to sardines in civilization, but was lost among countless other derelicts parked on Nowhere Street, Hel, U.S.A.

Hel.

Her lips parted in an unconscious sound, that spoke more eloquently than words, of all she fought to hide.

Mitch flicked a look at her, seeing that beneath a perfect cosmetic mask her cool, patrician face was haggard. Skillfully hidden circles lay under gray eyes that looked steadily and calmly through the windshield. The calm was only surface. Beneath the glacial aloofness writhed a searing pain. He, alone, knew Katherine carried the memories of their nights in the underbelly of the city in her heart.

She could walk past a painted child who might offer some obscene service without a noticeable flicker of expression. And stand by his side unperturbed by sly comments made to Mitch but meant for her. She endured catcalls and innuendo, or graphic narrations of what she inspired in men and what they would like to do to her in response, without so much as a flutter of an eyelash.

None of it had been easy, but she'd learned. Quickly, with agonizing effort.

As Mitch instructed, she was deaf and mute, and virtually blind, and never more than a touch away. She was to the most canny observer, a mannequin—remote, impassive. But he knew that every lecherous comment sickened, graphic speculations unnerved, and her gentle heart was left shredded and raw. A new stab of pity for each hostage. A new, silent wound for each child.

Yet Katherine played her role well, and only he could count the cost of it. Because only he held her in what was left of the fading darkness and listened to her anguish.

There weren't always nightmares, and these sleepless times were the worst. When she was quiet and withdrawn. Too quiet, too withdrawn, as she paced with a haunted look on her face. He couldn't connect with her then. No matter how often he reached out to take her in his arms, nor how tightly he held her, nor how desperately he tried, he couldn't soothe her. The ghosts of the children were too powerful.

So, remembering the vibrant, golden woman he'd met in a peaceful mountain valley, he'd watched her. He watched her eyes growing sicker, her slender body melting into greater slenderness.

Each evening he would have spared her, but he didn't fight the futile battle. And each evening she put on her costume, sometimes the black, sometimes a pale, glowing rose, other times, a midnight blue. Her accents might be gold, and the cosmetics she'd learned to apply of a tawny hue, but she never dressed in gold. Never her special color for her nightly stroll through terror. And Mitch was glad. Like so many other things he felt about her, he didn't quite understand his reason. It was simply there, some small and, per chance, meaningless essence of sentiment he hadn't explored. Perhaps because he hadn't the time. Perhaps because this wasn't the time.

For two weeks their routine had been the same, with the same intensely single-minded purpose. To be visible, to keep a high profile, to become a common presence in the crowd, until they were accepted fixtures among the melee.

No one really knew who they were, or what they did. No more than anyone knew where the handsome couple came from, when they arrived, or where they went when they left. The watchful man with dark auburn hair might be an entrepreneur, a racketeer, a procurer. Either or all. The still, silent lady might be his wife, or mistress, or simply chattel. No one cared so long as nothing the interlopers did or said involved them.

The strollers and stragglers would talk, in groups and singularly. To hear themselves talk, as much as anything. Around and about on vague, meandering subjects. In jive, in slang, in the vernacular of the street, but no one would talk *to* them. The instant Jocie's picture appeared, the mood changed. Tongues grew still, ears closed, eyes were sightless.

Two weeks and they were no closer to finding the girl, yet Mitch was as certain as Katherine that she was here. If she wasn't, she had been, and this was the starting place for finding her.

With an open palm he hit the steering wheel. "One more night. That's all we have."

All of the time Cam had promised him in their conspiracy to salvage Katherine's chances with the consortium. He thought of the land she loved, the aunties who depended on her.

Gran.

Especially Gran.

Dragging a hand through his hair, disturbing its slicked-back order, he clenched his teeth against a bitter curse, muttering again, "One."

Katherine turned to him, focusing on his frustration. "After tonight we have to admit this isn't working and we aren't one step closer to finding Jocie. That is what you mean, isn't it?"

Mitch nodded, absorbed in thoughts of more than finding her sister.

"Then we'll do our best in the time we have. A lot can happen in a day." Some of the coldness that was her salvation on the street left her face, fine lines that fanned from the corner of her eyes softened as she touched the curve of his jutting jaw. "A lot has happened."

Mitch turned his face into her hand, breathing in the sultry scent of her. The perfume of exotic lilies enveloped him, but it was the crisp scent of sun-warmed hay that filled his mind as he kissed her palm. "Yes," he whispered, letting the brush of his lips tease the trembling flesh. "More than a lot. Much more."

"It can again." Taking her hand away, trapping the warmth of his lips against her thigh, she stared out the window as she continued in a breathless tone. "So we put aside these fruitless moments and look to the next and hope for better."

"Is that how you've survived the last thirteen years? Taking one moment at a time? Coping with it, good or bad, then moving onto the next?"

"My life hasn't been so bad, Mitch. It's more than a case of sheer endurance for I've truly been blessed in many ways. I have my family, they love me and care for me. They do as much for me—more than I do for them. The grounds are mine to see to, but the household is theirs. A burden they take willingly and eagerly from me, with skills I could never hope to master.

"Bea is an excellent cook, and you sampled the wine she made. Violet is a born gardener and keeps our pantry filled summer and winter. Daisy keeps the house spotless and filled with flowers from her garden and greenhouse. Rose is an uncanny seamstress. No intricate design or difficult repair is too much for her. When I indulge my proclivity for vintage clothing and raid the trunks in the attic, she's as excited as I am about each new discovery. She enjoys restoring the gowns and loves fussing over precise little details of tailoring."

Mitch chuckled. "She would. She loves fussing over all of you."

"She keeps us in line, when she can. In her vague, fuss-budget manner, she does her share. Everyone does. At the end of a long day, when I step inside a fastidiously kept house, and sit down at a beautifully appointed table loaded with food that rivals the best of dining rooms, I'm reminded of my blessings all over again."

"If there are lemons, make lemonade. If it rains, dance in it," Mitch murmured. If a horse slams you into a fence, get up, kick your hat, curse, then dust yourself off. Levy a Hail Mary or two for the temper, and go back for more. But, above all, be thankful for the opportunity the beast represents.

"It would help if there were rain for the dance," she added in an undertone, referring to the drought that threatened all she loved, yet completely lacking in self-pity.

Mitch had no answer for that. He couldn't give her the weather she needed, but he would do everything else he could for her. Save her farm, with Cam's help. Find her sister any way he could. "So, we make our own luck, or turn our lack of it to our advantage."

"If we can."

Mitch was struck again by how very similar their very different lives had been. Turning whatever luck there was to an advantage had saved his life and the lives of his fellow agents more times than any of them could remember. But this time it wasn't just a life resting on the whim of luck. It was more than bringing Jocie back to this woman's strong, tender care. It was salvaging a heritage, a family, a way of life. All of them precious and alien to him. And more threatened each fruitless day.

"Maybe this was a mistake." He gestured to the garish lights beyond the windshield. "Coming here like this has been useless. No one will talk. I've been gone more than sixteen years, but I didn't expect this."

He felt he'd failed her, she saw it in his face. "It's more than the years. You've changed, Mitch. But I imagine the people here have, as well. You've said you were one of them, but one of whom? Recall one familiar face for me. One name."

He couldn't. On the surface everything had seemed the same, with only subtle differences. But the differences were more far-reaching than he knew, and far less than subtle. The mood was different, the timbre. Where once they'd spoken with variations of one voice, now there were many. He was a Cajun, but in his day the Cajun family unit had been uniquely strong for the most part. So strong their dialect had been rare on the street. So rare he hadn't heard it as a child, had never spoken it. Sadly, he heard it now, and many others.

Mitch slumped in his seat, wondering how she did it. All the torment locked inside her, her life in shambles, the burdens, the grief, the loneliness, yet that calm, reasonable center prevailed. It was overwhelmed at times, and buried deeper at others, but never compromised. In the end it would surface, and with it, strength, clarity, an infectious optimism.

She might bend beneath the weight of her responsibilities, or falter in the hurt of disappointments, but she wouldn't break. Mitch brushed a tumbled curl from her shoulder, remembering the shadow gathering in her eyes, and amended his certainty. She wouldn't break *yet*.

Maybe never, if he could work through this.

Taking his hand away, he addressed her challenge. "There are no familiar faces. But I didn't think there would be. I expected a type, not specific people. Sixteen years can be sixteen lifetimes out here. Some have moved on and out, out of whatever lives they'd lived. The rest just aren't here anymore."

"These people you knew, some have moved on, but some have died, haven't they?"

Mitch sucked in a breath, held it, exhaled heavily. He'd very carefully skirted the short span of these wretched lives. Katherine had gone bluntly to the heart of the matter, expressing a fear that would haunt any astute man or woman. She was thinking of Jocie, wondering how she coped. If she had. "Most of them are dead, I suppose. Maybe a few have stayed and survived." He shrugged and offered a splinter of hope. "New Orleans is a sprawling city, with good streets and bad. Just because I haven't found them, doesn't mean they aren't here."

"Who survives?"

"The toughest. The smartest."

"The children?"

Mitch followed the direction of her gaze. A boy of twelve or thirteen, with his thick hair coated with gel to cement it into dingy spikes, had taken his post at the corner of the block. The perfect place to approach and be approached by cruisers seeking what he had to offer. The boy was pale, his thin shoulders were beginning to stoop. His spine bending with the first stage of a diseased body, a jaded mind. He would be an old man before his voice finished the slide from soprano to bass.

He could have been Billy. He could have been Mitch. If circumstances and Simon had been different.

"The children aren't lucky, Katherine."

"They don't . . ." She stopped. The soft sound that rippled in her throat could have been a moan or a sob. A fracture in her icy composure, mended by a hard bite at her lips. The breath she drew after a minute was as steady as her voice. "They don't make it out."

"No." He brushed a knuckle down her cheek. Only a comforting touch, and all he dared. More would destroy her tenuous check on her fears. "They don't."

"You were only sixteen." The same as Jocie. Hope was reborn. "You made it."

"I owe that to Simon." Most kids don't have a Simon in their lives. He did what he could, but there were too many of them. Not many could be lucky like Mitch Ryan. Mitch considered the consequences of the tangling of his life with Simon's, and that it ultimately led him to her. "It's a long story, Katherine," he said quietly. "Too long for now."

In his voice she heard the promise that one day he would tell her. Then another part of the enigma that cloaked his past would be resolved. She suspected it would be the definitive part. The part that made him the man he was.

Mitch had Simon, now Jocie had Mitch. The ache deepest in her heart eased a bit.

A car stopped at the curb. The boy smiled and postured at the open window. The door swung open and he climbed in.

In less than an hour he would be back, waiting for the next car to stop.

A pall fell over the car while Mitch made one last sweep of the street. A tap at the wheel signaled that his study of its mood was complete and his decision about the evening made. "If this is our last night, we'd better make the most of it. Ready for our promenade, Katherine?"

"I'll never be ready." Each night it grew harder.

"Let me rephrase. Will you be going on our nightly promenade?" A rhetorical question, her response would be as rhetorical. A sure bet.

"I'm going." Her hand was already at the door and she was climbing out of the car as she spoke. By the time he'd crossed to the sidewalk, she was standing straight and tall, waiting for him.

Tonight she wore the rose. A softly clinging affair with a square-cut neckline. The knee-length skirt was draped, as all her costumes were, to reveal a gorgeous length of sheer stockings. For one almost totally lacking in vanity, she knew instinctively her legs were uncommonly beautiful.

She wasn't beautiful in the ordinary sense of beauty. But, God! She was lovely. Her hair was up, twisted into a loose coil at her crown and held by the customary single pin. This one was straight, long and slender. A thick piece of base metal with a rose-colored pearl of paste at one tip. He'd watched as she'd put her hair up. A sweep of her hand and a twist of her wrist and it was done, with the gaudy pin securing the bulk of the coil at her crown. But not all. As tendrils escaped and fell to curl loosely about her face, disheveled elegance was added to her mix of class and trash. The effect was astonishingly erotic, her intention was simply to please him.

Worn down, her hair was a magnet. Men, women, beggars, prostitutes, people who had forgotten what it was to see and feel clean, shining hair seemed compelled to touch her. Enough to risk his wrath by catching a flowing strand in their fingers, letting it trail from their grasp as if they were catching sunlight. Most were gentle in their awe. Katherine hated the reverent mauling, but tolerated it. Mitch couldn't bear it at all, and after the first few nights insisted she wear it up.

He hadn't bargained for the startling result. Especially tonight.

"Mitch?" She touched his arm, the lightest brush of her fingers over the nubby cloth of his jacket brought him back to the present.

"Sorry, I was thinking."

"Serious thoughts?"

"Yes." He couldn't take his eyes from her. Even with the theatrical makeup, purchased along with skillful instruction from the genial ex-hooker in the consignment shop, she was still a lady.

Sweeping lines and shadows of deepening shades of gold and rosy brown gave her eyes a smoky Gypsy aura. Mascara-feathered lashes completed the look, adding to the mystery, hinting at marvelous hidden secrets. A sheer dusting of tawny rose highlighted the natural contour of high cheekbones and accentuated the hollows beneath them. Her mouth was the most alluring of all. Almost bare, with only a whisper of color, it intrigued and invited. A perfect rose, dipped in dewy gold. Soft, lush, tempting.

The paint was stunning in golden tones for her golden skin, but for Mitch her loveliness lay beneath the flawless skin. Thirty years from now, when women who were more attractive than she had lost their surface beauty, Katherine would look the same. With a few wrinkles at her eyes and throat, a sag here or there, but the same. Nothing, not even time, could disguise the fine bone structure that would endure.

Mitch realized as he looked at her that he wanted to be with her when those thirty years were past. He wanted to be a part of her life, he wanted to be a part of her. He wanted it very much. An astonishing thought that terrified him. Little in his life had been permanent. He'd never understood permanence, never wanted it. He wasn't sure he was cut out for it. Would he feel the same next week, or next year? In ten years? Twenty? Thirty? Longer?

Katherine needed a man who was solid, to stand by her in good times and bad. She needed a man who understood her and himself and was content with life on a farm. Mitch had always lived in cities, and beyond the years of his schooling, had never stayed in one place for more than a few months at most. Even his home, the place he stayed when he was not on assignment, had a temporary quality. The walls were bare, the furniture functional, the bed comfortable. It was a place to drop his luggage and catch a good night's sleep, or two, or three, while he waited for Simon's next call.

He was committed to The Watch. His place in the world was wherever the next assignment took him. The women he encountered were simply passing through as he was. If along the way they found a moment of mutual gratification, it was never meant to be more than transient. He'd never wanted any more.

From the first time he'd made love to Katherine in the loft of the barn, he knew she was different. Yet he hadn't let himself look beyond the day when they found Jocie. Not even when Gran issued her ultimatum of sorts.

He never tolerated ultimatums. In his early life they were the prelude to losing control. His practice in adulthood was to change the situation, or back away.

Yet when Gran had challenged him, he hadn't gone. He couldn't. Not then. And the only feeble excuse he could offer was that he wasn't sure.

Mitch Ryan, hotshot agent who had his life firmly under control, wasn't sure! That was a jolt. He wasn't sure he could leave then. He wasn't sure he could stay now. How could he know the day wouldn't come when he couldn't stay, no matter how much he cared for her?

"Hey." Katherine tugged at his sleeve. When he turned a vague, unfocused stare at her, she laughed, weakly, and failed to hide her sudden attack of worry. "Good grief, where did you go?"

"I'm here, Katherine." He caught her wrist in his grasp. The bones were small, blue veins pulsed barely below the skin as the heat of her body blended with his. Holding her like this, her wrist manacled by his encircling fingers, she seemed deceptively fragile. Proof of her skill and command in handling a raging half ton of horseflesh with only a tug of the reins was evident only in the gentle power of her lightly callused hands. "I'm not going anywhere. Not yet."

"Your body is with me." The dim glow of a street lamp was mirrored in the iridescent pearl in her hair. "Your mind was light-years away."

"Years, but not light-years."

"Sounds like it could be serious."

He couldn't tear his gaze from her mouth, no matter how he tried. Not from the shadow that lay beneath the natural pout of her lower lip, making it seem fuller and irresistible. "It could be."

"Care to share?"

"What?" He knew she asked a question from the inflection of her voice, but the words were a jumble, lost in his sudden, aching need to kiss her.

"Your thought. What are you thinking, Mitch?"

"I'm thinking about you." Releasing her wrist, he blazed a slow path up her forearm to her shoulder to cup the side of her throat. "I'm thinking that, right or wrong, I'd like to kiss you." His thumb brushed over her mouth, tugged at her lower lip until her lips parted.

"I'd like to kiss you and not think of anything else. Neither the past, nor the future." He touched the corner of her mouth, the sensitive spot that always made her gasp. As her teeth parted with it, he stroked the perfectly aligned edge, feeling the moistness of her tongue. "I'd like to have your mouth open and warm like this under mine. I'd like . . ." He sighed and scowled with a sharp jerk of his head. "But we both know that if I began I wouldn't stop."

Abruptly he slid his hand across her cheek, burying it in her hair. The coil loosened more, but didn't fall. He stared at her, at her trembling mouth, in a look as passionate as a kiss. His chest ached with the need of a breath, his body sang its hunger for her.

His heart and mind said no.

The breath he finally drew was harsh, ragged. His hands tightened unconsciously in her hair. He lifted his head, his hard look probing, cold with bitter loathing. "And may God damn me if I sully what we have with this."

Releasing her, he stepped back. The mood was broken, the need quieted. The peculiar reluctance that had kept him sitting in the car longer than usual was back.

Nothing appeared different. The murky air hadn't changed, the stench of hopelessness and the evil that fed on it was no greater, no less. Quiet despair still ruled with a stark, corrosive power. There was sordidness and squalor, and emptiness. The usual blank-faced carrion plied the usual trade. The same vultures circled.

Nothing had changed, yet it didn't feel right. He was uneasy, but there was nothing he could pinpoint. Intuition? Were there eyes really watching them, or was the need to hunch his shoulders against some malevolent presence simply a reflection of his own mood? He'd scanned the street, scoured the darkness, and even lost himself in Katherine for a while, but the feeling never left.

He tried to shake it off, but it persisted. Like a snake, it slithered down his spine and coiled in his belly. Cold, heavy, warning.

Warning of what?

He almost called the night's venture off. He would have, if time weren't running out. Maybe he should, or maybe he'd been around the mystic Matthew too long.

He realized that Katherine was staring up at him. He was confusing her with his mercurial moods. He was confusing himself. Dear God! He wanted to walk out of here. He wanted to turn his back on all he saw, on all the memories it resurrected. He wanted to get drunk. Something he'd never done in his life. Getting drunk meant losing control, and losing control meant falling to the vultures.

Mitch stifled a shudder. He didn't want to think of vultures. He wanted to breathe clean air and see a clear, blue sky. He wanted to listen to music and dance with Katherine in the rain.

He wanted to walk with her over rolling green pastures and make love in clean, crisp hay. He wanted paradise. But paradise was a universe away.

Mitch reined himself in. He was back in hell, his hell, but he didn't have to stay.

He had to do this one more time. Just one. Regaining his hold on his normally tightly controlled emotions, he tucked her hand in the crook of his arm. Shifting moods again, he teased her, quieting her worry. The grin that creased his face was patented Mitch. Familiar, warm, boyishly wicked, and all for Katherine. "Business first, kisses later."

"Is that a promise?" Katherine didn't understand, not completely, but she wouldn't ask. Not now. Nor ever.

"A solemn one."

She squeezed his arm, playing his game, and her answering smile was almost real. "I'll hold you to that."

"Lord, sweetheart, I hope so."

"Count on it."

Mitch's grin faded, his hand rested over hers at the crook of his arm. His shoulders tensed, his eyes were the eyes of a man of The Black Watch again. "We'd better make this one count. Ready?"

Katherine nodded, echoing his thoughts again. "One more time."

Her foot hurt. The band at the heel of the sling she wore had grown tighter with each passing hour. Breaking a cardinal rule, Katherine stopped, bracing herself against a brick wall while she adjusted the troublesome buckle, hoping it would ease the tension on her heel. Mitch, who was a pace ahead, moved on, his attention too totally concentrated on their surroundings to know of her problem. He was far more than the decreed touch away when the grossly malformed beggar flowed out of the darkness of an alley. Half a face peered out of the rumpled pile of rags on a wheeled cart.

A scarred, gnarled hand caught at Mitch's, only long enough to detain him. A voice that came from a throat wrapped in ragged scarves, even in the torrid heat, wheezed a warning. "Watch for him."

Mitch went rigidly still, his attention riveted on the man crouched at his feet.

"Turn away! Don't look at me." Even with the effort it took to speak, the man scooted deeper into the obscuring alley. But not before Mitch saw fear in an eye too old even for the half of the ravaged face not covered with another scarf. "Don't let anyone see we are speaking."

Taking a step back, Mitch complied, realizing as he turned back that Katherine had lagged behind. For once it was good fortune in disguise. Any observer would think he'd paused to let her catch up. In a low voice, his lips hardly moving, he asked, "Who should I watch for?"

"You'll know him."

"How can you be sure?"

"Because we know who you are, and what you are. He will, too."

"We? Who do you mean by 'we'?" The skin on the back of Mitch's neck prickled. He didn't doubt that someone out there knew who he was. Who he had been. Because he knew his question wouldn't be answered, he asked one more pertinent. "What does this man want from me?"

"The woman." The cart inched deeper into the alley. "He will want her. Just like he wanted the other."

Mitch felt as if someone had slammed a sledgehammer into his gut. This could be the break they'd waited for. "Jocie?"

"Yes." Wheels rumbled over uneven concrete.

"Wait!" Mitch clenched his fist, barely restraining himself from turning to force the man to obey. But there was unmistakable danger in coming forward, and he wouldn't bring more trouble down on his informant. "What reason would this man have for wanting Katherine?"

"Blonde." The terse answer made Mitch shudder. He knew the rest before the rasping voice whispered, "His clientele likes blondes."

"Where?" Mitch spoke through gritted teeth as he watched Katherine, praying the shoe would occupy her a bit longer. "Where will I find this clientele?"

"We don't know."

"What do you mean, you don't know?" Mitch half turned before he stopped himself. "You knew enough a while ago."

"We know a monster when we see one, we know when he is among us, we know what he does. No more. We're glad when he goes, but we don't know where."

"Damn you, I don't believe you."

"Believe." The cart moved again, this time splashing through the foul-smelling liquid draining from a garbage can against the wall. The voice was faint, drifting from a greater distance. "He comes, he takes, and because we want to continue our life, pitiful and empty as it is, we keep silent."

Life. Not lives. The beggar spoke in a peculiar mix of numbers. "You kept silent until now."

"We prayed you would be gone before he came again."

"Why are you telling me this? Why take the risk?"

"Because of who you were, because you made a difference. If not to us, then to those before us."

"That was a long time ago and often too little, too late. And then I left."

"Not so long ago, and nothing is too little, or too late. But never feel guilty for leaving. You were too young to bear the burdens you bore—you wouldn't have survived if you hadn't gotten out. Even so, the good you did didn't end when you left."

"Talk sense, man, tell me what I need to know."

"A dream," the voice continued as if Mitch hadn't interrupted. "You left us with a dream that someday there would be another. Another like The Saint of Bourbon Street."

"There was never a saint." Mitch shrugged off the name he never wanted. "And if there were, what good is a dream here?"

"Where there is a dream, life isn't totally hopeless. Even here."

Katherine was walking toward them, the tap of her heels a muted warning.

"Watch for him." The voice drifted from the inky blackness, disembodied words, from a ghost who had never been. "You will know him."

Mitch waited as a long, gargling breath rattled the stillness, as if gathering strength for one more effort from ruined lungs.

"You will know him." A wheel creaked one last time. "And he will know you."

Then the alley was silent, and only Katherine's steps disturbed the stillness.

Seven

"That poor man!" Katherine faced the cavern that had swallowed the cart and its occupant. "We've seen him before." Or a dozen like him, calling for alms in prosperous areas, where there would be change jingling in pockets and guilt, if not sympathy, in the heart of the affluent. "What did he want? What was he saying to you?"

So much for Mitch's hope she hadn't seen. He hesitated as he separated fact from impression for there was more to this encounter than was apparent.

She studied him a moment. His hair rumpled from the latest, worried sweep of his hand through it. A face so dear, so familiar, a face that could keep secrets, but didn't quite manage to hide a keening tension and alarm. She touched him, only briefly, needing the contact, needing to be a part of his newest concern. "He didn't beg, did he?"

"No." With the back of his hand he stroked her cheek, trailing his knuckles over the satiny contour. "He didn't beg."

"Then, what?" She tipped her head to one side, a frown beginning as she sensed his rigid control. She'd never seen him quite like this.

"He brought a warning."

"Warning?" Her frown was in full bloom. "Why?"

"Someone is here, someone who has come back." Mitch scanned the street, his hot, roving stare like a laser. "A man he assures I will know." He brought his gaze back to Katherine, casting about for the kindest way to tell her the rest of the beggar's bleak discourse. Ultimately he chose to be straightforward with it.

Sugarcoating was a waste of time, and not her style. She might weep in his arms in helpless horror for the vile and abominable conditions on the street. She might carry her bruising grief for the children in her tender heart. But it was strength and love that kept her coming back to walk the brimstone of her private hell, night after night.

Strength that would allow her to face what she must. With his chest clenching with the ache of it, he took her by the shoulders and continued with the rest of what he had to tell her. "Most of all, his warning was for you. That this man will want you, as he wanted Jocie. That he will take you, as he took her."

"Take me?" She shook her head, assimilating the words that rattled in her head, then seizing on the only thing that mattered. "Jocie! He took Jocie?" She grasped the lapel of his jacket, shaking him as she was shaking. "Where did he take her? Why?" Then, as the answer to her question hit her, "Oh, dear God! No. No!"

She sagged against him, while every dreadful fear she'd harbored ripped and shredded her. Her body shuddered against his, but only for the space of a sob she couldn't quite hold back. She clung to him, her fingers twisted into the fabric of his shirt. One long, anguished breath drifted slowly from her. Then she was quiet, frighteningly quiet.

When she straightened, her face was composed in rigid lines of forced self-possession. She had dealt with the awful implications of what had been done to her sister, what conditions they might encounter when they found Jocie. "Who is this man?" she whispered, her voice hard. Bitter. "Where is he?"

"Shh, sweetheart. I don't know who he is, and I don't know where he is." He framed her face briefly with his hands, drawing her sorrowing gaze to his. "But I promise you I'll find out." When Katherine was well out of it, but not until. "I promise," he repeated softly. "Somehow."

"Find the beggar." Her teeth were clamped together to keep back a scream of anger and frustration. "He must know more than he said. Find him. Make him tell."

"He won't say any more, Katherine. This person, whoever he is, is obviously dangerous. The beggar risked a great deal by saying the little he did."

"Why did he wait until now to speak when we've been asking about Jocie for weeks?"

"The warning was for you. As far as he's concerned, Jocie's no part of this. The man comes, he takes, and when he goes those he's taken no longer exist for those who are left."

"Where do they go? What does it mean?" The hope that had blazed in her, that had blocked out everything else, was faltering.

"It means, first of all, that we need to get you off the street. Now."

"But, Jocie!"

"We can't think of her now."

Katherine balked. "We *have* to think of her."

"Sweetheart, we're no good to her unless we take care of ourselves," he explained with forced patience. "Taking care of ourselves means getting out of here. Now." His tone softened. "Can you understand the importance our own safety means to Jocie?"

She nodded numbly. After weeks of nothing, so much was happening so fast. "I'm sorry. I wasn't thinking."

Mitch took her arm to guide her back to the car, grateful that this time she didn't resist. Grimly he promised himself that whoever was out here, this lover of blondes, wouldn't have Katherine.

Their steps were hollow on the sidewalk as they moved as rapidly as they dared. No one accosted them. No one delayed them. No one eluded Mitch's cold, searching stare, but no one was more than recently familiar. No face leapt out at him from his past. Their escape, looking like a swift and purposeful stroll, went smoothly and without disturbance.

A half block from the car their luck ran out.

From a van idling at the curb, a tall, cadaverous figure emerged, his lean, bony frame unfolding like a jackknife. A malevolent Ichabod Crane with chalk white hair. From the back doors came two others. A man, a giant bowling ball in human form, as round as he was tall. Dark skin, dark beady eyes made more ominous by shaved brows and a glistening, hairless scalp. He was followed by one of the most exquisitely beautiful women Katherine had ever seen. She moved like silk, every muscle utterly attuned to the other in an utterly natural grace. A perfect face. A perfect body.

"Too late." Mitch cursed effusively under his breath. "Too damnably late. Be careful, Katherine," he muttered without looking at her. "As careful as you would be with a killer stallion."

He was warning her to expect the unexpected, but without his warning, Katherine instinctively knew this was trouble, and one of these men, the bowling ball or Ichabod, was someone Mitch knew. The woman never crossed her mind, she was too young.

Standing quietly where he'd pulled her to a halt, Katherine didn't speak or flinch from the cautioning force of his grip at her elbow.

The caution was unnecessary. If fear hadn't frozen her tongue, she wouldn't have spoken. She wouldn't distract him, or make an ill-advised move, even as a novice she could see they were in the presence of evil. Evil writhed in every feature, every look. Remorseless evil that profited on human misery. One of these depraved creatures had taken women and children, and Jocie.

Jocie.

Rage, sudden, savage, like none she'd ever known, swept through her, and her fear was nothing. She stood a little taller, her pale face was stained by slashes of violent color across her cheeks. Her eyes were hard and frosty. Katherine wasn't afraid; they were too despicable to fear.

Mitch felt the change in her. The trembling that coursed through her and thrummed beneath his fingertips lying tautly on her arm ceased abruptly. In its place was tension, and rock-steady quiet. With his years of experience in taut situations he sensed the shift in her reaction, gauged it correctly, and was grateful for it. But he didn't acknowledge it. He didn't look at her, he didn't move. He hardly seemed to breathe as he waited for the three to approach. His expression was bland, his demeanor aloof, but his stony stare never wavered.

A pace away, the trio halted. The thin one grinned, adding wrinkles to wrinkles on parchment skin, and waited for a reaction that never came. The Ball was sweating, it seeped from his pores, running in slow rivulets like glistening oil. His shorn head swiveled on a neck that bulged over the tight collar of his shirt and tie, but his agate eyes never turned from Mitch. The beautiful woman, with her perfect face and magnificent body, stood in a model's pose watching all of them with an amused smile.

After a long, dismissing appraisal of Katherine, she turned the full blast of her attention to Mitch. Her voice was deep, smoky, reeking of sex. "Hello, handsome. I've heard a lot about you."

Mitch didn't respond.

With a low laugh she tossed her black hair over her shoulder and posed provocatively, offering a generous glimpse of spectacular cleavage. "I've always wanted to meet a red-haired saint." A subtle shift, a slight hunch of the perfect posture, and her plunging neckline bucked, offering more than a glimpse. "Now that I have, I'd like to know you better. Wouldn't you like to know me better, Red?"

Her gambit prompted no reaction. Mitch gave no more credence to her performance than if he were a saint and she singing prayers, muffled in a muumuu from head to toe. His attention was too carefully riveted on the tall one, waiting for his first move.

An angry flush spread over the dark-haired woman's face, her black eyes blazed. Hissing like a cat she lunged forward, her fingers curved stiffly, clawlike nails only inches from Katherine's face. "You like this one, hey? I can fix it so you won't."

Katherine closed her eyes, the vivid color rage had given her blanched away leaving her even paler. Yet she held fast before the onslaught, never doubting that Mitch wouldn't let this woman hurt her. This was show, she told herself. Only that. For now.

A barked command from the round man brought the hissing woman back. She settled again into her model's pose, the amused smile broader. But the hot, dark eyes glittered with cunning and craven lust.

Mitch was quietly immune to the calculated distraction, and the underlying reality of lust and jealousy.

The incident was like many others that played constantly on the street and should have caused at least a ripple, but sidewalks that teemed with flotsam were suddenly deserted. Derelicts and hookers and vagrants melted into doorways and alleys. Bedlam turned to eerie silence.

Only the tall one stirred restlessly, tired of the game of wills. "Say, Mon?" With a beaming smile he wagged his fingers, directing attention to himself in a sweeping gesture. "You been gone so long you don't recognize an old friend?"

"I don't see an old friend," Mitch answered coolly.

"You don't recognize The Mentor, hey?" The smile didn't change.

"I recognize you, Isaac, but I—"

"He is The Mentor." The bowling ball threatened with his voice.

"I recognize you, Isaac," Mitch continued patiently, shrugging aside the menacing interruption as if it were nothing. "But I don't see a friend."

"So that's how it is to be, now?" Black brows arched up toward the drift of chalky hair. A subtle hand signal leashed his huge companion.

"That's how it always was, and how it always will be," Mitch said with little inflection as memories of Billy and countless others came rushing in. "Nothing has changed in that."

"Nothing?" The smile altered. The friendliness turned sly. "You don't remember the last time we met? You don't see ironic similarity to the last time we saw each other?"

"I see you, Isaac. Older, skinnier, and I'm sure, meaner."

"Meaner than all the others," The Mentor declared proudly. Then he laughed, showing that one of the sharp, pointed eyeteeth Mitch remembered had been replaced by a shiny gold replica. As sharp, as pointed. As much like a vampire as the real tooth. "Mean enough that I'm the one who's here and not moldering in some pauper's grave."

"What do you want, Isaac?" Mitch was tired of the game, as well. He wanted to take Katherine far away from this man's evil. "State your business or get out of the way."

"My business? Ah, yes, that little matter." He chuckled, all good humor. "This is almost like old times. Almost. That, you see, is the irony of this."

"Get to the point." Mitch's hand tightened on Katherine's arm, a signal to move when he did.

"Once you were the buyer and I the seller. Now our roles are reversed."

"Yours, maybe."

"Ah, that means you aren't selling."

"Smart deduction, Isaac."

The gold-toothed grin turned malevolent. "I could take her."

"You can die trying."

"My, my, my. Still the same tough, uncooperative bastard."

"Right on all three counts, Isaac, so why don't you chalk this one up as no sale, and get the hell out of our way?"

"No," Isaac mused as his glance ran over Katherine, lingering on the shining disarray of her hair. "I don't think so. I have clients who would sell their souls for an hour with this lady."

"And you want their souls."

Isaac beamed at Mitch. "Their dollars, too. But their souls above all."

"Then these so-called clients will be keeping what masquerades as souls. The lady's mine, she's staying mine. You need blondes, send Tootsie over there out for a bottle of bleach."

"You always had an answer."

"For you I did."

Isaac swept him with a mocking glance, giving grudging approval to the gambler's vest, the fine silk shirt, the perfectly knotted tie. And most of all the sleek trousers that fit like a supple glove, leaving absolutely no doubt of the masculinity so closely encased in them. "At least your taste in clothes has changed."

"Yours hasn't." Out of the corner of his eye Mitch saw the fat man begin to drift to his left under the cover of the intended distraction of Isaac's chatter. He moved as so many grossly obese men did, gracefully, almost femininely. A silent, deadly man, on tiny, booted feet.

A tap on the soft inner curve of her arm alerted Katherine. She had no idea what Mitch planned, but a catch in her breath, held and softly exhaled, signaled she wouldn't be unprepared.

His hold was loose on her arm, but she felt the coiling readiness in him.

Isaac beamed. The woman glared. The fat man continued his slow move.

Mitch stood stock-still, his hand still lying on Katherine's arm. When he moved, he moved fast, sending her spinning out of the path of a vicious backhand that sent Isaac reeling. In a continuation of momentum his foot connected with the fat man's crotch. The kick bent the man double, the second blow stood him erect as it smashed into the multiple chins, clamping the open mouth closed on his tongue and his whistling struggle for air.

"Go, Katherine. Run!" Mitch didn't look at her as he closed in with pent-up fury, fighting for his life and Katherine's.

Climbing to her feet from the gutter where she'd fallen, she turned to obey. Ignoring her bleeding knee, she began her sprint to the car. A gesture, a move, something her rattled mind registered in her subconscious, stopped her cold.

Isaac lay where he'd fallen, eyes rolled back in his head until only the white showed, his hand twitching at his jaw. But the woman, the beautiful, vicious woman, advanced toward Mitch's back, the glinting steel of a switchblade poised to plunge into him.

"No," Katherine cried, and launched herself at the woman. Her strong hands caught at the long black hair, dragging her away as she would have dragged a wayward horse down by its mane. The woman fought and snarled, trying to turn, to gain leverage. Katherine was smaller, but her years as a trainer made her quicker and stronger. The woman bucked and twisted, but nothing she tried hadn't been tried by a bigger, more powerful horse.

Their battle became a battle of tenacity and guile. Katherine hadn't brawled in the streets, but she'd battled in the corral. Tonight that was better. She had no idea how the pin from her own hair came to be in her hand, or where she found the nerve to promise it as permanent decoration for a certain beautiful throat, if the knife didn't hit the concrete immediately.

"That's it," Katherine murmured as the switchblade clattered at her feet. She kicked it away but didn't release her tight grasp on the wealth of black hair. Nor did she ease the pressure of the pin as it drew a trickle of blood from a swanlike neck. "The quieter you stay, the less damage this will do. The choice is yours."

"You won't stab me," the woman snarled. "You don't have the guts."

"The hell I don't." The pin pricked a little deeper. "The hell I won't."

As the woman wilted in defeat, Katherine risked a look at Mitch in time to see The Ball succeed in refilling his lungs and steadying his legs. Head down, howling like a demon, he charged. Mitch sidestepped as gracefully as a bullfighter and met the careening force with an axlike force of his own. The fat man went down under the chop at the back of his neck, staggered to his feet and charged again. This time Mitch didn't sidestep, but stood firm, bringing the larger man to a grinding halt with a short, powerful jab followed by a punch that flattened his nose and sent blood spurting.

Feinting left, then right, while The Ball shambled stupidly in a circle, Mitch rained short, quick, damaging blows deep into soft blubber. Moving constantly, dancing out of the path of charge after charge, he pounded his attacker without mercy.

This was for Katherine. Each battering blow was earmarked for her, to keep her safe. With a few for Jocie.

Finally he stepped back, waiting for another attack. The Ball stood, head down like a tired bull, arms hanging, nose dripping red as he swayed back and forth staring through unfocused eyes.

The fight was done.

Mitch lifted his own head, allowing himself to look for Katherine. It took a second for his tired brain to assimilate what his eyes saw. When he understood, he didn't know if he should be angry or grateful. The switchblade lying at her feet tipped the scales toward gratitude.

"Let him go, Katherine," he said softly. "He won't hurt anyone now. Not without the protection of the watchdog here."

Katherine backed away, the pin still in her hand, her gaze moving feverishly over Mitch, searching for injury. He had the makings of a bruise under his eye, and his chin had a scratch, but given the disparity in size, he had defended himself and her more than adequately.

Adequate! A hysterical laugh bubbled in her throat at the paltry choice of words. He defended like a tiger, a wolf, a Viking. Like the man he was.

If he hadn't... All of what could have happened to her came rushing down on her. Much to her disgust, she discovered she was shivering.

Isaac groaned and jacked himself upright with the support of his arms. He had become an old man, a fragile pile of bones, guided by a mind steeped in wickedness.

"Get up, Isaac," Mitch commanded, wasting no misplaced sympathy for age. "Get up and help Tootsie here take your human tank to the van." He stepped to the man, grasped the white hair to lift a face as ghostly pale to his. "You should have marked this one no sale and gone away. Do it now, and don't try a second time."

Mitch backed away again, his hands raised, as if the stench of Isaac clung to them. "Get up." This time the command was low, guttural, a threat threading through it. "Go. Now!"

As mute as stone he watched the old man struggle to his feet. Arms hanging loosely at his side, hands curled into fists, and his weight resting easily on the balls of his feet, he waited while the two of them led the nearly comatose round man back to the van. Doors closed with a thud, the engine revved, and the massive machine screeched from the curb. Its dirty taillights blinked out of sight before Mitch turned to Katherine and opened his arms.

She flew to him, clutching his shirt, dropping her forehead against his chest. He was all right. Thankfulness lanced through her heart and tears burned in the back of her throat. Thank God, Mitch was all right.

He felt her gulping struggle to hold back the tears. With a finger under her chin, he lifted her face. "Sweet Kate," he murmured tenderly, "what's this?"

Katherine lost her battle and wiped at the tears that spilled down her face. "You know damn well what it is, and you know damn well for who."

"Whom," he corrected with the beginnings of a grin.

"You know damn well for whom, then."

"Tears for me from a woman who fights like a warrior, whether her foe is a four-legged creature or a man?" There was awe beneath the teasing, and something more even he couldn't define. An elemental pride that this woman was his.

"Four-legged creature or a woman." It was Katherine's turn to correct as she stemmed the emotional flood.

"That was no woman, sweetheart."

"But she had . . . um."

"Breasts?" He almost laughed at her shock. Sobering he agreed, "Yes, he did."

"But they were . . ." She made a helpless gesture.

"Spectacular?" Mitch supplied.

"Exactly."

"Yes they were, and about as real as a three-dollar bill." When she still looked perplexed, he added with no little amusement, "Surgery, love, and more to come. Tootsie isn't completely Tootsie yet, but he will be."

"Oh." Then, with a dawning memory. "But she, uh, he liked you." A half beat later she tagged on, "Red."

"Don't remind me."

"That your hair is red?"

He grinned down at her, and was pleased to see that some of her color was returning along with her sense of humor. "Witch." He gathered up a handful of her flyaway hair and shook her gently before he wrapped his arms around her. To hell with the fact that this was the street. It was the best place to hold the amazing woman, who gave without thought of receiving. Who, in all probability, saved his life. The thought of the danger she'd risked for him made him quake with fear for her, down to his toes.

"Tell me," he muttered into her hair. "What were you really going to do with the hairpin?"

Her answer was quick and casual. "Skewer her. Him. Whoever. Like shish kebab, if she hurt you."

"He."

"He."

Mitch's laughter filled the street. He pulled away to capture her face between his hands. "What a woman!" He kissed her mouth long and lingeringly, then pulled away to laugh again. "God! What a woman."

Flinging an arm across her shoulder, he continued their aborted trek to the car. The street was coming alive behind them, but their night was done.

"There's nothing more we can do tonight. Let's go back to the hotel, Kate, our home away from home. There are promises I desperately need to keep."

When Katherine stepped from the bathroom, Mitch was sitting at the edge of her bed speaking in a low voice into the telephone. Signing off abruptly, he looked up at her as he dropped the receiver back into its cradle.

He'd bathed the scratch, ignored the bruise, shed the vest and changed his shirt. If she didn't look too closely he seemed unaffected by his skirmish. He'd had worse from a friendly barroom brawl, he'd assured her. A closer look found the beginning of new bruises, and a weariness in his eyes. The discoloring hand that had held the receiver still toyed with the cord, as if there were other calls he wanted to make.

"Am I interrupting something?" She made an indecisive gesture toward the door she'd just closed. "I can always finish at the vanity mirror over the bathroom sink."

Her hair was wrapped in a towel and her body in a matching white terry robe that verged on swallowing her, but she looked scrubbed and vulnerable, and wonderful. He knew that under the voluminous robe, she sported a flesh-colored bandage on the knee she'd scraped when he pushed her into the curb. He'd applied the bandage himself, hating the need.

He took his hand from the telephone, scrubbing his palm against his thigh. "You aren't interrupting. I'd finished that bit of business."

"Successfully, I hope."

"Temporarily." Too temporarily. He'd just bartered with Cam for more time. He wanted two more weeks and settled for one, maybe ten days, if Cam could stretch it. If luck smiled on them, and this break panned out, between them they could set Katherine's world right. Jocie would be back and Katherine would still have her chance with the consortium.

If the lady called Luck smiled.

God! If she smiled.

Tonight the lady had been two-faced. Giving with one hand, taking with the other. Giving their first real clue, then taking its effectiveness away by destroying the best contact. If Katherine hadn't been with him, if the threat to her hadn't existed, he could have dealt with Isaac, cajoling the information he'd needed from the man.

But Katherine had been with him, and he'd done what he had to do. What he would do again. All the ifs in the world wouldn't change it.

She was safe here with him, and so lovely, his heart ached.

"Come here." He stretched a hand to her. When she came to him, he pulled her between his knees. Taking the towel from her, he dried her hair, carefully, thoroughly. When it was done to his satisfaction, he led her to the bench in front of a dressing table. Standing behind her and taking up her comb, he worked through the tangles. Next came the brush and the traditional one hundred strokes. Drawing the brush slowly from crown to tip, he was mesmerized by the changing colors, by the shine. As it dried it seemed to spring to life.

From his vantage, in the mirror he saw as her lashes drifted to her cheeks, in pleasure, in peace. The night had been rehashed time and again, completely, and laid to rest. He hadn't lied, but he hadn't been totally honest about how difficult it might be to follow up on the information. Just this one time her hopeful happiness justified the omission.

"Two times," he muttered, remembering his conversation with Cam and another omission. Two lies by omission. "Just two."

"What?" Katherine blinked sleep from her eyes and tried to focus on him.

"Nothing, sweet Kate." He bent to kiss the side of her throat, breathing in the clean scent of soap and shampoo. "Relax and say your Hail Marys."

She leaned back against him. "There are none to say."

"I distinctly heard a couple of damns." He stroked down her arms, then back to her shoulders, massaging the last tiny tension from them. "Maybe even a hell."

"Justified." Her eyes were growing heavy again and she sighed slowly, deeply, under his soothing care. "Completely justified."

"Yes." Mitch was smiling. This was his lady, tough, sweet, reasonable.

His.

Still smiling, he laid down the brush. Sweeping her hair from her shoulders, he slipped the robe from her. With one hand he snagged her gown from a chair and slipped it over her head. As he would a child, he guided her arms through the proper openings and adjusted straps. That done, he gathered her into his arms and took her to bed. Lying with her, holding her against his clothed body, he watched the unrelieved blackness of the sky begin to pale. When her breathing was deep and quiet, he eased from the bed, intending to take his own shower before he joined her for what was left of the night.

"Mitch?"

Her drowsy voice stopped him. Fingers still at the buttons of his shirt, he returned to sit on the edge of the bed. Tucking the sheet over her, he murmured, "I'm here, love."

"What if Isaac had succeeded in abducting me? What would you have done?"

Mitch thought for a minute, though there was never any doubt what he would do. He considered lying, then saw the uselessness of it. "I would have tracked him down, to the end of the earth if necessary." In quiet dispassion he added, "Then I would have killed him, slowly, with my bare hands."

Katherine caught her lip between her teeth, horrified, yet pleased, as she believed every syllable of every word. "That's what I thought."

"So, tell me, if Tootsie had slid his pig sticker into me, what would you have done?"

Katherine didn't think for a minute. She didn't consider lying. The truth came swiftly, certainly. "I would have made shish kebab of her."

"Him."

"Him."

"That's what I thought." Mitch kissed her and ruffled her hair. How many times had he discovered that, with nothing in common, they were so much alike? He wondered how that could be, and if it would be enough. Enough for what? he asked himself, but no answer was forthcoming. Perhaps this wasn't the time to think of it. "Sleep now, Kate." He wanted to kiss her again, but resisted and settled for a fleeting caress with the back of his hand against her cheek. "Sleep."

"Not yet." Her eyes were open, and soft, and inviting. The heartache of fear and worry banked for a while. "You won't be long?"

A rough sound rumbled in his throat, quiet, startled, suddenly filled with smoldering passion. His voice was a low, hoarse whisper, reflecting a spiraling desire. "No more than five minutes."

"Five minutes." She made it seem like forever. "Then there are promises to keep."

His pulse stuttered. It always did when her voice took on the low, sexy drawl. It always would. He kissed his fingers, then passed them gently over her trembling lips.

This wasn't selfishness. Jocie wasn't forgotten, nor the newest difficulty. The hurt and the worry were only tucked away while she reached out to him, needing solace and offering it.

"Three minutes," he said, making another promise he would keep, as he rose to go. "Only three. Count on it."

"So." Katherine laid down her fork, forgetting the sugared *beignet* she'd been arranging and rearranging on her plate. "We begin all over again."

"In a manner of speaking." Mitch leaned back in his seat, admiring the play of light over the spill of her hair as it tumbled over the shoulders of her dressing gown. It was morning and, thanks to their rare early night, the first time they'd shared breakfast at a reasonable hour. "But not until you do more than nibble at food the chef made especially for you."

"Especially for me? Why would he do that?" Momentarily distracted, she touched the flowers that looked as if they were freshly picked from a dew-laden garden. A cheery splash of color against the perfectly appointed table set by the uniformed waiter from room service.

"He likes your smile." The whole staff was half in love with her, with her quiet graciousness, and her strength. Gossip traveled like wildfire among them and each was privy to real and imagined reasons the sad and lovely lady in the penthouse suite searched the streets of New Orleans. Each giving his or her own romantic twist to the growing legend.

"He hasn't seen my smile."

"Then someone must have told him. So—" Mitch nudged her plate a fraction closer "—don't disappoint him. I suspect he went to a lot of effort to encourage your appetite."

Katherine laughed. "You sound like a father trying to coax a stubborn child to be nice."

"Will it work?"

"When you do it so wonderfully well, how could it not?"

"Prove it." Mitch settled back in his chair, sipping a second cup of coffee, watching her over the rim of the fragile china. She'd begun her day with a call home. Bea had assured her Cam was taking excellent care of them, that she needn't worry. In turn, each aunt had spoken to her, and even Rose had been cheerful. Only Gran hadn't come to the telephone. Not to worry, Violet reassured her again, Jocelyn Rivard was only sleeping in, and surely she was entitled to one day in nearly a hundred years when she didn't rise with the sun.

For the aunts' sake, Katherine pretended to accept the excuse, but she'd brought a poorer appetite than was usual to the table. She didn't discuss her concern for Gran, but a new shadow was added to the darkening gray of her gaze.

Mitch wondered what her eyes would be like without that shadow lurking in the background. Without the worry of Jocie and Gran and the aunts touching every thought. When this was finished he would like to take her away somewhere. Away from her cares. An island, perhaps. An island that belonged to a friend. Patrick McCallum's Eden. Where there would be only sun and sand, and lazy days on the beach. He'd show her Jordana's special garden where the laughter of children, happy children, could be heard on the ocean breeze. And nothing bad could touch her.

He wanted to swim with her in the sea, and lie with her on the warm sand. He wanted to laugh with her, and love her. When this was over. When they found Jocie.

He took her hand in his, brushing his thumb over her bare fingers. And reality swept a foolish fantasy away. She wore no jewelry now, but the untanned circle where the signet ring had been was still visible. A reminder, as undeniable as the ring had been, of their differences. Katherine Rivard wore rings bearing a prestigious family crest; Mitchell Ryan had no family at all.

For a moment his grasp tightened in regret. Then, catching her puzzled glance, he only shook his head and shrugged, making light of his mood as he released her. Something altered between them then as he backed away, the first step of many.

He wouldn't be taking Katherine to Eden. When this was done, he wouldn't be part of her life at all. And now every instinct told him that time had nearly come. The search was almost over. The plain white note card slipped under their door in the night, summoning them to a meeting, was tangible proof.

Pulling the card from the back pocket of his trousers, he laid it on the table for Katherine to read. "This was lying on the floor in front of the door this morning."

She picked up the card, her puzzlement increasing. "Who sent it?"

"I don't know."

Her gaze flicked over the message written in a decidedly masculine script. She read it twice then laid it carefully aside. Folding her hands tightly to stop the sudden tremor in them, she said softly, "He says he can help us find Jocie."

Mitch nodded, but said nothing.

"He wants to meet with us."

"It could be a scam." As disastrous as the night had almost been.

She studied his face for a long while. "It could be. But you don't think so, do you?"

Mitch didn't hedge or evade. "No."

"So what do we do? Do we accept the invitation, or refuse?"

"It's your call, Katherine."

She tapped the card, the message suggested a meeting on the worst of streets at midday. "We've come too far to turn back now."

"Then we go?"

"Yes." She was rising as Mitch was. "We go."

Eight

Katherine was astounded. She stood on the sidewalk at the garden gate, staring at the tiny clapboard building tucked between taller, larger buildings. An air of decay permeated the neighborhood, and though someone had fought valiantly for it, the clapboard hadn't escaped. Not completely. The building was weathered and gray, it tilted and sagged, the door was crooked and the roof a patchwork of colors and odd shapes. But the arched, lead and stained glass windows were perfectly set, perfectly intact and magnificent. An equally tiny lawn divided by a hand-laid brick walk was a miniature masterpiece of horticultural splendor. She felt as if she were looking at a painting, a master's attempt at creating a cleansing breath in the stench of squalor.

"What is this place?" She realized she was whispering and knew it was because the aged structure inspired reverence. "This can't be right. We must've mistaken the address."

"We aren't mistaken," Mitch said as quietly. "This was a chapel once, a place where sailors came to pray. It was abandoned years ago. One of the old landmarks that slipped by the historical society's notice. But, obviously, not of our informant."

"You think he's here? That he lives here?"

"There's one sure way to find out." Mitch opened the garden gate and stepped inside. He paused. "It isn't too late to change your mind. We can still go back."

Katherine stepped into the garden. "We won't be turning back."

Mitch touched her shoulder briefly in encouragement before he turned to continue to the door. A small iron bell hung by a sign that welcomed them in faded letters, but he chose to knock.

The first rap drew no response, nor the second. To curb her tension Katherine slid her fingers into the back pockets of her jeans. "Maybe he's not here. Maybe he changed his mind. Maybe—"

A bolt slid away with a smoothly oiled thud, and the door opened. Though it was midday and the sun bore down unmercifully, the interior of the chapel was dark and cool. The figure that loomed in front of them was dressed in a hooded robe and stood well in the shadow as he motioned them in.

As they advanced, he retreated with a crippling limp, never allowing a glimpse of his face, never speaking until they were beyond the light of the sun. "Please." A breathless voice wheezed and struggled to find more breath to continue. "Close the door." A second fisted gesture indicated chairs by a roughly constructed table. "Be comfortable."

Never taking her attention from the hooded figure, Katherine fumbled for a chair and found Mitch there before her, pulling it from the table, steadying it while she sat.

"A wise move." Wheeze, breathe. "But sturdier than it looks." Another gesture to the close interior. "Everything is. We made sure."

As Katherine did, Mitch followed the direction of the gesture. Somehow he wasn't surprised that the single room was spotless, that the floor was scrubbed and the bolt holes that once held pews in place had been filled with wooden pegs. "You've made a nice home of the chapel."

The figure bowed, hands tucked again inside the belled sleeves of the robe. Katherine was reminded of Gran, who hated to be pitied for her gnarled, twisted fingers.

"The windows are your work?" Mitch ventured.

"Yes, ours." Wheeze. "How did you know?"

"I remember this building. You've done an excellent job restoring what could be, but even I know that some were beyond repair. The replicas are faultless." Then, taking a different tack, Mitch said softly, "What changed your mind? What made you decide to tell us the rest of what you know?"

What was meant as a laugh issued from the darkness of the cowl. "We should have guessed." The ruined voice stopped, but Mitch knew he wasn't through. "Should have guessed The Saint would know."

Katherine was turning from one to the other, as astonished by what was occurring inside the sanctuary as with the outside. "Mitch, you know this man?"

"Forgive us, dear lady." The figure turned to her, the cowl falling away from one side of a grotesquely scarred face. The left side. "We assumed you would know."

"The beggar!"

The beggar bowed again. "In the flesh, charred though it is." Another struggle for breath followed the long speech. There were only two fingers and a thumb on the hand he offered her. "Trevor Hamilton, at your service."

Without blinking or cringing, she took the hand and shook it gently. "Thank you, Trevor Hamilton, for what you did for us last night. For what you did for me."

"It was our pleasure."

Even with the struggle for air, and the distortions of the grating rasp, his words were those of an educated, cultured man. Katherine glanced again at the leaded windows. Trevor Hamilton, whoever he was, wherever he had come from, was an artisan without peer.

"Last night you would only risk a warning," Mitch interjected, repeating a question, "why have you changed your mind?"

"Your lady changed our mind." Trevor kept his face carefully in profile, keeping the right side constantly covered. "Before we didn't know if she was truly worthy of the risk of more." A long, patient, wheezing pause. He'd grown too accustomed to the fight to be frustrated. One eye blazed like a laser at Mitch. "You wouldn't be alive if it weren't for her."

Mitch looked away from the beggar to smile at Katherine. Sliding his palm under her hand as it lay on the table, he lifted it to his lips. "No one knows that better than I."

"Because of that, and because of who you are, we have decided to tell you..." Mitch and Katherine sat in distress through a paroxysm of coughs. When Katherine would have risen to help, Mitch stopped her with a deterring shake of his head. "Forgive us," Trevor murmured, recovering at last. "We haven't much strength left."

"Why don't you sit down." Katherine pulled out the chair next to her own. "It might be easier."

"We thought . . . we were afraid you would find us—"

"Please," she interrupted the fumbling apology. "I would be honored if you would." She saw the grimace that was intended as a smile as Trevor sat by her. It was then she realized how beautiful his eye was, as clear and blue as an arctic lake, lost in craters of ridged and distorted flesh. She wondered how awful the right side of his face must be. The side so terrible he hid it even in this world.

"We've written out what we have to tell you. Things we dared not risk in the note we gave the bellboy to slip under your door."

Mitch took the folded page Trevor offered. "You're tired, we should leave you to rest."

The hooded face turned to Katherine. "Before you go, does the lady know who you are?"

"She knows."

"Who you really are?"

"No." This time it was Katherine who answered. "I know it will be hard, but could you tell me?"

"Katherine, don't," Mitch said forcefully. "Who I was or what I did in the past doesn't matter anymore."

"It matters to me." She turned from Mitch and found Trevor staring at her, a sudden softening in one clear, beautiful eye.

"Katherine," Trevor whispered, a strange note in his voice. "A beautiful name."

"Dear Heaven! I didn't realize." She touched a scarred hand beneath the voluminous sleeve before he could pull back. "I'm sorry, I didn't think to introduce myself."

Trevor was staring down at her hand on his wrist. When he looked up there was a glitter of tears in his eye. "An oversight. It isn't important."

"But it is, and unforgivable. My name is Katherine Mary Rivard, and meeting you has been my privilege, Trevor Hamilton."

Slowly, as if he couldn't bear her touch any longer, Trevor pulled away from her. One eye blazed at Mitch with the same keen probing quality. "Do you know what you have in this woman? Do you have any idea?"

"I know," Mitch said quietly.

"But you have doubts, we see them in your face."

"The doubts are for myself," Mitch said, again quietly. "Never for Katherine."

"Don't be a fool, man." A dire struggle to pull oxygen to starving lungs turned his drawn lips blue and triggered seizure-like tremors in asphyxiating muscles. When the spasms finally ended, Trevor was pale and flaccid and on the edge of consciousness. In the unguarded ordeal the cowl fell from the right side of his face, and it was Katherine who rose to slip it painstakingly and unobtrusively back into place.

With her head bowed she backed away, her arms clutching at her sides. "No! Dear God, no." For a long while she didn't move, then slowly, careful to draw no attention to her ministrations, she slipped back into her chair. She made no other betraying sound, but there was horror in her face and tears in her eyes when she looked at Mitch.

"We should go, Katherine, and leave Trevor in peace."

"No! Not yet." The poor effigy of a human struggled to sit erect. "She needs to know. Katherine must know."

"What must I know, Trevor?" Her hand was on his again, holding him, offering the warm personal contact that did not exist in his life. "Tell me."

"The Saint. Do you know The Saint of Bourbon Street?"

Tootsie had called Mitch a saint, but Katherine had dismissed it as another meaningless name heard on the street. "I've never had the pleasure or the opportunity."

"Then I'm giving it to you now." The single eye turned to Mitch was clear now and crystal blue. "Miss Katherine Mary Rivard, may I introduce Mitchell Ryan, The Saint of Bourbon Street, and all of New Orleans."

The next half hour was the most agonizing Katherine had ever spent, as she listened to a man struggle to tell her of another man. The man she loved. When Trevor finished after many starts and many pauses, each longer than the last, he was drained and nearly lifeless as he slumped in his seat, head down, his body swaying from fatigue. Mitch, who had stood to pace the small confines of the chapel in claustrophobic tension, was as grim and pale as a ghost. And Katherine, who had sat transfixed throughout the revelation, let tears stream down her face without shame.

Long after Trevor had fallen silent, she rose to go to him. With the gentleness she would have given to a hurting child, she eased his head to the table and slipped the cowl securely over the right side of his face. The side he would not want her to see. When he was as comfortable as she could make him, she looked to Mitch for the first time since the awful story had begun. "I think he'll sleep now."

Mitch came to her. He wanted to take her in his arms and tell her he was sorry for who he was, and what he'd been, but he didn't touch her. Instead he bowed as Trevor had, and gestured to the door.

"Will he be all right, Mitch?"

Mitch looked down at a scarred hand that had slipped from the bell sleeve of the robe. "As all right as Trevor Hamilton can ever be."

It was dubious assurance, but the best anyone could give her. At the door she halted to look one more time at the splendid glass the crippled hands had fashioned, and her heart ached for a man who had been beautiful once, and who was beautiful still, on the inside.

The door had almost closed on them when the croaking voice called out. "Ryan?"

Mitch nearly didn't turn back, he'd heard enough for one day. More than enough. But the man had risked his life and his pride for them. He deserved every courtesy. "I'm still here, Trevor."

"When you find The Mentor's hellhole, you can't be the one to go in. It must be someone he doesn't know."

"That isn't a problem."

"A guide. You will need a guide unless you can track water moccasins across swamps."

"I can't," Mitch answered. "But there is someone who can."

"This someone, this tracker, he is the one Isaac will not know?"

"One and the same."

"You trust him?"

"I trust him, I have trusted him for years. With my life."

"Good." Trevor seemed to drowse, then roused. "Ryan?"

"Yeah?"

"Take care of her. Guard her."

"I will. We will, with both our lives."

A labored breath rattled in scorched lungs. "I wish I had."

"I know." Mitch waited for more, but there was nothing. "So long, Trevor," he whispered. "May God ease your tortured soul."

When there was only silence, Mitch closed and locked the door and walked with Katherine to the street through the garden. The small bit of beauty created by a man who had destroyed the most beautiful part of his life.

Katherine was still staring out the window. Still standing exactly as she had when he'd left her to go to his room. His telephone call to Matthew Sky hadn't taken long, but he thought... Mitch hunched his shoulders and clenched his hands in his pockets, admitting he didn't know what he thought.

The light streaming through the window was harsh, turning her to a featureless figure. But even shadows couldn't disguise the taut angle of her head and shoulders, the taut control. She hadn't spoken, not once since she'd stepped from Trevor Hamilton's chapel.

What was she thinking? What did she feel? About Trevor. About Mitchell Ryan. Mitch's lips curled in disgust as he added The Saint of Bourbon Street. He didn't want to know, yet he couldn't leave it alone. "Katherine?"

She didn't turn or speak, and only held up a staying hand. A signal that clearly said, *Don't. Not yet.* Slowly her fingers closed into a fist, her hand dropped to her side. Mitch watched helplessly as she struggled for composure.

Her shoulders heaved. She dragged a hand through her hair, pushing it impatiently from her face. Then she was rigid again. When she spoke, her voice was low, rough, barely a whisper. "He was beautiful."

"There was no one more handsome. Once."

"No!" She faced Mitch then, dry-eyed but with the evidence of her tears still on her face. "He still is. The right side of his face hasn't one single scar." She pressed her fingers against her eyes, trying to force the memory of what she'd seen from them. Her face was bleak when she lifted it from her hands. "The right side is perfect, yet he covers it."

"When he can."

"Why hide the handsomeness and expose the . . . the . . ."

"Say it, Katherine, the hideous side."

"All right, the hideous side."

"Maybe he can't stand the pity."

"That makes no sense, Mitch. None at all."

"Doesn't it?" He moved closer, but didn't touch her. "You felt sorry for him from the first, but once you saw, once you knew what he kept hidden, what did you feel?"

Katherine probed her reaction. The heartbreak. "It was worse," she whispered. "Much worse. Seeing what he'd been and what he'd become was far worse. So awful."

Mitch made no comment. None was needed, his point was made.

"What happened to him? What terrible thing could leave him like that?"

"Trevor Hamilton was a pilot, Katherine. A lucky pilot and a damn good one. One day his luck ran out. His plane crashed and burned, and all on board died."

"Except Trevor."

"If you call what he's doing now living, then, yes, all 'except Trevor,' " Mitch repeated.

"Who was Katherine? The way he said my name, there was a Katherine in his life. Someone special."

"Katherine was his wife. She rarely flew because she hated it. When she did, it was because Trevor insisted. She died on the plane, along with their two baby daughters."

"And Trevor consigned himself to hell." Katherine didn't express her grief, for it was unspeakable. "Did you know him?"

"Not personally, but I knew of him because he was a pilot. The sort who made news."

"Do you fly?" It would explain his interest and knowledge of another pilot.

"I can. I have." All agents of The Black Watch could and did. Simon required it.

She accepted his answer with no surprise, her mind ranging. "What will become of him?"

"No one can say, Katherine. Just as neither of us knows what will happen to us, today, tomorrow, the next day."

"Is he mad?"

"I think he'd like to be, but, no, he isn't mad."

"But when he speaks in plural terms it's only of himself, isn't it?"

"Trevor has divided himself into two people. The unscarred man he hides, and the man he has become. In rare instances, the two merge into one."

"But it isn't because he's insane." She was considering Mitch's explanation, understanding. "He's too rational in every other way to be insane."

"Think of it as a safety valve, a device."

"A device that preserves his sanity," Katherine whispered. "We all have those, don't we, in difficult situations." She looked at Mitch. "How did you cope? You were so young and the burden of what you tried to do so heavy."

There it was, what he'd dreaded, his wretched past lying between them.

"What I did was no more than what anyone else would do. The Saint of Bourbon Street was a silly romanticized name tagged to rumor and legend that grew out of proportion. I was a kid, just a kid, doing the best I could to survive, and helping others do the same when I could. There was nothing saintly about it. My methods were hardly that. And, most ridiculous of all, what I did had little to do with Bourbon Street. I was rarely ever there, my life was in other parts of the city."

She'd put together bits and pieces of his life, and Trevor had filled in the blanks about his birth and the accomplishments he chose to deny. The encounter with Simon and its result were part and parcel of the legend and well-known. Then a curtain had come down, dividing Mitch's life as surely as Trevor divided his, leaving a void that stretched to the day she drove her aging Rolls into McKinzie's Valley.

"Your life was here, until Simon McKinzie took you off the street and into his organization." When he started to protest, she stopped him with a finger slanted across his lips. That was the void, his work with Simon. "I know what you do is secret, and that you can't speak of it. I know you don't wish to speak of the past, so I won't question you any more about either. Someday, when you trust me more, perhaps you'll tell me what you can about the life that made you who and what you are."

"There's nothing to tell, that you don't already know."

"Sketchy bits and pieces garnered from strangers, from strangers' perspectives." Even Isaac had told her more than

Mitch. Even Tootsie. Yet Mitch was determined to shut her out of that part of his life.

"There's nothing more to tell," Mitch repeated grimly.

"Then we needn't discuss it ever." Hiding her disappointment, sure she was losing her last chance to understand the moods and silences of this rare man, she closed the door on his past.

"There's something more important we need to discuss." Glad for an opportunity to change the subject, Mitch produced the paper Trevor had given him. On it he'd scribbled a list of names of people and of places. Dozens of them, where Jocie might be. "The trick will be to find them."

"Why?" Katherine frowned down at the list, then returned it to Mitch. "I don't understand the problem."

"Most of these people will be swamp rats and trappers, who move about constantly. Going where the game is, sleeping and eating on the first high ground or abandoned shack they find. The establishments could be flatboats, maybe even tents and lean-tos. Either can be picked up and moved on a whim." He pointed to the name of an establishment. "This one, for instance. It might be upriver tonight, and next week twenty corkscrewing miles downriver. It would depend on the weather and the trade."

"The trade," Katherine muttered hoarsely, thinking of her sister and what had become of her. "My poor Jocie."

Mitch didn't try to ease her worry—it wouldn't be fair to paint a pretty picture with lies. Instead he put his arm around her and pulled her close. "We'll do all we can to find her, I promise."

Katherine leaned against him, absorbing his strength, his warmth, blocking out the appalling images of what might have befallen her sister. "You said you know a tracker."

"He's on his way. In fact he'll be here by midnight."

This didn't surprise Katherine, either. When Mitch moved, he moved fast. "How can you be so sure he can find Jocie?"

Now that she'd disappeared into the bayou country, Mitch wasn't half so sure that he could find the girl. Only that if she *could* be found, Matthew would do it. "Come sit down. Let me tell you about Matthew Winter Sky."

"An unusual and interesting name."

"No more than the man. Technically, Matthew is a half-breed, born of a French mother and an Apache father. But his heart is one hundred percent Apache. Best of all for Jocie, he's a throwback, attuned to his surroundings, and a tracker like no one has ever seen before."

Mitch settled her in his arms, and leaned back into the soft cushions of the sofa. In the next quarter hour he regaled her with stories of Matthew's prowess, and his mystical understanding of people and things. If the stories sounded embellished, maybe they were, but only a little. And all were part of the ever-growing lore of Matthew.

"Matthew doesn't make friends easily, but a true friend is a friend for life. I'm fortunate that he's been mine for years." He drew his story to a close as he led Katherine to her bed for the rest she needed. "He'll be yours, too, if you'll let him."

Leaning over her, he kissed her forehead and pulled the sheet to her chin. "Sleep if you can. I'll be in the next room if you need me."

"If I sleep, you'll wake me before midnight, won't you?"

"I'll wake you," he promised, hoping with that assurance she would truly sleep. "Then we'll meet Matthew together."

She had rested and slept deeply, and sleep had swept the darkest of the gloom from her. Her trademark optimism and resilience were back as she stood in the airport concourse waiting for Matthew to deplane.

"There?" Katherine indicated a swarthy man dressed in worn jeans, a fringed vest, with a knapsack thrown over his shoulder. Before Mitch could respond, her choice was gleefully bombarded with hugs and kisses bestowed by half a dozen children. The oldest couldn't have been more than nine, and the youngest three. A very pregnant brunette added her greeting.

"No, guess not." She laughed and returned to her vigil. After a while an uneasy frown began to form. "Do you suppose he missed the plane?"

"Katherine, Matthew didn't miss the plane. He's standing by the door, speaking with the stewardess."

Only one man stood by the concourse door courteously suffering the delaying grasp of a uniformed flight attendant. He was tall and lean and darkly attractive. "That's Matthew?"

"You expecting breechclout and war bonnet?"

"I don't know, but certainly not a three-piece suit worn by a man who's...good Lord! There's no way to describe him except to say he's gorgeous."

"That's Matthew's cross to bear."

"Some cross."

Mitch dodged a harried woman arguing with her equally harried companion without missing a beat. "Watch it, Kate, you'll wake the green devil who sleeps within me."

"We both know there's no such animal in you."

"Don't be so sure."

Katherine only grinned as she studied Matthew Winter Sky. He was taller than Mitch, and darker. He wore the elegantly tailored suit and subtle tie as if he were born to them. As he spoke pleasantly to a clearly smitten stewardess, the only evidence of his heritage was his copper skin and sleek black hair drawn severely back from his face then tied at his nape. The last could easily have been more in keeping with fashion than a statement of his heritage.

She had no inkling of the color of his eyes, but darkest brown was a good bet. He was lean and rangy, leaving an indelible consciousness of the honed and finely tuned body beneath the sartorial excellence. Her first perception was that he would be far more suited for the tennis courts of some exclusive country club than tracking through snake-infested swamps.

Until she noticed how totally focused he was, with an intense readiness coiled and waiting beneath the apparent ease. That he listened a great deal more than he spoke. Most of all she remembered her first misconceptions of Mitch. Quiet danger with a quick smile, a gentle hand, and a baby bottle tucked nonchalantly in the hip pocket of his jeans. Appearances did, indeed, deceive.

In an undertone, hardly aware she'd spoken out loud, she murmured, "I hope he tracks even half as good as he looks."

"Try better." Accustomed to this reaction to Matthew, Mitch cast her an amused look and took her arm, a courteous gesture that came naturally. "Why don't we interrupt the little tête-á-tête, and take him home?"

"Before he breaks her heart?"

"Matthew doesn't break hearts. He never gets that involved." A quick move pulled her from a direct hit by a suitcase carelessly shifted. "This is like running a gauntlet," he grumbled in an aside, but dismissing it even as he sidestepped again. "No one ever gets close enough to Matthew to harbor any illusions about a future with him. He keeps too much to himself."

A common failing among friends, Katherine decided. And when she turned her welcoming smile on Matthew, it held a shadow of melancholy.

If she'd ever truly doubted his abilities, it wouldn't have been for long, Katherine admitted to herself as she watched Matthew in action. For two days before their departure from New Orleans, he'd studied maps and spoken endlessly with native Louisianians. He listened to speech patterns, absorbing accents and tonal nuances. He watched the sun rise, and he watched it set. He studied the sky. He made lists, and gathered equipment. He suggested once that she should stay behind, when she refused, giving her reasons, he said no more. Matthew Sky understood intuition. It was as much part of him as his Apache heart.

Katherine didn't think anything could surprise her once he'd shed his modern persona for canvas jeans, a shirt of supple chamois, and moccasins laced below his knees. When he stood, unrepentant, in front of her and the world a proud Apache warrior down to the beaded turquoise feather tied in his hair, she was sure of it. Until their last day in New Orleans, when this man who might have stepped out of the pages of a cruel and bloody history book turned to the last of his agenda. A visit to Trevor Hamilton.

"To thank him for his help," Matthew had said in his deep, quiet voice. "And discover if there is anything he might remember in retrospect."

There had been nothing, and their journey had begun. It would become a watery door-to-door investigation of shacks and cabins standing on pilings and surrounded by more water. But first there were the outlying settlements and the Cajuns, a warm and lively people whose existence ·evolved around the rivers and streams. Displaying the same facile ease, Matthew moved among them, still as focused, still as heedful, still listening, solemnly, far more than he spoke. He was a man of the desert, but he mingled with the Cajuns as if he were one of them, speaking as they spoke, with the same inflections, the same nuances. In French, his mother's tongue.

Mitch did not mix and mingle as if he were one of them, he became one of them. He *was* one of them, discovering a life he'd been denied, traditions he'd never known. While people stood a little in awe of Matthew, they were drawn to Mitch. For his quick smile that had grown more at ease with every mile he distanced himself from the city; for his unabashed delight in everything Cajun.

Tongues that might have stayed silent spoke to Mitch. Secret knowledge and suspicion that might have stayed secret were imparted. A generous people offered more than information. They offered their time and their possessions for his disposal.

Mitch and Matthew were a mighty combination. Invincible. Katherine's hopes, which had risen and fallen like a tide, were suddenly soaring.

"That's it, then, we begin." Matthew crouched by Katherine's side as she sat in the shade of an ancient and massive oak. After a day in a small settlement, they'd found that Trevor's information was correct as far as it went, and for the time. But nothing stayed the same in the bayous. What wind and weather and wild creatures didn't change, man did.

"Where do we begin?" she asked.

"Out there." Mitch looked to the bayou, at gnarled cypress veiled by drifts of moss, rising from still, black water. "There are hundreds of hunter and trapper cabins, in hundreds of curves of creeks and streams. Isaac has set up shop in more than one of them, but none are static. He moves on a whim and follows the trade."

"So we look where he was, and follow his trail to where he is?"

"We look for a pattern." Matthew answered, not Mitch. "And hope Isaac is a creature of some habits." He looked beyond the bayou, at things only he saw, invisible and far away. "Then we stalk him, until he leads us where we need to go."

"But will he?"

Matthew turned his rapt attention to Katherine. His eyes were as dark and mysterious as the still and silent water. "Yes. Perhaps not directly to Jocie, but to someone else who will. Every creature leaves some mark of its presence, especially man. Our task is to find that mark. We start our search tomorrow."

"Tomorrow!" She looked from Matthew to Mitch. "Why tomorrow? Why not now?"

Mitch came to kneel by her. He caught the end of her single braid in his hand, curling the silky strands around his finger. "We leave tomorrow because today is nearly done. Dark will come soon and there are final preparations we need to make. I thought you'd like to call home before we go."

"We'll be completely out of touch, won't we?"

"Not completely, but contact could be difficult."

"You're right." Her fingers brushed over his arm with a tentativeness that hadn't been there before their encounter with Trevor Hamilton. "I should check the situation at home before we vanish into the swamp."

Matthew stood to watch as she wandered to the general store, the only place in the small village that boasted custody of a public telephone. As she crossed the broad porch, without looking at Mitch, he speculated quietly, "Trouble at home?"

"The lady has more to contend with than any lady should."

"Want to tell me about it?" He crossed his arms over his chest. The sleeves of his shirt were fringed, a black bandanna was tied at his throat; he was perfectly at home as he leaned against the trunk of the tree. "Should I get more comfortable than this?"

"No need, the story's short, and at the moment, not so sweet." Mitch didn't lean, he didn't relax. He didn't turn his gaze from Katherine's receding figure. "Katherine is sole support of her family, four generations of women. Six of them whose ages range from rebellious sixteen to an amazing ninety-one. She's struggling to keep up a farm that must be half the size of Rhode Island." He ignored Matthew's raised brows noting the exaggeration. "At the moment, to complicate matters and keep it fun, mile upon mile of magnificent Rivard pastureland is shriveling and turning to dust with the worst drought in history.

"Katherine might curse the dust and a cloudless sky, but she doesn't complain. Instead she digs in her heels and fights to survive. She does all the outside work on the place, boarding and training horses on the side. One came close to breaking her ribs just before we left. It wasn't the first time." Mitch raked an agitated hand through his hair. A gesture that spoke volumes. "The hell of it is, I'm afraid it won't be the last."

"So." Matthew watched his friend as his friend watched the door that closed behind Katherine. "The lady trains horses in what would laughingly be called her spare time."

"Yeah, sure, spare time," Mitch growled around a bitter smile. "She had a shot at a deal to train for some high-class consortium. A 'show us what you can do and we might just give you the time of day, even though you are a woman' sort of arrangement."

"She *had* a shot. What happened?"

"Jocie happened. A neighbor is watching over the Rivard ladies, and training the horse on the sly. Each time I ask for more time he busts his butt to do it. This time he thinks he can hold the consortium off another week, maybe ten days. Then the deal's lost. And now I think there's a problem with her great-grandmother. She was the mainstay of the family until Katherine, and Katherine adores her. I don't know what will become of her if Gran should die while she's away."

"In that case, we'd better make sure we do what we came to do, and get Katherine home."

"She won't go without Jocie."

"Then we'll find her." Matthew pushed away from the tree and straightened to his full height.

"If she's still alive."

Matthew looked out over the bayou again. Rippling water glittered like black diamonds in the evening sun. "She's alive." His eyes focused again on a distant point. "She's alive and we'll find her, but it won't be pretty. Stay close, then. Jocie will need her and Katherine will need you."

Mitch didn't question. What Matthew said was all he knew. Nor did Mitch scoff—he'd seen these premonitions before, they were rare, and never wrong.

Matthew pulled his thoughts back to Mitch. His black gaze swept over his friend, lingering on the secret hurt that lurked in his eyes. No one knew better than Matthew how difficult it was to return to the place where life had been only trauma and chaos. He knew memories could rip and shred at a man until they nearly destroyed him.

But he knew Mitch, too. Enough to recognize it was more than returning to a pain-filled past that tormented him. More than Trevor Hamilton's tragedy. More than the lost girl. Mitch's disquiet had to do with Katherine. Not just with her trouble, but with Katherine, the woman. He saw it in Mitch's overwhelming need to touch her, when his hand was drawn to her with a will and mind of its own. He saw it in the swift and bitter withdrawal, in the disgust for the weakness.

Most of all, he saw it in Katherine. In her tentativeness, as if she'd found that Mitch was two men and she was never really sure which she was confronting.

Matthew knew something heavy had happened between Mitch and Katherine. Then it had changed.

Laying a hand on Mitch's shoulder, he gave it an encouraging slap. "You see to your lady, make sure she gets a good night's sleep. I'll see to the supplies. We're going to find Jocie Rivard and reunite her with her sister. After which you and I are going to sit down by the river while you tell me what your trouble is with Katherine."

Mitch turned his concerned study of Katherine as she crossed the dusty road back to them. "There's no trouble. At least nothing that ending this won't cure." He hesitated, only a minute break in the flow of his conversation, but it didn't escape notice. "She isn't my lady, Matthew."

"You wouldn't kid an old friend, would you?"

"This isn't a matter to kid you about."

"Then, maybe you're kidding yourself." When Mitch didn't answer, Matthew smiled grimly. "We'll find the girl, I promise you. Then we'll talk."

Nine

They made camp on high ground. A blatantly euphemistic term for the small clearing that rose a bare few feet out of still, murky water. The air was thick and humid, a cloying blanket. Each breath was so filled with moisture it was almost like breathing water.

It was hot. As hot as hell, but the only fire that burned was the campfire that was ever present each time they stopped. Dark was falling, and here in the swampland it came down like a curtain in one swift, silent, impenetrable instant. Night collided with day, and the world and its creatures stood still while they got their bearings.

In that millisecond of still silence Katherine sat by the fire, as still, as silent, staring into its flames, letting its copious smoke billow around her. Her eyes burned and her throat closed in choking gasps, yet the caustic cloud was blessed added relief from mosquitoes that swarmed in a black tide. She swatted one more persistent, then with unthinking resignation rubbed at a stinging swelling just beginning on the back of one hand. Even with the smoke and though she stank of Matthew's pungent concoction that Mitch insisted she smear on her face and neck, and any other parts of her body exposed to sun and insects, there was always one, or two, or a dozen whose craving for her blood was undaunted by any protection.

She turned her gritty gaze to the garish smear, all that was left of the swatted insect, a blue-black blob reaching from knuckle to wrist. As her mind filled with thoughts of human vampires who fed on human misery, she clutched at her sides, folding into herself, shivering. She was sweltering, but there was a coldness in her the heat couldn't touch. Sickness at the horrors she'd seen and some she could only imagine was mounting, and nothing could ease it.

In a watery wonderland, where exotic flowers grew in profusion, and magnificently plumed birds soared; where countless trapper cabins stood, quaint and dilapidated, on pilings rising from riverbeds; where even the deadliest creatures could claim an ugly beauty, she saw only misery and danger. She hadn't thought anything could be more ghastly or more savage than the streets of New Orleans.

She was wrong. So wrong.

A hand curled around her shoulder. In spite of its familiar and beloved tenderness, she cringed from it, haunted by hands that were touching Jocie. Strange hands, hands that made tenderness and love a travesty.

As he sat beside her, a frown on his face, Mitch took his hand carefully away. "Sorry. I didn't mean to disturb you."

Katherine relaxed and managed a smile. "Don't be sorry. I should thank you."

Mitch touched her again, drawing the back of his hand down her sooty cheek. "Bad, huh?"

"I keep thinking about her. Imagining..." She stumbled over images too awful to explain.

"Shh." Mitch gathered her in his arms. She was sooty, and reeked of smoke and Matthew's insect repellent, and the ever-souring mud of the swamp, but so did he. "Don't imagine, sweetheart. Don't think of it." He stroked her back, feeling muscles drawn in knots beneath her thick shirt. "Why don't you try to eat something and then turn in?"

Katherine only shook her head, her cheek brushing his throat with the small effort. The hammock Mitch had strung between two saplings and its mosquito netting would be a claustrophobic cage, not respite from fatigue. She couldn't sleep, she couldn't rest. Not now. Not when a second tip whispered behind a shielding hand offered the first real hope in days.

She pulled away, lifting her head, lifting her gaze. Blinded by the fire, she saw only unrelieved darkness, but she didn't need to see to know that out there in the moonless night, lamplight danced in the unshuttered windows of another shack Isaac had taken as his. In those peculiar moments when the swamp fell silent, the sound of music and laughter drifted through the motionless air. Jubilant music, deep, rich, masculine laughter. The sound of fulfillment, the aftermath of sexual pleasures taken from The Mentor's stolen chattel.

With a fresh wave of pain sweeping through her, Katherine lurched to her feet, turning away from the lights. And when the chorus of swamp creatures returned to full cry, even the scream of a panther was not as frightening as her thoughts. Her hands clenched into fists, she stood rooted, wanting to move, to act, to do something. Anything was better than this waiting. But what could she do?

Mitch recognized her restless tension. "Take it easy." He moved behind her, but this time managed not to touch her. "There's nothing we can do to make this go any faster."

Katherine whirled to face him, frustration spilling out in anger. "How can I take it easy when Matthew might have found Jocie by now? How can I sit here doing nothing, a useless lump wondering when he'll come?"

As quickly as it came, her anger died. The bleak look on Mitch's face cut her to the core. He felt as helpless as she. As useless. As frustrated. "I'm sorry." She reached out to him, stopping short of contact. "I didn't mean . . ."

"Katherine." He tried for a smile and didn't quite make it. "I know what you meant and I know what you didn't mean." He knew how she felt, too. He knew too well. Matthew had gone to do something he couldn't. In his mind, Mitch accepted that they'd chosen to broach Isaac's security the only way possible. Isaac's henchmen, The Ball and Tootsie and others, would be looking for Mitchell Ryan. Expecting him. Mitch acknowledged he wouldn't have gotten past the door and any hope of more information on Jocie would have been lost.

Matthew had gone to do what only Matthew could. It was the only sensible course, but being sensible didn't ease the bitter sense of uselessness or hurry along the long hours of waiting.

"How much longer do you think he'll be?" Katherine regretted her outburst, but something in her couldn't be silent. "Do you think they've hurt him?"

"These things take time. Matthew has to move cautiously." He drew a long, slow breath. "And we have to be patient."

"I know. I'm sorry, I'm being foolish."

"Not foolish, natural. Now—" he offered his hand palm up "—come back to the fire before a legion of greedy mosquitoes decides to make a meal of you. And try not to worry about Matthew."

She took his hand, a rare voluntary physical closeness. Accepting his need to care for her, to feel a little less helpless, she went where he led, sat in the caustic smoke, ate and drank to please him. Then, keeping within the small circle of light and quietly grateful for the camp chores that were hers, she moved with practiced ease through the evening routine. Mitch's conversation, as he attended his own chores, was deliberately subdued and unperturbed. She responded in kind, letting him set the mood and the pace, resisting only when he suggested again that she should sleep.

The evening dragged by slowly and seemingly peacefully for there were no further incidences. But the calm was only a sham. They were players in a deadly game and no amount of pretense could hide their concern for Matthew and his journey.

Seconds became minutes. Minutes, hours. Each creeping by slower than the last. Katherine's patience was unraveling, her steel control beginning to fray when Mitch's staying hand on her arm brought her to a freezing halt. Her head came up, but only her eyes turned, scanning the thick shadows beyond the camp.

The swamp was silent again. A trembling, heavy silence. Expectant. No leaf stirred in the undergrowth or crackled underfoot. There were no smooth, gliding disturbances in the still water. No glittering, staring eyes caught the light. Nothing moved, yet something was out there. Waiting, as the darkness closed tighter around them. Watching.

Katherine didn't speak, or question, or acknowledge the leap of fear that set her heart racing.

"Go back to your seat by the fire," Mitch murmured on a breath. "But don't look into the flames, protect your vision. Stay ready. If I say go, make a run for the dugout, don't take anything, and don't look back. If I'm more than a pace behind you, shove off. Don't wait." His fingers curled painfully into the soft flesh of her arm. "Hear me, Katherine." There was no arrogance in the command, only stark authority. "No matter what happens, or what you hear, don't stop or turn around. Just go."

Katherine nodded. What Mitch might have to do, he could do better if she was out of harm's way. "I won't wait."

Mitch released her. "Sit. Act natural. But be ready."

She did as he commanded, and was surprised when he joined her by the fire, pouring a cup of rich, fragrant coffee, leaning back in leisure to enjoy it. He was the epitome of cool detachment. No one knew better than Katherine that it was a lie.

He was tense, ready, his roving gaze avoiding the blinding flames as they flickered into embers. He knew this small patch of ground like a blueprint. He knew where the egret roosted and the owl hunted. He knew where the muskrat swam and what creatures burrowed and prowled at the river's edge. He knew the vines that twined in the underbrush and the Spanish moss that wreathed the limbs of the bald cypress. He knew when silent passage stirred the drifting gray veils and glided by the vines.

He knew after a while that the stillness that reached beyond the camp was truly still. The empty silence truly silent.

A bird called. A soft, sleepy, grousing note heard only because there was no other. Mitch drew a deep breath and straightened to reach for the coffeepot to fill another cup. Before the shimmering liquid touched the rim, a hard slender hand reached from the darkness to take it.

"Matthew!" Katherine barely stifled her shock to a whisper at the menacing but familiar figure. She hadn't heard the splash of a paddle as he'd crossed the bayou, or the rustle of underbrush as he'd made portage. But it wouldn't have been Matthew if she had. And Mitch wouldn't have sat quietly but carefully monitoring his trail back, as she realized now he'd done.

They worked as a team, personal affinity and years of training melding them into an efficient unit. Words weren't needed, before or now, as silent messages seemed to emanate from the quirk of a lip or the arch of a brow.

A thousand questions leapt to her tongue, but she forced herself to keep her peace. Matthew was exhausted. It was there, not in the lithe, easy moves of his body, but in the grim flicker in his jaw. Mental fatigue, the strain of witnessing human suffering, and far more taxing than physical labors.

He gulped down the scalding brew, as if it warmed some dank cold spot the cloying heat couldn't touch. The cinnamon hue of his skin was deeper in the flickering shadows, his hair sleeker. Blacker. In his trapper's clothing he could've been a roving Choctaw or native Chitimacha, as proficient in the skills of their land as his own.

Feeling her probing stare, Matthew lifted his own gaze above the rim of the cup. A slow shake of his head left her rising hope in the dust. "She wasn't there." His next words, delivered gently in a voice as unaccented as Mitch's, lifted them again. "But I know where she is."

For one suffocating instant, when her heart somersaulted in her chest and her breath was lost in shock, Katherine wasn't sure if she'd really heard the simple, wonderful phrase or imagined it. Only the cautious smile that touched his lips, but not his eyes, told her she hadn't imagined it.

"Where? Matthew, where is she? Take me to her." She caught his hand, nearly spilling the heated liquid on her arm. "How far is it? Where is it?"

"Katherine." Mitch's fingers circled her wrist, bringing her back to sanity with the compassion and concern in his tender warning. "It won't be quite as easy nor as simple as just going for her."

"Why?" She turned to him. "Where is she?" Then crumpling. "Oh, God! Not another of Isaac's places."

Gripping both her hands in his, Mitch looked to Matthew, his eyes as sick as Katherine's. "Where is she, Matthew?"

"There's a small settlement downriver, and a small chapel. She's there. Isaac took her there when he knew you would be coming for her."

There was more to the story, an uglier side. "How is she?"

Matthew didn't flinch or look away. There was no sugar-coating for Jocie's condition. "Not good."

"What do you mean?" Still gripping Mitch's hands, Katherine swung around to face Matthew squarely. "Tell me what that means."

"It means she's had a rough time of it," Matthew answered carefully. He didn't say that Isaac's usual way to rid himself of useless human baggage was to dump it into the swamp for the gators. That Jocie had only escaped the same fate because of the certain knowledge nothing on earth would have stopped The Saint of Bourbon Street from coming after The Mentor then. A grim avenger, meting out judgment for judgment given.

"What..." Katherine began and caught her lip cruelly between her teeth, stopping the outpouring of questions.

"She's safe, now. Safer than she's been in a long, long time." Matthew brushed her braid from her shoulder, resting his hand in brief encouragement on her shoulder. "Soon she'll have you. I'd think that's the best medicine of all."

Katherine searched his face, knowing there was more, much more, behind the cautious answer. Misery she couldn't imagine and shouldn't try. Swallowing the knot of fear that threatened to choke her, she clung to Mitch, taking desperate comfort from his strength. "Falling to pieces now won't help her, will it?"

Neither answered. No answer was necessary.

There was no jubilation in their camp. No celebration. Matthew waved away an offer of food, taking only another cup of coffee. For hours he stared beyond the high ground to the winking lights that appeared to float in a black void. His face was grave, his mouth taut and grim. He didn't speak of where he'd been or what he'd seen. After gentle persuasion from Mitch, Katherine had gone to the hammock to try to sleep in preparation for the next day's journey. Worn down by the heat and the long hours of waiting, contrary to her protests, she was nearly comatose in a matter of minutes.

Mitch settled in for the night and lay staring with gritty eyes at the starless sky. The second watch would be his. Scorning fatigue, Matthew insisted on standing the first. Mitch watched as he paced the perimeter of the camp, always coming to stand, staring out at the lights.

He hadn't spoken for hours, though he knew Mitch didn't sleep. A small wind rose, skimming the surface of the water, bringing again the alien sounds to the hush of their distant encampment. Raucous, drunken sounds. Too merry. Too hearty. Then, as quickly as it had come, as if only intended to bring a reminder, the wind died away and all was quiet again.

Matthew stood as he'd stood so often, feet apart, shoulders back, every inch taut and barely controlled. "Stay with her, Mitch," he muttered without turning or looking away. "She'll need you tomorrow. More than either of us could have imagined."

Mitch nodded, and though Matthew couldn't see, he knew.

When Mitch took his watch, he hadn't slept. When Matthew sought his bed, neither did he. It wasn't the first time for either of them. It wouldn't be the last.

The settlement was a half day of hard paddling, with the two dugouts, chosen in the beginning for their silence, moving carefully in tandem through twisting, currentless channels. The small cluster of buildings, crouched on a surprisingly dusty curve of the river, took its name from the chapel. The latter, a small structure endowed by the wife of a Spanish governor in 1851, its true name long forgotten in the annals of history, was called in her honor, simply, The Chapel of the Spanish Lady. Thus the village came to be The Village of the Chapel of the Spanish Lady. Then, fondly, even more simply, Spanish Lady.

It appeared on no maps or tourist brochures. Travel to it was hard, and visitors rare and likely to be nomadic trappers or hunters. Even time appeared to have forgotten it.

Its inhabitants were solitary and self-sufficient, living off the land and the swamp, buying the little else they needed in infrequent visits to the next, more progressive settlement. The chapel was tucked away at the end of a narrow avenue lined by oaks drifting with moss. A simple edifice, reflecting the Spanish influence, better suited to arid lands but oddly at home in a little cove where the river curled and wandered like a peaceful brook.

As Matthew strode in his loose-limbed step down the black-green tunnel created by the joining of the massive branches of trees, only he among them knew how unintentionally fitting Isaac's choice for Jocie had been. The Chapel of the Spanish Lady was a sanctuary. A place for the wounded and the lost to hide.

Left alone, Jocie would choose to hide for the rest of her life. It would be up to Katherine, first, and then to time and the professionals to show her she had nothing to be ashamed of. Nothing at all to hide.

At the end of the leafy tunnel the chapel sat in a pool of broiling sunlight. The door was of rough wood, strong, sturdy, a crudely forged circle of iron mounted in its center to summon the sisters. Once more the Spanish influence was serendipitously in harmony with the village and the land.

Katherine was visibly nervous, scrubbing her hands on the sides of her trousers. As Mitch rapped three times, she flinched and paled. It was Matthew who took her arm and guided her a few steps away to shade. "Easy," he soothed. "You've been to hell and back and never faltered. Never lost faith or courage or allowed yourself the luxury of weakness. You've been stronger than any woman I've ever known. Don't lose it now. Not when you're so close."

"But what if I can't do this?" She looked into his stern but steadfast features and wondered how she had ever questioned him. "What if I can't face what we find?"

"You can. You will. Haven't you always?"

"Nothing like this, Matthew. Never anything like this."

"Maybe not," admitted the tracker, the man she trusted second only to one other. "But this time you're not alone. You have Mitch."

"Do I?"

"What do you question? His courage? His commitment to this?"

"I . . ." She stumbled, searching for her answer, then shook her head. "No. How could I question either after all he's done?"

"Yet there's something."

"It doesn't matter."

"I think it does, Katherine, and it will. To you and to Mitch."

"I wish..." Her response was lost, forgotten, as she spun in reaction to the creaking of massive hinges swinging the door inward.

At first there was only a square of darkness. Then a face framed by a wimple peered beyond the edge of the door. Gradually, as if she were materializing bit by bit, she became a whole person dressed in black from head to toe. She was tiny and plump, with the face of an angel. When she saw Matthew, her pleasant smile wavered. "May I help you?"

It was Katherine who stepped forward, surprising even herself. "We apologize for disturbing you, Sister, but we're looking for someone. A young girl. We were told she was here."

"A girl?" Aged hands clutched at the door, she couldn't take her gaze from Matthew. "I'm sorry." Evasion, not a lie. "So sorry."

"Please." Katherine stepped closer. "She has to be here. Look at me, Sister. She's blond like me, and her eyes are as gray. Her name is Jocie and she's my sister. These gentlemen are my friends, they've helped me find her. Please don't tell us she's not here."

"These men—" the wimple turned from Matthew to Mitch and back again, not missing a detail of their rough dress "—these gentlemen are your friends?"

"Yes," Katherine said firmly. "We've been searching for weeks. First in the city, then here in the bayous." She pulled her wallet from a back pocket. "Look, this is my identification. Jocie's last name is Rivard, so is mine."

The old woman took the wallet, but only held it. "You do look like her."

"Then you've seen her!"

There was still doubt in the old eyes.

"Sister." Mitch stepped forward. "We aren't from The Mentor. We haven't come to take her back to him."

"Let them in, Sister Agnes." A taller figure moved from the shadows. "I think we can trust them."

"Then she is here."

The taller figure turned to answer Katherine. "Jocie is here— The Mentor brought her here a few days ago. But before you see her, we should talk. If you and the gentlemen will follow me, we'll have something cool to drink and decide how best to handle this."

After weeks of walking dangerous streets, among dangerous people, Katherine was more afraid than she'd ever been. "Mitch."

"I'm here, Katherine."

She managed a wan smile as he laced his fingers through hers. "Matthew said you would be." She realized only then that they were alone on the front step. The tracker had faded away like a ghost. "Matthew! Where is he?"

"Now that we know for certain Jocie is here, he has another matter to take care of. Someone who will need him."

"His informant." Katherine surmised the obvious now that she'd come to know the caliber of these men who were her companions and her friends.

"He'll bring her out, if he can, before Isaac learns who she is and what she's done."

"Will he bring her here?"

"If there's no place else, and the sisters will have her."

"We'll have her, young man," the little nun piped in. "We have before, many times. But for now, shouldn't Jocie be our main concern?" She gestured down the cool, Spartan hall. "Sister Marie will be waiting in the sitting room."

"Then let's not keep her waiting any longer," Mitch suggested. Giving Katherine's hand a squeeze, smiling when she squared her shoulders and lifted her chin to its fighting angle, he walked hand-in-hand with her to hear the bitter truths about Jocie.

One hour, thirty-six minutes and seventeen seconds after the end of a devastating conversation that had left them all drained and hollow, Katherine had bathed and changed as Sister Marie had insisted she must. Much to her surprise, even as she'd counted every interminable second, she'd managed to rest a bit in the cell-like room she'd been assigned. The narrow, spotless cot had been no harder than the ground and less confining than the hammock, and if she hadn't slept, the strained look had eased around her mouth and eyes.

Though knowing the truth, however awful, was a relief from greater fears, she'd worried about what she would see in Jocie. Sister Marie had worried about what Jocie would see in her.

"You look like death," the sister had pronounced bluntly, giving no quarter in her critical study. "Jocie has enough to contend with, without thinking she's done this to you."

The sister was a psychologist to rival all psychologists, instinctively waging the argument that would convince Katherine to rest. The only argument she would have heard.

Now the promised hour had arrived. Dressed familiarly, as suggested, in tall polished boots, a fresh cream shirt and fawn riding pants retrieved from her pack and pressed by Sister Agnes, she looked as she would in the paddock at Stone Meadow. As Jocie had seen her almost all her life. Even Sister Marie had given her choice a surprisingly worldly thumbs-up gesture. Now, Katherine thought feverishly as she smoothed back her braided hair, if Jocie would only react as positively.

The expected knock at her door had her whirling nervously from the scrap of mirror scrounged from heaven knew where. It was time, at last, to go to Jocie.

When she stepped from her room, Mitch was lounging against a wall, leaner and more handsome than she remembered. He'd followed orders, shaving a two-day growth of beard, and changing into freshly pressed clothing, as well. Once more Sister Agnes had plied a relentless iron.

He straightened from the wall to look down at her in the cool, somber hall. "Ready?"

Katherine only shook her head.

"Hey—" his fingers closed around her elbow "—you're worrying too much about making a mistake with Jocie. She's fragile now, and a long, long way from being the girl you knew, but you'll still know what to say to her and what to do. Just listen to your heart, Kate, and go with it." He pulled her closer, their bodies not quite touching, and kissed her forehead. "It won't be easy, but you'll both be okay," he murmured against her pale skin before he moved away. A smile tilted one corner of his mouth. "The Ryan intuition is betting on it."

Laying her fingers at the corner of his mouth in a caress that garnered a small measure of his strength, she found her voice. "Thank you." Blinking back tears, she struggled with an answering smile. "Thank you for more than I can say."

There was no time for anything else as Sister Marie appeared at the end of the hall to escort them to the infirmary where a single patient waited in solitude.

The infirmary was well-equipped. Isolated from any other medical attention, the villagers had naturally turned to the sisters for aid. A plaque on the wall attested that what was lacked had been supplied by a grateful wealthy patron. An artist who had come to paint the bayous and suffered the good fortune of falling ill in the village rather than in a hunter's cabin on some isolated stream. His gift was ultimately good fortune for the sisters, the village, and for Jocie.

Sister Marie led them through the main area, then to one of three closed doors. At one she rapped and waited. When there was no answer she opened the door and stepped in. "Jocie," she said softly as she would to a frightened child, "you have visitors."

A thin shape huddled in blankets showed no sign of response, a hunched back remained turned to them. Though the single window opened to a vista of steaming swamp and water like hot glass, the thick walls of the chapel protected it from the heat. Not enough to warrant blankets, yet Jocie was wrapped in two and still shivered as if she were cold. Even their bulk couldn't disguise the mummylike thinness of her body. Hair that once had been long and golden had been hacked away, short tufts that stood in a wreath of dirty spikes around her head were dark and oily.

"Wouldn't you like to say hello, Jocie? They've come quite a distance and have searched long and hard for you."

Only silence greeted Sister Maric's cajoling.

"Jocie." Katherine took a step closer, and blinked back a fresh wave of tears as the thin shoulders hunched lower, cowering as if they'd been struck. "It's Katherine."

No response, the stick figure shrank deeper into the blankets.

"I talked to Justin's flowers a few days ago. They all send their love, and so does Gran. Cam's looking out for them for a while." Katherine took another step forward, this time not expecting a response. "There's someone I'd like you to meet, when you're feeling better. His name is Mitchell Ryan. He and a friend, Matthew Sky, helped me find you."

"Why did you bother?"

For the space of a somersaulting heartbeat Katherine wasn't sure she'd really heard the hoarse whisper. Or that the lifeless voice was Jocie's. Yet there was no one else it could be. Regaining her equilibrium, and gathering her strength, she moved another step toward the wreck that was her sister. "It wasn't a bother, Jocie. It was something I had to do and wanted to do."

"Had to? Wanted to? Why?"

"Because I love you. Because we all do. We miss you, Jocie."

"Don't call me Jocie," the voice was a toneless murmur. "I'm not Jocie anymore."

"You are. Nothing that's happened can change that." Katherine advanced again, slowly, carefully, gratefully aware that Mitch stood in silent support by the door.

"You don't know. You can't know." A calm observation, too calm, too resigned. "What I've done. What's been done to me."

Katherine felt her stomach churn at the depravity that would strip hope and life from the spirited girl her sister had been. "I'm sorry for all that happened, but it can't keep me from loving you." Raking a hand through her hair, sending the braid into a state of disarray, an edge of frustration at her own inability crept into her. "I wish I knew the right words, words that would make you understand how important you are to us. All of us."

"Why would you love me when I hated you?" The cry was filled with the first emotion Jocie had shown. Vicious, pent-up rage.

As if she'd turned to stone, Katherine stopped her subtle advance. A hand clapped over her mouth to stop any outcry, she stared at the thin, shivering back, hearing the words with a mind not capable of understanding.

"That one stopped you, did it, Miss Perfect?"

"I'm not perfect, Jocie."

"Yes, you are. Always doing the right thing. Sacrificing yourself. Never having any fun. Never complaining. Why do you think I ran away the other times? Or insisted on going away to school?"

Katherine swayed on her feet, realizing for the first time that Jocie had truly been running away, not just imbued with the wanderlust of their father and so many Rivards before her. "You were running away from me?"

"My, my, my, give the smart little lady a rose, she got it right the first guess." The mocking voice fell silent. When Jocie spoke again, the lackluster tone had returned. "The funny thing is, even a school hundreds of miles away didn't work."

Katherine was close enough to touch her. She wanted to, needed to, but dared not. Not yet. "Why not, Jocie?"

"Letters! From the flowers, and Gran, always about you."

"I'm sorry," Katherine whispered. "I didn't know."

"Of course you didn't know. Truly perfect, perfect people don't know they're perfect."

The gibberish made sense to the tortured mind of this suffering child who had been her sister. No, Katherine corrected, this suffering child who *was* her sister. "I'm not perfect, I never was," she insisted gently. "There are calluses on my knees for all my sins."

"Ah, the famous Hail Marys. Would you like to know where my calluses are for all my sins?"

"Jocie, don't!"

At Katherine's cry of anguish, Mitch took a step toward her and was stopped by Sister Marie's hand on his sleeve. He wanted to tear away, but deep within himself he knew he must not interfere.

"Sweet, innocent older sister doesn't want to hear about my adventures? My escape from one monster at the bus station, only to find another was waiting on the street for a girl exactly like me. It doesn't matter, you won't have to hear. I wear the evidence on my face." Jocie was rising, weaving weakly on her feet. "Wouldn't you like to see?"

"Jocie!" Katherine reached out to steady her, but the blanketed creature scuttled away.

Spinning drunkenly, Jocie dipped and swayed, and regained her balance. Feet planted, and spine straight, she hesitated only a second before flinging the blankets away in a curiously graceful gesture. Then she lifted her face to stare into Katherine's eyes.

"Don't you think I'm pretty, perfect Katherine?" She laughed softly, a cold, punishing sound, and shook her shorn head. "Because I cut my hair, ruining my selling point, The Mentor did this." She stroked her cheek. "This was my punishment, a lasting reminder. Do you still insist on calling me Jocie? Do you insist, even now that I look like this?"

To her credit, and testament to the power of her love, Katherine didn't flinch or turn away. She didn't gasp or cry out as her heart shattered for the beautiful girl Jocie had been. "I call you Jocie because you are Jocie. Nothing that you've done, or nothing that's been done to you could change that.

"Scars can be repaired, wiped away." She prayed the internal scars would be half as simply dealt with as the ragged X carved in Jocie's cheek. "There are surgeons," Katherine said almost desperately. "We'll find the best."

"Surgeons cost money." The life, welcomed even if it was anger, was snuffed out again. "Money we don't have."

Perhaps she was grasping at straws in her eagerness to establish some little rapport with Jocie, but the inclusive "we" sent Katherine's hopes spiraling. "Money is no problem. I can get all you will need."

"How? Why?" A sneer lifted Jocie's lips. Only a little one as her bravado and her strength were failing.

"I can sell the farm, as much of it as is needed. All of it if it's needed."

Jocie's drooping head jerked up, surprise rounded her eyes. "Sell the land! Rivard land! You would do that?"

"Every acre," Katherine said levelly, and no one who heard could doubt her. If it took every penny or every grain of red clay every Rivard had in the past, or would have, it would be offered for Jocie's well-being.

"You would do that? Give up everything you've worked so hard to save? For me? Even after..." Jocie swayed and shook her head. "It makes no sense."

"It makes perfect sense." Katherine risked touching her, cupping her palm over the scar. A touch that was as much a caress, a touch that spoke of love. And Jocie didn't pull away.

"Because you love me." Wonder trembled in her voice and tears softened eyes that had been dry and hard.

"Yes, because I love you. But it's more than that. You're a survivor. Sister Marie told us that no matter what was done to you, you always rose above it. You weren't defeated—you are the winner. A survivor! I don't think I've ever been prouder of anyone than I am of you, here and now."

Jocie stiffened, her breath coming in labored efforts. Her eyes blazed into Katherine's, searching for the lie. Then slowly she crumpled and, with a mewling cry, went into her sister's waiting arms.

They were one shape in the dim light—two people joining to be the strength of one—when Sister Marie touched Mitch on the arm and pulled him quietly from the room.

What Jocie would tell Katherine, what Katherine would say to Jocie until the small hours of the morning, no one would know for a long, long while. Some things, perhaps never. But when exhaustion overtook them and Jocie slept at last, Katherine left her in the quietly insistent care of Sister Agnes who appeared like a guardian angel at the perfect instant.

Katherine had her own guilt to deal with. Undeserved, but real nevertheless. When she stepped from the infirmary, closing the door softly behind her, Mitch was there. Without a word he opened his arms, and when she went into them, he held her close to his heart.

Katherine cried. Once she let down her rigid guard, she cried as she did everything else, with all her heart. Her sobs were wrenched from her throat and would not be silenced. Her tears were a flood that would not be stemmed. Mitch held her, letting it happen as it would. Understanding this one expression of profound grief must follow its course before the mending could begin. When her sobs grew quieter, her tears fewer, he did not break his silence. When Katherine needed his words he would give them, and not before.

Finally, the storm ended. She pulled away, wiping her cheeks. "All of this," she whispered. "Because of what I am."

"No, Kate." He lifted her face to his with thumb and forefinger. "Because of what she perceived she was not."

"I should have known! I should have done something to help!"

"You couldn't know. Jocie didn't want you to know. And anything you might have done would only have made things worse. Jocie had to work it out for herself. Her choice was nearly disastrous, but awful as it was, I have a gut feeling that when this is resolved, she'll be a better person for it."

At Katherine's skeptical look, he smiled that same crooked smile. "Call it Ryan's intuition again. That and the fact that I know a stubborn older sister will make it so."

He pulled her closer, tucking her under his arm as he led her to her room. The chapel corridors kept the secret of what he whispered as he walked with her, giving the solace she needed. Solace he had promised Gran and himself he would give her no matter what else he could not.

Ten

―――――

"How is she?" Matthew leaned against a gate that led from a walled garden to a path by the river where Katherine and Jocie walked. His keen eyes followed every tottering step accompanied by one surer, absorbing every subtle nuance, every comforting gesture.

"That depends on which one you're asking about," Mitch responded, his gaze, like Matthew's, only on the women.

"Does it?" Matthew shot him a quizzical look. "Isn't the well-being of one of them almost solely dependent on the other?"

"Katherine's fine, Matthew. It was a shock discovering how Jocie felt about her, and she still feels twinges of guilt for it, but deep down, she knows she only did what she had to do. For all of them. To survive. If Jocie had trouble accepting and measuring up to that, it was her problem."

"Katherine's that objective about it?"

"Not completely. Not for a while yet, but she's getting there. She knows she must if she's going to help Jocie."

"She's quite a woman."

"You won't get any argument from me on that."

"So, how are you?"

"Okay." Mitch shrugged, but didn't look away from Katherine. "Better than okay, really. How else would I be?"

Matthew turned another look at Mitch, a piercing study, with a question hovering on his tongue. A question he would save for another time. After a three-day absence, he'd come in at dawn, battered, bruised from a skirmish with Isaac's henchmen, but with his informant in tow and carefully protected. The sisters had gladly taken in the girl who was only a little older than Jocie, seeing first to her care, then to Matthew's injuries. Their meticulous attention, once they'd grown comfortable with his fierce veneer, hadn't kept him from hearing a complete account of the encounter between Katherine and Jocie.

At the moment he was as concerned with what had transpired later between Katherine and Mitch. A new and easy rapport had emerged, but one with scrupulously guarded boundaries. So carefully guarded, he knew that once they hadn't existed.

He wondered why they must now. What foolish reason was driving two lovers apart?

He turned abruptly from his thoughts. This wasn't the time. Other matters, urgent and critical, were pressing down on them. "How soon do the sisters think it will be before Jocie can travel?"

Mitch was too engrossed in the women to note his disquiet. "A few weeks at the earliest."

"That long?" Matthew shifted restlessly, a rare reaction.

"Our one blessing has been that since Isaac works the bayous instead of the streets, he was too stingy to buy drugs, so addiction is no problem. But now she's developed pneumonia. She insists on these short evening walks but they're almost more than she can manage. The trip back through the bayous would be impossible for her. The only alternative would be by helicopter. For some reason she's deathly afraid of that. If Katherine insisted, she would try, but her emotional state is too precarious for the risk."

"And Katherine? Could Jocie deal with letting her go?"

Mitch looked sharply at his friend and fellow agent. "What is it, Matthew? What's wrong?"

"I stopped by the last settlement and made a call from the general store to Stone Meadow." He shook his head, the feather twisted in his hair drifting over the taut, bare flesh of his upper arm. "The news isn't good."

"Gran?"

"Cam Halsey says there isn't much hope. If Katherine wants to see her great-grandmother one last time, she should leave as soon as possible. I arranged for a helicopter to be here by seven tomorrow morning, in case she can go and wants to go."

"Tough decision." Mitch faced the river and the winding path again, a bleak expression recarving the lines around his mouth. "Who needs her most now? The choice will tear her heart out. It shouldn't have to be made, dammit, yet it's the sort she's spent her life making."

"Can she go?" Matthew asked. "Does she truly have a choice?"

Mitch sighed heavily. "Maybe. Jocie's grown more comfortable with me. Contrary to what I would have expected, given her recent experiences with men, she trusts me. She might agree to let Katherine go if I stay."

"You would do that?"

"Yes."

"Then we'll both stay. If it works out, I'll see Katherine to the airport, and come back here." There was a dangerous fire deep in Matthew's black eyes. "I hadn't planned to leave just yet anyway. There's a small matter of unfinished business to be taken care of."

Mitch had no need to ask the nature of Matthew's unfinished business for it was a task they would share. When it was done, Jocie's captor would not cruise the streets of New Orleans. There would be no dens of revelry that moved along the bayous at his whim. Neither Mitch nor Matthew fooled themselves that there wouldn't be others who would take his place. But there was grim satisfaction in the knowledge that none of the new scourge of vultures would be Isaac, The Mentor.

Mitch knew Matthew had a second reason for staying. He would stay to help the girl who'd helped him. And Jocie, if she would allow it.

Jocie didn't know Matthew yet, but when she did, when she'd spent some time with this young man who was wise in the ways of his people, and beyond his years, her life would be better for it. Matthew, with the quiet wisdom of an Apache medicine man, could bring an added depth to the healing Katherine had already affected. He would teach Jocie to look to nature and life beyond herself. In unraveling its mysteries and discovering its value in the universe, she would unravel her own mysteries and recognize her own worth.

In his simple Apache way, Matthew could teach her as few others could. He could show her the way to peace that would allow her to put aside memories that haunted her and scarred her mind. When he had taught her she must not mourn for the Jocie who was gone forever, nor to hide from the new, he would lead her to the strength to find her place in the world.

Mitch looked beyond the garden with the perception Matthew had taught him over the years. He saw the sinking sun. A great ball of fire casting down elongated pools of darkness as it etched ghostly cypress in stark relief against a brilliant sky. He smelled the delicate scent of flowers drifting from tended beds, blending with the richer, heavier perfume of wildflowers blooming in tangled profusion beyond the garden wall. He heard the nearly silent rush of the current that moved beneath the still surface of the river. A bird sang an ode to nightfall and somewhere deep in the swamp a cougar padded. There was beauty here, and danger, and the absence of evil.

The Village of the Chapel of the Spanish Lady was an exquisite relic from a gentler era. A much-needed sanctuary, but one that must be temporary if Jocie was to flourish.

A bell high above the chapel began to toll the hour of sunset. Sweet, clear notes that called the weary to rest, the thirsty to drink, and the lost to shelter. Mitch waited, listening, watching as Katherine and Jocie turned back from their wandering path, answering its call.

"I'll speak to Katherine," he promised when the bell was still again. "I'll speak to both of them, after dinner."

"Then I'll leave you to it." Matthew turned away from the wall. He had other responsibilities. One was another wounded child, a waif from Isaac's den of evil. Corrie, who had risked grave consequences to help him, who hadn't the family support that blessed Jocie. Corrie, who had only the sisters and Matthew.

"You'll be in the infirmary?" It was a question that needed no answer. "If Corrie is recovered enough, I'd like to come by for a visit later. To thank her for what she's done."

"She didn't do it for thanks, but she'd like that. I'll tell her you're coming." With a small wave, Matthew faded into the shade of trees that marked the path to the infirmary.

Mitch's thoughts returned to Katherine and the grave condition of Jocelyn Rivard. He would have to tell her soon, but not just yet. He wouldn't spoil this hour of the day when the sun was kind and the shadows long, and The Village of the Chapel of the Spanish Lady was its most peaceful. Sad news couldn't be changed by hurrying its telling.

The soft murmur of voices floated on the evening air. Close in conversation, two blond heads glittered in the light, one with hair long and flowing, the other chopped and ragged, but more alike than either of them knew.

Opening the gate, he stepped through it, going to meet them, to share this tranquil interval destined to end too soon.

"Mitch." Jocie reached out to him with a thin, clawed hand as he drew near. "I wondered where you were."

"I was no farther away than the garden." He put an arm around her, fitting her comfortably to his side. Though he marveled at the resilience of youth and her ease with him, he didn't delude himself that she would be as relaxed with other men, or as unafraid beyond the security of the chapel.

"I saw your Indian friend. Katherine told me about him and how he helped you find me."

"He's an interesting person. Would you like to meet him?" He felt her step falter. The hand that curled at his waist stiffened into a fist. Mitch's gaze met Katherine's over the shorn blond head that bobbed at his shoulder. He saw misgiving cloud her gray eyes and knew his speculation that Jocie's trust of men was truly trust of man. One man. Mitchell Ryan. "There's no hurry." He pulled Jocie closer and kissed her forehead. "We'll wait until you're ready."

"What if I'm never ready?" Jocie's voice was hoarse with her cold, but the tremor was fear.

"You will be, in your own time." Katherine caught her hand in hers. "Mitch meant it when he said there was no hurry."

"How about dinner?" Mitch asked. "Sister Thumbelina was stirring up a wicked gumbo when I checked by the kitchen. Let me warn you, she expects you to bring a ravenous appetite to the table."

Jocie laughed at the name he had given the tiny Sister Agnes, as it was intended she should. If there was a forced note in the sound of it, no one was discouraged. That she could even pretend to laugh so soon was a miracle.

As he walked with them through the sunset, Mitch hoped the night would not destroy even the pretense of laughter.

The helicopter hovered over a field behind the chapel. An incongruous sight as it swayed and dipped and fought to keep its cumbersome body aloft. Jocie hid her face and shivered as the force of the wind plastered her clothing to her thin body. Katherine wrapped an arm around her, wishing she could spare her even this little discomfort.

When the machine set down and the rotors slowed, Katherine kissed her cheek and wiped away her tears. A bond had formed between them. In the face of the tragedy Jocie had survived, petty differences and jealousy had been put aside. The future wouldn't be without its problems, but for the first time Katherine understood this wild fey creature, and knew what it was like to have a sister.

"Time will pass before you know it. Then you'll be home, with all of us, and this will only be a memory." Lifting Jocie's face, she promised, "Memories fade."

"I know," Jocie said, but for once in a great while her mind was on something other than her troubles. "About Gran..."

"I'll tell her," Katherine offered when the young, hoarse voice failed. "I'll tell her you love her and that you'd like to be with her. That you will as soon as it's safe for you to travel. I'll tell her, but she already knows."

Neither admitted that Gran might not be there when Jocie could finally travel.

"I wish things could have been different."

"So do I, Jocie. I have a lot to answer for, don't I?"

Jocie shook her head, a vehement denial. "Not you, Katherine Mary." She stepped out of her sister's embrace, her head lifted, for once unmindful of the scar. There was the beginning of a new maturity in her, the willingness to accept the consequences of her own behavior. "What I said about hating you. I don't. I never did."

"I never believed that you did."

"Don't!" Jocie's gray eyes brimmed with fresh tears. "Don't be kind. I'd feel better if you'd get mad at me. Yell, or something."

"I will." Katherine laughed and kissed her lightly one last time as the motor revved and dust whipped around them. "That's a promise."

Mitch touched her shoulder. Leaning close, his mouth nearly touching her ear, he warned the chopper was loaded and waiting.

Torn between her duties, Katherine fought back the rush of her own tears. She hated to leave Jocie, who looked so lost and forlorn without her. Yet she was desperate to go to Gran.

"It's time, Katherine." Taking her hand, Mitch walked with her to the helicopter, stopping just short of the worst of the wash from the propellers. Conversation of a reasonable decibel was still just possible. Resting a hand on each of her shoulders, he looked deeply into her eyes.

"Take care," he half spoke, half mimed. When she shook her head in agreement, his grim face grew grimmer. "Tell Gran I'm sorry."

"Sorry?"

"She'll understand."

"Mitch?" Katherine was confused and hurt. After telling her of the gravity of Gran's condition and Matthew's plan, under the guise of allowing her to spend the last precious hours alone with her sister, he'd avoided her. Now he seemed almost relieved that she was leaving. Katherine didn't understand, and a new stab of pain nearly defeated her. She knew he cared. It was there in every look and every touch. He made no effort to hide it.

Mitchell Ryan cared deeply for her, yet he was pulling away.

As time was counted, he'd only been a part of her life for a short while. Destiny promised he would live in her heart forever. Lifting her hand, she stroked his face, to take a memory with her.

Mitch flinched and caught her wrist, circling it in his grasp, as if he couldn't bear her touch. There was pain in his look as he raised her palm to his mouth. His lips lingered, caressed, unwilling to let her go. Yet abruptly he backed away.

"You'd better go." His voice was rough with strain. "Matthew's waiting."

Katherine wanted to run into his arms and hold on to him. Instead she squared her shoulders and lifted her chin. "You'll watch out for Jocie?"

"With my life."

She knew he would. He had. There was more she wanted to say. More she wanted to hear, but Mitch was already signaling the pilot she was ready to board. ''Three weeks?''

''Three, at the most,'' he promised.

Then Matthew was at the door, offering his hand. The journey to Stone Meadow and to Gran had begun.

The lumbering helicopter was ancient, far removed from the cutting edge of technology. Lifting off was an effort. As it swayed and struggled, Katherine stared down at the ground, at the shrinking figures of those she'd come to love and respect. The sisters with their dark habits fluttering like raven's wings in the turbulence. Jocie, who was becoming a stronger and better person with each minute in their company, and with Mitch.

Mitch.

A hand slipped over her hand, strong fingers laced through hers. When she lifted her gaze to Matthew he was watching her gravely, reading every broken dream.

''He loves you, Katherine.''

''I know.''

''And you love him.''

''Yes.''

''This is new to him. Nothing in his life has ever been as precious as you. Mitchell Ryan has never been afraid of anything in his life, now he is.''

Katherine couldn't pretend to understand, and Matthew wouldn't presume to. He would leave that to Mitch.

The chopper finished its grinding climb and turned to the mainland. The field and the waving figures were swallowed by the thick growth of trees. The morning was bright and clear, in a bit more than an hour they would land at the airport and Katherine would take a flight home.

''Give him time, Katherine. That's all he needs.''

Katherine didn't answer. No answer was necessary. She would give Mitch all the time he needed.

The rest of her life, if he wanted it.

Eleven

***

Matthew put aside the strips of leather he was braiding. He'd promised Jocie an ornament for her hair, like the one he'd made for Corrie and like he wore, as soon as she had one single tuft long enough to hold it. In two weeks more had changed than just the length of a young girl's hair.

With the aid of Simon McKinzie and The Black Watch, Isaac's operation had been destroyed. Isaac, himself, sat in a jail cell awaiting trial for a number of charges, among them, kidnapping. Corrie and Jocie, bare acquaintances in the past, had become fast friends. A friendship that benefited both girls.

And Mitchell Ryan had become a quiet presence, given to brooding moods. He could hide what he felt and its cause from the sisters and the girls, but not from Matthew. On this bright afternoon as they sat together at a table in the shade of the garden, the Apache decided enough was enough.

"You're missing Katherine."

Mitch pushed away an untouched glass of lemonade, forgetting that it was Sister Thumbelina's specialty and that her feelings would be hurt if he didn't drink it. He didn't bother with denials that wouldn't fool Matthew for a minute. "It's difficult not to miss her."

"Jocie's better and could travel by the middle of next week. You could go on to Stone Meadow and we could follow then."

"The last time you called, Gran was better. Katherine doesn't really need me now."

"Jocelyn Rivard's condition is a long way from stable, and whose decision was it that you could only go to Katherine when she needs you?"

"The decision is mine, Matthew. It's the only time and place for me in her life. We have no common ground. I couldn't ask her to lead a life like mine, and I'm not sure I could adjust to hers."

"Family life, you mean. Staying in one place, an unchanging routine day in and day out. Year after year, always the same. Something you've never known."

"I see you haven't lost your powers of observation, particularly for the obvious." There was an edge of derision in Mitch's tone.

Matthew refused to take offense, nor would he let the matter slide. "You know how it is with Indian mystics, we see things. But I wouldn't have to be a mystic to see that you're miserable without Katherine."

"If I am, then it's a condition I'll have to learn to live with."

"Because you don't like Katherine's life-style?"

"I didn't say that, Matthew."

"You don't like Stone Meadow. It's ugly."

"You know that isn't true. I've never seen prettier country in my life."

"Then it's the old ladies," Matthew continued in his role as devil's advocate, and relished it. "Five of them would be quite a responsibility. I imagine they're cranky."

"They can be. Even then, they're delightful."

"Ah, you like them?"

"Of course I do. You will, too, when you meet them."

"I see." In a gesture familiar because it was one employed habitually by Simon, Matthew raised his hand, fingers splayed. "You're leery of her life-style, but you don't hate it." A finger folded into his palm. "You like where she lives, in fact it's pretty." A second finger folded. "The ladies wouldn't be an unpleasant responsibility." Another point, another finger folded to his palm. "You like them, I suspect you love them." One finger remained to complete the fist. "That leaves Katherine."

"What about Katherine?"

"You love her, but not enough to take the risks that loving her completely would demand."

"Katherine isn't the risk. I am. For all the reasons you've named, except the last. Too many people she's loved have left her, Matthew, and if the bucolic family life was beyond me, I would be another. I don't want that."

"You're choosing to step out of her life because you aren't certain you could always be a part of it?"

"That's a simplistic explanation, but, yes."

Matthew leaned his chair back, balancing on two legs. His arms were crossed over his chest, his piercing stare never leaving Mitch. "So," he said after a time, "you're going to leave her alone and miserable all her life on the off chance that someday, twenty or thirty years down the road, you might not be in her life?"

The chair crashed down, Matthew's fist slammed against the table, rattling ice in the forgotten glass of lemonade. "If that sounds like hogwash, there's a reason. It is hogwash! You're asking for guarantees, Mitch, and there are few in this life. All you have to do is look at Corrie and Jocie over by the river for proof of that.

"Anything could happen at any given time, for any reason, and one of you would be without the other. There might be a bullet out there with your name on it. Or a plane waiting for you before it crashes. But that's you, isn't it? Let's talk about Katherine.

"If you knew there was a horse not even born yet that was destined to trample Katherine twenty, thirty, forty, or even fifty years in the future, would you back away now to keep from hurting then?"

"That isn't the same, Matthew," Mitch said, struggling to keep a level tone.

"Isn't it? It all goes back to guarantees, Mitch. That rare entity in this life. But if I were asked to pick a sure bet, it would be that once committed to Katherine, nothing short of death would pry you loose. You've never in your life broken your word. But the real truth of it is you're too damn stubborn to ever quit, and you love too deeply to ever stop."

"People change. I have. Have you forgotten I nearly killed a man on our last assignment? I would have, if you hadn't stopped me."

"For what he did to the baby, he needed killing."

"No, I lost it."

"You were too close, too involved. You always are when there are children. In any case, you would have stopped yourself if I hadn't."

"We don't know that."

"I do." Matthew was implacable.

Mitch shrugged. "In any case, it's proof that I'm unstable."

"All it proves is that you've a lot of love to give, to a lot of people. Especially Katherine." Brushing aside Mitch's argument and leaning forward, Matthew made his final point. "You've a chance not many of us get. Take it, man. Go to her. Take what happiness you can and don't ask for guarantees."

With a sweep of his hand Matthew gathered up the leather braid and stood. "The not-so-silent savage rests his case."

"You don't understand," Mitch began, but he was speaking to Matthew's retreating back. "You don't understand," he muttered again. Then buried his head in his hands.

The sun was low, the bell had fallen silent, and Spanish Lady was cloaked in long shadows when he lifted his head and muttered, "Maybe you did understand, Matthew, better than I." He slid back his chair to stand looking out over the village one last time as he whispered, "But not anymore."

The rented car sped down the steep incline known as Saluda Grade. Its curves were wide and sweeping and plummeted ever downward. The wilting valley that lay beyond the sharply dropping ledge to which the road clung was wreathed by clouds that teased with the long-awaited promise of rain.

Mitchell Ryan felt the prickle of exhilaration. He knew what the rain would mean to Katherine and to the sprawling farm she loved. She had promised Jocie she would sell every inch of it to find a surgeon to repair her scarred face, but it wouldn't be necessary. This morning, Simon, in his wisdom and generosity, had listed both Corrie and Jocie as casualties of an operation of The Black Watch. Their mental and physical needs would be attended to by the best physicians the profession offered.

Jocie's surgery would be under way as soon as the pneumonia was resolved. No one of her family but Katherine would ever see the bitter punishment levied for her rebellion. Jocie had learned she was a fighter like her sister. Resentment and jealousy had been laid to rest and, in time, she would be completely healed. The healing had already progressed beyond belief in Matthew's hands.

And Isaac, The Mentor, thief of children's souls, was no more. Even in jail there were those who hated what he was, and what he'd done. Hatred violent enough to drive a knife into his heart.

Jail cell justice.

Mitch grimaced and put Isaac from his mind as he took the turn from the interstate that would lead to Stone Meadow. He flashed through well-tended fences and over unpaved roads. He didn't cringe when the airport rental wallowed in sand and trickling streams as he had when it was the marvelously aged Rolls. At the last fence he was tempted to drive on through, leaving the gate open, then decided better of the impulse and closed it as emphatically as Katherine had.

If he was going to be a farmer, he'd better learn to do it right.

"Mitchell Ryan, a tough from the street, a farmer!" He laughed, then sobered. "A farmer if Katherine will have me."

She would. He knew it and never doubted. When a woman loved as Katherine loved, it was with all her heart and forever. Loving so completely didn't make her a martyr. Katherine Rivard was the strongest woman he'd ever known. The only woman who could make him believe he could return to the streets of New Orleans and walk away unscathed. The only woman without whom he could never draw a happy breath.

"I almost threw it away." Dust boiled behind him as he negotiated the last twist in the tree-lined drive that led to the house. He absorbed, again, the sheer size of it and of the barns and corrals where a horse gamboled and pranced. His gaze swept over the hills rising behind, assessing the damage of the drought.

The grass was brown and brittle. Leaves hung like limp handkerchiefs from massive trees. Even the hardiest wildflowers barely survived. Only the unwanted vines flourished, coiling thickly over any surface in their path. Trees, shrubs, the fence that circled the family cemetery where more than a century of Rivards were buried.

Where a solitary figure stood alone beneath the threatening sky.

Katherine.

He was too late after all.

At a slower pace he drove to the steps that led to the balustered veranda. Lace curtains twitched over gleaming windows as he climbed from the car. Girlish shrieks and laughter preceded what could only be called a stampede of elegantly garbed old ladies. As they lined up to stare down at him, a curious hush fell over the yard and the veranda. Then one strong, aged voice broke the silence in classic fashion.

"Well, hell, Mitchell Ryan, I thought you weren't going to come."

"And I thought you were dead, Jocelyn Rivard."

"Not quite. There's too much to be done for me to die."

"Then why is Katherine at the cemetery?"

"I sent Katherine Mary to explain to my Byron that I'll be a while longer yet."

"I take it you plan to hang around to ride herd on the rest of us?" Mitch braced a foot on the first step as lightning split the sky and thunder shook the ground. The smell of rain was thick in the air.

"Ride herd and dandle red-haired Rivard babes on my knee."

"I don't think there can be babies, but if there are, they'll be Ryans, not Rivards."

"No babes! Ha! What does some fool country doctor who only looked at Katherine Mary once after a fall from a horse know about her innards?" A gnarled hand normally hidden away waved impatiently before falling heavily back into her lap. For just a moment the frailness of age and the long illness showed on her face.

"Gran," Rose cautioned.

"Be quiet, Rose, I'm all right." The old lady turned a blistering gaze to her granddaughter and then her daughter. "You be quiet, too, Bea."

"But I haven't said anything, not even hello to Mitchell," Bea protested.

"Then keep it that way. You have years for your hellos and goodbyes, and to hover over me." She swept the rest of the gathering with a fond but stern glance. "Violet. Daisy. That applies to the two of you, as well."

"I wouldn't dream of saying hello to Mitchell," Violet said around a chuckle. "Or hovering."

"Nor would I," Daisy echoed, a ghost of a wicked smile tugging at her mouth.

"Good." Gran turned back to Mitch. "Now, about these babes. If you think I care what name you call them by, you're mightily mistaken. Just give me strong boys and stronger girls. One or two of each before I die."

Mitch grinned. "Either I'm going to have to work fast, or you're going to need to make Byron wait quite a while."

"He's waited this long, I imagine he can wait a little longer. But unless you're a bigger fool than I think you are, you won't keep Katherine Mary waiting any longer.

"It's going to rain, young man, and from the looks of the clouds rolling in, I'd say it's going to be a doozy. A doozy is exactly what we need, but someone should remind a certain young lady that she shouldn't tempt fate by standing under trees in a storm." With a gesture, Jocelyn Rivard summoned her daughter to her wheelchair. "The rest of us are going to hide under our beds until the storm is past."

"You've never hidden under a bed in your life, Jocelyn Rivard, and you aren't going to start now," Mitch ventured.

"Maybe I'm not, but you're wasting time."

"Just paying my respects."

"Ha!" She waved him away, the gnarled hands visible again. "Enough of your foolishness. We all know you have more important matters to attend to. Such as my great-great-grandchildren, and the sooner the better. Neither you nor Katherine Mary is getting any younger, you know."

A final gesture set the elderly procession in motion. It was not until the last had disappeared into the cavernous foyer of the mansion that Mitch turned toward the hill.

The cemetery was deserted. The winding path was empty. Nothing moved but the leaves rustling in the stirring wind and the horse that nuzzled at a tuft of grass beyond the fence.

Mitch didn't hesitate. Spinning around, he hurried to the barn. Stepping inside the open door he was enveloped by silence and blinded by the cool darkness. "Katherine," he called. Then again. "Katherine."

"I'm here, Mitch." She stepped from the shadows. Lightning flickered weakly, and in its light she was the most beautiful sight he'd ever seen.

"Juggernaut is in the corral," he said lamely.

"He'll come in when he's ready."

"Cam succeeded with him?"

"He'll be a champion."

"Jocie isn't with me."

"So I see."

"She's making great progress."

"I know, Matthew has kept me informed."

"He sends his love."

"Is this why you came, Mitch? To make small talk and deliver messages?"

"I came for this, Katherine." His hand curled at her waist pulling her against him. "Only for this."

His mouth was hot and hungry over hers, saying without words all she'd ever wanted to hear, and a lonely heart lifted and soared. Her arms crept around him, holding him fiercely, answering his need with all the love within her.

This was her man. The only man she would ever want. He had given her back her sister, and along the way taught her to laugh and to cry and to love.

There was much she had to tell him. Gran's resurgent good health. The contract Cam had managed to salvage by convincing the power among the consortium Juggernaut was such a spectacular horse only because he was trained by Katherine Rivard's methods, if not by Katherine herself. Now the consortium was asking for as many horses as she could train. Simon McKinzie's recent and clandestine midnight visit with a proposal to make a part of the farm a haven for children like Corrie and Jocie. A place where they could learn to live new lives, with guidance from men like Mitch and Matthew. Simon's men, who called themselves The Black Watch. And from Trevor, if he would come.

Best of all was her secret. The fruition of love. A child, a miracle, growing inside her. The first of the family Mitch had never had.

There was so much to say. So much to tell and to hear. But first . . .

Katherine pulled away from his kiss, away from his embrace. Her smile was only a flash in the darkness as she took his hand. The steps to the loft lay in deep shadow and only lightning marked their way.

The hay was deep and fragrant.

Mitch caught her in his arms and kissed her again. "Tell me," he whispered, winding her hair in his hand. "Have you done this before? Seduced a stranger in your barn, I mean."

"Once." Turning her lips to his palm she trailed kisses over the callused flesh. "Only once."

"What sort of man was he?"

"A kind man, a gentle man. For a while, my friend." She smiled softly. "Always my love."

"No Hail Marys because of him?"

"No Hail Marys. No regrets."

"If he came back? If he wanted to stay, not just a day, or a week, but forever? Would it matter what he'd been?"

"What he's been is a wonderful child who grew to an even more wonderful man. This is his home for as long as he wants it to be." Katherine laced her fingers through his, pulling him down with her to the hay. "For a day," she murmured. "A week . . ."

"Forever," Mitch finished for her. "And a little longer."

"Mitch, I have so much to tell you," Katherine whispered as clothing fluttered over the hay.

"I know, sweet Kate. I know." Mitch hardly heard as he discovered another delight, and another.

Thunder rumbled and the heavens opened. Rain drummed on the roof and splashed on parched earth. The day grew darker, and the scent of the hay sweeter. Once Mitch gathered his wits enough to promise himself he would dance with Katherine in the rain.

"Later," he growled as he took her again with him to paradise.

Katherine heard the grumbled word. She didn't understand, but didn't worry. Later, like forever, sounded like a promise.

Mitchell Ryan, man of The Black Watch, and keeper of her heart, *never* broke a promise.

Rising over her, he stared down at her, storing away another memory. "I will always love you, Kate."

She was smiling as she pulled him back to her again, murmuring cryptically, *"Never."*

The rain fell harder, pounding its life-giving rhythm against the tin roof. There was hope in the sound, and happiness. For the first time in weeks Katherine slept peacefully.

When she dreamed, she dreamed of Mitchell Ryan. Quiet danger with a quick smile, a gentle hand, and a baby bottle tucked in the hip pocket of his jeans.

A man who had no concept of how special he was.

The Saint of Bourbon Street.

* * * * *

SILHOUETTE® *Desire®*

COMING NEXT MONTH

#955 WILDCAT—Rebecca Brandewyne

October's *Man of the Month*, wildcatter Morgan McCain, wanted every inch of city slicker Cat Devlin, but there was no way he was going to let her womanly wiles lure love into his hardened heart.

#956 A WOLF IN THE DESERT—BJ James
Men of the Black Watch

Patience O'Hara knew she was in trouble when she felt more than fear for her dangerously handsome kidnapper. What was it about Matthew Winter Sky that had her hoping her rescue would never come?

#957 THE COWBOY TAKES A LADY—Cindy Gerard

One night with irresistible Sara Stewart had rough-and-tough cowboy Tucker Lambert running for cover. Because falling for Sara would mean saying "I do" for this confirmed bachelor!

#958 A WIFE IN TIME—Cathie Linz

Kane Wilder was driving Susannah Hall crazy! But when they were both sent back in time to solve a mystery, Susannah's only chance for survival was to pose as the stubborn man's wife....

#959 THE BACHELOR'S BRIDE—Audra Adams

Marry Reid James? No way! But Rachel Morgan's pregnancy left her no choice but to accept the infuriating man's proposal— even if it was *just* for her baby....

#960 THE ROGUE AND THE RICH GIRL—Christine Pacheco
Premiere

Prim and proper Nicole Jackson was desperate, and hotshot Ace Lawson was the only man who could help her. Now if she could only be sure he would never discover her secret....

Take 4 bestselling love stories FREE

Plus get a FREE surprise gift!

Special Limited-time Offer

Mail to Silhouette Reader Service™

3010 Walden Avenue
P.O. Box 1867
Buffalo, N.Y. 14269-1867

YES! Please send me 4 free Silhouette Desire® novels and my free surprise gift. Then send me 6 brand-new novels every month, which I will receive months before they appear in bookstores. Bill me at the low price of $2.44 each plus 25¢ delivery and applicable sales tax, if any.* That's the complete price and a savings of over 10% off the cover prices—quite a bargain! I understand that accepting the books and gift places me under no obligation ever to buy any books. I can always return a shipment and cancel at any time. Even if I never buy another book from Silhouette, the 4 free books and the surprise gift are mine to keep forever.

225 BPA ANRS

Name	(PLEASE PRINT)	
Address	Apt. No.	
City	State	Zip

This offer is limited to one order per household and not valid to present Silhouette Desire® subscribers. *Terms and prices are subject to change without notice.
Sales tax applicable in N.Y.

UDES-295   ©1990 Harlequin Enterprises Limited

It's our 1000th Special Edition and we're celebrating!

Join us these coming months for some wonderful stories in a special celebration of our 1000th book with some of your favorite authors!

Diana Palmer   **Nora Roberts**
Debbie Macomber   **Christine Flynn**
Phyllis Halldorson   **Lisa Jackson**

mini-series by:

Lindsay McKenna, Marie Ferrarella, Sherryl Woods, Gina Ferris Wilkins.

And many more books by special writers.

And as a special bonus, all Silhouette Special Edition titles published during Celebration 1000! Will have **double** Pages & Privileges proofs of purchase!

Silhouette Special Edition...heartwarming stories packed with emotion, just for you! You'll fall in love with our next 1000 special stories!

Four talented authors make their Silhouette debut—
and you are invited to join the celebration.
Don't miss any of these exciting titles:

HONEYMOON SUITE
(Romance #1113) by Linda Lewis

A prim-and-proper lady must find her way into a confirmed
bachelor's bedroom—any way she can.

THE ROGUE AND THE RICH GIRL
(Desire #960) by Christine Pacheco

After setting out to seduce a serious-minded lady, a sexy
rogue discovers how hot a plain Jane can be.

AND FATHER MAKES THREE
(Special Edition #990) by Laurie Campbell

One single mom and one rebellious teenager meet the man
who just might make their family complete.

ONE FORGOTTEN NIGHT
(Intimate Moments #672) by Suzanne Sanders

With no memory of her past, a woman suspected of a crime
must trust a handsome detective to clear her name—and give
her a future.

PREMIERE: The stars of tomorrow—making their
debut today!

Only from ▼ *Silhouette*®

Become a
Privileged Woman,
You'll be entitled to all these Free Benefits.
And Free Gifts, too.

To thank you for buying our books, we've designed an exclusive FREE program called *PAGES & PRIVILEGES™*. You can enroll with just one Proof of Purchase, and get the kind of luxuries that, until now, you could only read about.

BIG HOTEL DISCOUNTS

A privileged woman stays in the finest hotels. And so can you—at up to 60% off! Imagine standing in a hotel check-in line and watching as the guest in front of you pays $150 for the same room that's only costing you $60. Your *Pages & Privileges* discounts are good at Sheraton, Marriott, Best Western, Hyatt and thousands of other fine hotels all over the U.S., Canada and Europe.

FREE DISCOUNT TRAVEL SERVICE

A privileged woman is always jetting to romantic places. When <u>you</u> fly, just make one phone call for the lowest published airfare at time of booking— <u>or double the difference back!</u>

PLUS—you'll get a $25 voucher to use the first time you book a flight AND <u>5% cash back on every ticket you buy thereafter through the travel service!</u>